I reckon this is where I'm expected to tell you how I lived a life of towering adventure, saddle-broke a hundred wild mustangs, pitched a tent in Tibet, hunted Cape buffalo, served with distinction, rode with the wind, tramped the wild places and the crooked highways... oh, heck with it. That's not me.

I was the kid in the front row of the balcony of the movie theater who spent every Saturday afternoon with the likes of John Wayne, Burt Lancaster, Kirk Douglas, Lee Marvin, Charlton Heston, Gregory Peck, and the list goes on; a kid who thrilled to the sight of charging Comanches, saloon brawls, shoot-outs in dusty streets, not to mention sword fights, heroic last stands, dueling pirate ships, and chariot races. And when I wasn't at the theater I was reading the same, yondering by way of the written word, finding the lost and lonely places, and dreaming I would one day be the tale-teller, spinning legends on the wheel of my imagination.

Back in the mid-eighties, I wrote **Texas Anthem**. It was the first of a family saga set against the western frontier from the ending of the Mexican-American War to the turn of the century. I am pleased that St. Martin's is reprinting all five novels in the series.

The Anthem family is a robust collection of men and women shaped by the land, a strong and independent breed, often flawed and perhaps too headstrong, but the kind of folks who will stand for justice, live life to the fullest, and cast a tall shadow.

Sure, I've done some things, been some places. But

so have you. All that matters now, my friend, is the story we share. I have tried to craft these books with a sense of legend as well as history, finding just the right blend of thrills, drama, romance, and a dash of wit. Whether or not I have succeeded is in your hands.

KERRY NEWCOMB
MARCH, 2000

RIP-ROARING ACCLAIM FOR KERRY NEWCOMB'S
THE RED RIPPER

"A sizzler! Newcomb brings to life a larger-than-life frontiersman who strode boldly into legend. One helluva good book by a storyteller working at top form." —Matt Braun, Golden Spur Award–winning author of *The Kincaids*

"THE RED RIPPER bounds along with unrelenting vigor. This is historical fiction crafted by a writer who never loses his sense of pace, drama, adventure, and fun." —Cameron Judd, Golden Spur Award–nominated author of *Confederate Gold*

"With the historical accuracy of a L'Amour novel, the characters are well drawn, leaving the reader to feel the openness and harsh challenges of the Texas frontier . . . Don't expect to get any sleep when you start this one. A compelling mix of passion, revenge, and a gallant people's quest for freedom." —John J. Gobbell, bestselling author of *The Last Lieutenant*

"An entertaining tale of high adventure and low villains." —*Booklist*

"The ornery, pugnacious and legendary William 'Bigfoot' Wallace, a sometime Texas Ranger and full-time knife-fighter, strides through early 19th-century Texas history in this rangy, fast-moving historical novel. [An] action-filled plot, [with] broad-brush sagebrush scenes and the romance of the Texas republic." —*Publishers Weekly*

ST. MARTIN'S PAPERBACKS TITLES
BY KERRY NEWCOMB

The Red Ripper
Texas Anthem

TEXAS ANTHEM

KERRY NEWCOMB

(PREVIOUSLY PUBLISHED UNDER THE
PSEUDONYM JAMES RENO)

St. Martin's Paperbacks

PUBLISHER'S NOTE

This novel is a work of fiction. Names, characters, places, and incidents either are the product of the author's imagination or are used fictitiously, and any resemblance to actual persons, living or dead, events, or locales is entirely coincidental.

TEXAS ANTHEM

Copyright © 1986 by James Reno.
"Just a Note From the Author" copyright © 2000 by Kerry Newcomb.

All rights reserved. No part of this book may be used or reproduced in any manner whatsoever without written permission except in the case of brief quotations embodied in critical articles or reviews. For information address St. Martin's Press, 175 Fifth Avenue, New York, N.Y. 10010.

ISBN: 0-312-97682-8

Printed in the United States of America

Signet edition / July 1986
St. Martin's Paperbacks edition / November 2000

10 9 8 7 6 5 4 3 2 1

For Grandparents,
who make special the days
of Amy Rose and P.J.
in ways this mere papa never can

I would like to acknowledge, with affection and gratitude, Aaron Priest—agent and friend—and Maureen Baron, my wonderful and patient editor. Thank you for believing in me. Books may be part inspiration and perspiration but they don't get written without faith.

While the earth remaineth, seedtime and harvest,
and cold and heat, and summer and winter,
and day and night shall not cease.

—GENESIS 8:22

But I, being poor, have only my dreams . . .

—W. B. YEATS
"He wishes for the
Clothes of Heaven"

TEXAS ANTHEM

PART ONE

APRIL 1849

1

★

The dream began where it always did . . . Chihuahua, Mexico, July 4, 1848. Nine months past, on the borderline. Johnny Anthem had spent his twentieth birthday, and his country's seventy-second, riding for his life.

With gunfire for fireworks and his galloping black mare's hoofbeats for cadenzas, Anthem was his own parade. Wishing himself and America many happy returns, Anthem hunched low in the saddle as a musket ball whistled past his head. He glanced over his shoulder in time to see Vin Cotter thumb a shot at their pursuers.

A year older and two sizes smaller, Vin presented less of a target than Johnny Anthem's broad burly frame. Vin twisted around and wasted a second shot from his Walker Colt at the dozen Mexican dragoons who had been chasing them for the better part of an hour.

Sunlight glinted off drawn sabers. And the narrow walls of the canyon rang with the answering exchange of musket and small-arms fire. The war with Mexico had ended with the declaration of peace five months ago. Peace, sweet glorious peace at last. Johnny and Vin had been mustered out of the Texas Rangers and were heading for home. It just didn't make any sense to get killed now.

"Ride!" Johnny shouted.

Vin holstered his gun and, hunkering over the neck of his horse, spurred the animal unmercifully, raking the sorrel's flesh until blood oozed. "Come on, damn you," Vin growled, leaning over his horse.

Johnny had the faster mount, and given his lead, the black mare couldn't be caught. The mare, which Johnny had raised from a foal, had been a gift from Vin's father, who had also given the orphaned boy a home. Well, Johnny Anthem might be like a brother, but "like" didn't mean he was one. It was a distinction Vin regarded with importance as he looked jealously toward the black mare leading the way.

The sun-glazed walls of the canyon swept past as they veered into a narrow gorge that plunged them into disorienting shadow. Johnny suffered a moment of blindness, but he trusted the mare's instincts. With jagged limestone ledges closing in on either side of him, Anthem held the mare to a gallop. A single false step meant disaster. Johnny pushed his luck. The hoofbeats on the limestone rubble echoed off the shadowy walls, became a crunching battering noise that increased as the Mexicans swung their mounts around and filed into the passage the two Anglos had taken. Sunlight and the walls of the file receded thirty feet. Ahead, framed by the limestone battlements where the passage through the mountain opened up unto the plains, the Chihuahuan grasslands rolled down to the Rio Grande. He pulled back on the reins to slow the mare. The animal fought him. The black wanted to run.

Johnny lifted his battered broad-brimmed hat and wiped his forehead on his torn sleeve. His thick red hair was matted with sweat. His square-jawed features were caked with dirt, and he noticed his arm was streaked with blood. He remembered riding too close to an ocotillo. Its slender spiny branches clawed at the gringo riding past. Even the land wanted to be rid of him. Johnny Anthem was only too happy to oblige. He'd had a bellyfull of war.

Vin Cotter burst from the shadows, his narrow, thin-veined features flush with fear. He had lost his hat in the gorge. His flesh was sunburned and peeling away, even as the veneer of respectability had peeled away since he had ridden south with Johnny Anthem and the other newly conscripted Rangers. His eyes were wide with panic as he galloped up to the man on the black mare.

"They're right behind me," Vin yelled, his voice rising in pitch. "My horse is about played out."

"It isn't far now," Johnny replied. "Hang on. We ought to reach the Rio Grande by noon or so." He pointed toward the mouth of the valley, then swatted the black mare's rump with his hat. "Come on, Vin. I'll race you to Texas."

The mare took the lead again, leaving Cotter's sorrel in its dusty wake. A fine, refreshing spray of cold spring water showered the men as their horses followed the creekbed. With empty canteens rattling against their saddles, the spray was better than no drink at all. The two young Texans rode hard and reached the mouth of the gorge as their pursuers poured out of the narrows. Johnny Anthem loosed a wild yell as the grasslands spread out before him. Here the rolling landscape was splashed with chino and tobosa grasses in hues of faded green, stretching as far as the eye could see. The colors darkened against the bluestem-covered slopes. The Chisos Mountains shimmered in a blue haze, and at their base, like a spool of glistening gold, the sun-dappled surface of the Rio Grande—Río Bravo to the Mexicans—gleamed like a beacon of hope.

"Texas!" John shouted, ignoring the fact they must race death to reach it. Not twelve Mexican soldiers, not Santa Anna's whole blamed army were going to stop them now.

"Anthem!"

Texas in the mist, so close. The black mare glistened

with perspiration. Johnny knew she had enough heart to carry him home.

"Anthem!"

Johnny wheeled his horse around and saw Vin Cotter standing in the dust, the canyon walls rising overhead, dry harsh battlements on the outskirts of hard scrabble country. The sorrel was down, its legs flailing at the earth as it endured its death throes. Vin was afoot and running for all he was worth. Behind him, the pursuing Mexican soldiers spread outward in a single file to bring every gun to bear on the Texans.

Texas in the mist . . . so far away. Johnny spurred his horse. The mare bolted forward. They wouldn't make it, riding double. The mare couldn't carry both men home. Johnny's hopes plummeted. There were too damn many to stand against, but stand they must. Because there was nothing else to do. They had ridden into Mexico together and Johnny intended to ride out the same way. Or not at all. For such was the promise he had made Everett Cotter. The words of Vin's father echoed in Johnny's mind. "Look after my son. Look after my son. Look after . . ."

Johnny leaned low in the saddle and stretched out his arm as he rode back at a gallop toward Vin. It was no place to make a stand. They needed cover, anything to hide behind; Johnny wasn't proud, a rock, a stand of timber, anything would do. Geysers of dust spewed upward to either side of Vin, lead slugs whined through the air, whistling their high-pitched tune of death. Vin ran with his arms outstretched, face pale with fear, his battered boots digging into the shallow topsoil. He stumbled and Johnny thought he had been hit but Vin regained his footing as the shadow of the black mare fell across him. The Mexican dragoons charged. Some with sabers drawn, others with carbines brought to bear.

Twenty, fifteen . . . ten feet away, and riding at a gallop came Johnny Anthem on his black mare.

"Hurry, Vin, hurry! Swing up behind me," Johnny shouted. He holstered his pistol and leaned down, stretching out to clasp Vin's hand. The smaller man caught hold. Johnny lifted his eyes and glanced toward the charging line of soldiers, then back to Vin. He saw Vin's Colt drawn, held by the barrel, saw it swinging upward in a savage arc, saw the desperate fear in Vin's eyes. Vin knew the mare couldn't carry them both home. The wooden pistol grip slammed against Johnny's skull, opening a gash at his temple. The world shattered into sunlit splinters and Johnny toppled from the saddle, dragged free by Vin Cotter, who swung astride the mare and turned the animal around. Johnny tasted dirt, spat out a mouthful of clay, and lifted himself upon his elbows. The world tilted crazily. But he could see Vin riding hell for Sunday toward the Rio Grande. *Adiós, Vin, vaya con Dios*, you son of a bitch. Johnny rolled over on his back and stared up at the flat, hot, cloudless Mexican sky. In Texas it probably looked exactly the same.

The earth trembled as half a dozen horsemen galloped past in pursuit of the mare. Forget it, boys, you haven't a chance. As light as Vin is, not a chance. You'll eat his dust all the way to the Bravo.

A figure shaded Johnny, a man on horseback. One of the soldiers. Vision cleared enough to make out a black sombrero stitched with silver thread. Johnny saw a face like a hawk's, the look of a predator in that dark-skinned visage. Aztec blood was there, too. And pride . . . in the man's bearing, and later in the tone of his voice. He wore a cruel excuse for a smile, more like a livid scar beneath the black scrawl of his mustache.

"Good day, my young friend. It seems you have not chosen your companions wisely or well."

Johnny groaned at the pain in his battered skull and dug his fingers into the dirt, bracing himself for the gunshot he expected at any moment, the bullet that would end pain and life as well.

"The war is over," Johnny managed to say. "Peace treaty's been signed in Mexico City." The very effort of speech made him shudder. His head felt as if it were coming apart. Oh, Vin, you were like a brother . . .

"A treaty?" came the silken reply. "But I, General Andrés Varela, have signed no treaty."

Several silhouettes on horseback crowded into view. Johnny heard a carbine being cocked. But the man in the sombrero snapped an order and the weapon was lowered.

"You will have many days to consider such a peace." Andrés Varela chuckled. "Many days to regret you ever crossed the Río Bravo and invaded the land of our fathers." His men laughed too. But Johnny couldn't hear them anymore. He closed his eyes and sank back against the wild grasses and drowned in their sweet fragrance.

That was the way the dream ended and the next began.

In the nine months he had been imprisoned at Varela's hacienda, Johnny had learned to tame his nightmares. Sanctuary and peace existed in a single name, Rose McCain. Sweet Rose. They had endured tragedy together, suffering the massacre of both their parents at the hands of the Apache. They had cowered together in the same cave while the braves searched for them. They lived, survived, and were taken in by Everett Cotter and raised in Cotter's household, as brother and sister.

Later, when toys and pranks and carefree hours were traded for the ambitions and desires of adulthood, Johnny Anthem and Rose McCain found their emotions deepening. He could see her now, forming her out of the stuff of dreams, watching as yellow-gold hair replaced the hurt of

Vin's betrayal. Yellow-gold hair and tawny limbs and a taut tender body. He remembered a pond with weeping willows hugging the water's edge. He had surprised her, swimming alone. He felt again the stirring as he had then, remembering how she looked as she climbed out of the shaded pool, her cotton underskirt plastered to her legs, her cotton bodice soaked, revealing the ripened thrust of her breasts only partly concealed by the soft fall of her hair. Rose . . . my Rose . . . my Yellow Rose . . . And always would be. She promised to wait. She was waiting still, he knew, beyond the Río Bravo, across the Rio Grande, waiting for him, in Texas.

He called her name in his sleep. His own name returned in an echo, then a hand upon his shoulder was rousing him, robbing him of his vision of peace. His right arm shot up as he came awake. His right hand closed around the throat of the man leaning over him. His grip was iron—after nine months of swinging hammer and pickax in the silver mines of Andrés Varela, a man grew strong as iron, or died.

"No, Johnny," the voice hissed, the man struggled to free himself. "It's me!" Johnny recognized the voice and loosened his hold. Almost twenty years older than Anthem, Pokeberry Tyler was also a *norteamericano*. Tyler had spent the last five years toiling in the mines of Varela, the price for prospecting on the wrong side of the border. Imprisonment had taken its toll on Tyler. Not even forty, he looked sixty. His teeth were blackened, and only a few strands of straw-colored hair clung to his skull. He was nursing a fractured ankle that Johnny had applied a splint to. While the bone healed, Tyler had been unable to work. The only reason he hadn't been driven off by Varela's guards to die in the desert was that Johnny did the injured man's work, taking Poke Tyler's place in the mine. Varela's vaqueros and guards and even the landowner himself had bet on how long Johnny could work the double shift.

No one had expected the youth to last the day. He had lasted weeks. He had endured. He had become iron.

Johnny blinked and rubbed his eyes and looked around. The courtyard where the peons and prisoners were quartered was a veritable beehive of activity. He bolted upright and asked Tyler, "What's happened?"

Guards were hurrying from pillar to pillar, unshackling the prisoners and snapping instructions, pointing toward the dark slope that rose behind the hacienda, where the mine shaft shown in the moonlight like a lurid scar upon the hillside. Men with torches scurried up the slope. Smoke gutted from the shaft and Johnny heard the earth tremble and groan. Poke didn't have to answer. Johnny knew.

Cave-in. And there must be men trapped in the bowels of the mine. Poor slave bastards and their keepers, Varela's guards, buried in the bowels of the mountain. Lights burned in the window of Casa Varela, the general's two-storied, sprawling home. His precious silver ore was in danger, not to mention a full complement of slave labor.

A vaquero on a brown gelding galloped past. His whip cracked and Johnny felt the tip sting his back, drawing blood. He whirled around, fists clenched. The vaquero ignored such defiance.

"Go on, gringo. Up the slope. We need your strength in the tunnels. You too, old one." The whip cracked again, but with surprising agility Poke hopped aside, favoring his leg. Poke knew the whip well—its sting and the way the tip lapped and darted like a rattler's tongue. As far as Pokeberry Tyler was concerned, it had tasted enough of his blood over the years; his shoulders were scarred to prove it.

Johnny looked down at his legs, free from the iron tethers that had chained him to the post. All the workers were free in the courtyard. Vaqueros rode among them, their whips flecking out, some with lances prodding the already startled conglomeration of peons, Negro and Yaqui slaves and criminals. General Andrés Varela, as judge and military governor, had sentenced all of them to labor in his mine until he deemed them rehabilitated. The air rang with a raucous chorus of cries and shouts, gruff orders, bellowed commands, and the weary frightened protests of Varela's hapless captives.

Pokeberry tugged Johnny's tattered sleeve. "We better go." He ran a trembling hand over the silver stubble covering his jaw.

Johnny fell into step with the older man, running side by side and taking care not to lose him as they joined the other prisoners streaming out the courtyard gate. The gravel-littered ground slowed the procession of men and horses. A hundred yards up on the hillside, a handful of men were gathered around the opening to the mine shaft, and the screams of the wounded living seemed to rise from the very earth like the spirits of the dead. Johnny melted deeper into the confusion of guards and men, leading Tyler through the clamoring throng. The vaqueros with their torches were spread thinly now and the hillside was cloaked in patches of darkness. Bending double so as not to stand out from the rest of the prisoners—for he stood taller than most of the men around him—Johnny gauged the distance to the approaching shadows and began drifting toward the fringe of the column, motioning Poke to follow him.

Johnny had climbed this hillside a hundred times and more. He owned it in his memory. He knew every fissure and seep, every cluster of ocotillo clinging to the slope, every ledge thrusting out from the earth. He glanced over his shoulder and marked the position of the nearest vaquero, then did the same with the man riding just ahead. The prisoners around him paid him no heed, for their attention was rooted on the mine ahead. The word came that a section had collapsed and men were dying there, that the timbers might not hold and more men might die, probably some of the ones being herded up the slope.

Now. Johnny grabbed Poke by the scruff of his ragged shirt, propelled the older man under a stone outcropping, and scooted in behind the old-timer. Lying prone alongside him, Johnny put his hand over Poke's mouth to choke off the startled man's protest. Anthem's homespun breeches and shirt were the color of the earth and left him all but invisible to the casual glance. He lowered his head as the flickering glow of a passing torch passed across them. Then darkness returned.

"God in heaven," Poke muttered.

"Shh."

Another horseman carrying a torch. Then another. The two prisoners suffered through each second, each excruciating minute, a lifetime in half an hour. Discovery meant being shot outright or lassoed and dragged across the brutal soil with its razor-sharp granite ridges and spiny plants. And when it seemed neither man could stand the tension a moment longer, the press of men lessened. The last rider passed and the obscurity of night returned to the hillside.

Johnny slowly exhaled in relief. "Quickly now. We'll steal a couple of horses and make for the border. Trouble at the mine ought to give us a good start."

"Damnation," Tyler muttered.

"What is it?" Jonnny asked, alarmed, crawling out from under the ledge.

Pokeberry Tyler scrambled out after him and dusted himself off. "Look here, younker, the next time you shove me in a hole in the ground and crawl in on top of me, you be sure to take a bath."

"You aren't exactly a nosegay yourself." Johnny grinned.

"Are we gonna stand here jawin' or hit the breeze?"

Poke asked, sniffing defensively, a wounded expression on his face.

"Reckon you can keep up?" Johnny started down the slope without waiting for an answer.

"Keep up? I was leadin' the way when you were haulin' about in diapers," Poke retorted indignantly. But he had to hurry because the younger man was almost out of earshot.

Johnny and Poke skirted the courtyard where the workers were fed and quartered, and clinging to the darkness below the stone walls, they headed for the hacienda and the low-walled stockade. There, Varela quartered his vaqueros and the small army of dragoons who helped him exert authority over much of northern Chihuahua. Goats bawled from a nearby pen. Dogs barked. The men moved as quietly as they could. Ahead, beyond another system of walls and an aqueduct that brought water down from the mountains, the horses circled in their corral. A woman could be heard crying within the squalid confines of a nearby jacal. The prostitutes who serviced Varela's soldiers lived in these adobe-walled thatched-roof huts. The woman stopped crying, as if she feared calling attention to herself. A moment later Johnny understood why. He heard two voices: one haughty and strong, giving orders; the other tempered with subservience and nervously attempting to explain how an accident had happened.

"I should have been notified at once."

"Jefe, no one told me you were among *las putas*."

"Idiot!"

The voices drew closer, the tramp of boots on the gravel street echoed down the alley.

Johnny didn't care who the shadowy figures were as they stepped into view. He saw two men leading two horses saddled and ready to ride. That was enough for him. Before Poke could caution him, the younger man bolted from the narrow alleyway. The approaching pair halted, their sombreros tilted back as they struggled to identify the burly silhouette bearing down on them. In the moonlight, a saber gleamed as Johnny closed in. He rammed his shoulder into the closest of the two and knocked the man against the wall of the jacal. His sandaled feet digging into the stones underfoot, Johnny swerved, allowing his momentum to propel him into the second man, the one brandishing a saber. He caught the man by the arm, driving his knee into the vaquero's groin. As the Mexican doubled over, Johnny slammed his forearm across the man's neck. The iron bracelet circling Johnny's wrist crushed flesh and bone, and the vaquero dropped facedown in the alley.

"Younker, behind you!"

Johnny Anthem ducked and scooped up the saber as a gunshot boomed amid the confines of the jacales. A lead ball fanned Anthem's unruly red hair. In the powder flash he saw a face that had a special place in his heart, right next to Vin Cotter's.

Andrés Varela cocked the Walker Colt and leveled the heavy-barreled weapon. Varela had recognized the *norteamericano* as well but was shocked to discover his prisoner here among the brothels.

"Die, my friend. As you should have long ago." Varela squeezed the trigger as Pokeberry Tyler collided with him, sending the general's second shot crashing through the waxed paper window of the jacal on the other side of the alley. Tyler banged off the wall and limped after the horses which were trotting back to the corral. Three women, all of them naked, burst out of a hearby hovel to spew their venom at the brawlers. Varela, his back to the wall, stood framed in the lamplight flooding through the open doorway. He cursed and raised the revolver for the kill.

But Johnny had closed the distance. The saber slashed down, its wicked blade slicing the air with a whisper Andrés Varela would never forget. Varela felt the impact, a vicious sting, and squeezed the trigger. Nothing happened. The general glanced down past the crimson stump of his arm to the Walker Colt on the ground and the quivering hand, his hand, writhing in the dust. Andrés Varela groaned and pitched forward in a faint.

Johnny grabbed the Colt as one of the harlots ran shrieking for help. The others began to pelt him with stones. Johnny ran their gauntlet of verbal and physical abuse and raced down the winding path that led between the jacales.

A shot sounded and a chunk of mud wall flew away from the side of a hut. Not all the vaqueros were at the mine, Johnny realized with a sinking heart. He spun as a horse and rider bore down on him and thumbed the blood-slick hammer on the Walker but held his fire when he realized it was Poke.

"Light a shuck, boy. I think you have worn out our welcome hereabouts." Somewhere off to the side, a voice barked an order. Another gunshot sounded from a rooftop as Johnny Anthem swung his big frame into the silver-tooled saddle.

"Reckon you can keep up?" Johnny shouted at the old prospector.

"If I can't, I don't wanna know," Poke replied. He dug in his heels and the horse leapt forward. He took the lead at a gallop.

Johnny holstered his gun, slapped his stolen sombrero across the rump of his stolen horse, and rode to freedom.

2

★

"Vengeance is mine," Pokeberry Tyler intoned. He knelt by the pool of springwater, glanced over at his younger, more headstrong companion, then filled his sombrero and raised it overhead and doused himself with icy cold water. "Texas!" he roared, unable to contain his joy. His voice reverberated in the narrow little canyon, ringing out and upward to the starlit sky.

"Texas," Johnny shouted in return. He lowered himself facefirst into the pool. Two days and fifty miles into Texas . . . Some men said it just looked like more of Mexico, but such men had no eyes. Johnny Anthem stood, water droplets gleaming like diamonds streamed from his bearded features. Rose wouldn't recognize him. He needed a shave. Soap and water, a hot bath, yes, just the thing. And soon, he calculated, soon.

"You hear me, boy?" Tyler asked. Being free of Varela had infused Poke with new life.

"I heard. And agree. Vengeance *is* mine." Johnny walked away from the spring and followed the aroma of cooked meat over to the campfire. He reached down, picked up the saber, and carved a morsel of venison from the quarter roast skewered on a spit over the leaping flames. He plopped it in his mouth and exhaled sharply as the sizzling meat burned his tongue. The buck he had shot was lean and old, but hunger is always the best seasoning and the venison tasted fine, real fine. Tyler joined him at the fire, unable to wait any longer to eat.

"What day you figure it is?" Johnny asked.

"I know. It's April 1849 . . . my God, 1849." The older man shook his head, then sighed. "Injuns call it the muddy-face moon. As for the day, does it matter?"

"No," Johnny said. "But it'll be a holiday by heaven when we reach the Bonnet."

"That's what Cotter calls his ranch?" Poke asked. Johnny nodded. Tyler spat, then chuckled to himself. "Naming kids is one thing, but land . . . Hell, land is land. It's either yours or it ain't."

"It is only yours if you make it so," Johnny said. "If you take it and hold it with all the strength you can muster, with your sweat and blood."

Pokeberry carved another portion of meat and sat with his back against a boulder of granite, stretched his legs before him, and continued to eat. He was the picture of contentment—albeit ragged contentment. He jabbed a sizzling morsel in Johnny's direction. "This here Everett Cotter is like a father to you. And yet you're going to kill his son."

"What else is there to do?" Johnny growled. He wanted to change the subject.

But Tyler held tenaciously to the point. "Ride away. Let it be."

"Away? Where?" Johnny snapped back.

"With me," Tyler said, leaning forward. "I been stalking this country longer than you are old, younker. I come here with Moses Austin. Only I was too fiddle-footed to stay in one place, I had to see what lay beyond the next hill. Well, these past five years in Varela's mines sorta killed my wanderlust, boy. I promised myself, if I ever sprung loose, I'd settle down. Sink my roots deep. And never wander again."

A coyote howled. Johnny pulled the Walker Colt from his holster and studied the surrounding cliffs. He motioned for Tyler to remain quiet. Poke glared defensively and reached for the musket he kept close at hand. Johnny stepped out of the firelight and ambled down the canyon, his eyes slowly growing accustomed to the night. A shape detached itself from the underbrush a few yards off to his left. Johnny thumbed the hammer back and hesitated, eased it down slowly as the ghostly shape became a coyote scampering toward the mouth of the canyon. Johnny relaxed and started back to camp.

"I could of told you that weren't Apaches," Poke remarked.

"Oh. How?" Johnny asked sarcastically.

"Easy," Poke said, eyes twinkling. "If it was Apaches, we'd be full of arrows about now."

"I'll remember that," Johnny replied. He took another helping of meat and squatted by the fire to eat. He glanced over at Tyler, then looked down at himself. Two men clad in threadbare cotton trousers and shirts, serapes to keep them warm. Two vagabonds. He lifted his gaze to the horses, ground-tethered twenty feet away. Good horses, though. And a saddle with a silver pommel.

"Pop Hitner's Trading Post's another day's ride from here. We can outfit there and decide what to do," Johnny said, hoping to end Tyler's prying. "Maybe we'll split up, me for San Antone and you to west Texas. But I wouldn't stay too close to the Rio Grande if I were you. Varela has a long reach."

"You trimmed it considerable the last I saw," Poke said. "Anyway, I got me a place all picked out. It's waiting for me. And maybe you, John Anthem, if you got the stomach to reach out and take it."

"Chances are somebody's already there ahead of you."

"Not this place. No, sir. Ain't a white man seen it but me." Poke Tyler's eyes took on a dreamy look. "It ain't far neither. Not for a couple of men like us, who bearded the devil himself just recent. A grand place, fresh water, good graze and soil." He tilted his sombrero back from his forehead and looked at Johnny. "We get us some clothes, maybe a stake at the Bonnet. Then head out. Forget this Vin Cotter. Just take your gal and we'll head west. If she's got the salt, she'll make it. And she's bound to cook better than you. Been a while since I seen a yellow-haired gal. Of course, maybe you're afraid I might steal her plumb away." Poke chuckled, wet his fingers and slicked down the remaining wisps of his hair.

"Vin Cotter owes me for these past nine months," Johnny said bitterly.

"And you owe his pa your life." Poke wagged his head, picked a piece of meat from between his blackened teeth. There were gaps in his smile and his gums were sickly red in spots. "A killing never sets things aright. It has a way of sticking to a man. You can't ever shake it. And one day, it comes back at you when you least expect it. A man can't put down roots in the soil of revenge and retribution. You think on it, younker." Tyler's seamed, leathery features became deadly earnest. "Fetch your Yellow Rose and come with me."

Johnny shrugged and ran a hand across his face. Suddenly he felt as if all his strength had left him. He was bone-tired. Thinking, he walked past the campfire to the shallow pool that had formed at the base of the cliff. He knelt in the moist sand, knees digging into the tender green shoots of grass sprouting in a tenuous border around the spring. He placed his hand flat against the seep and, leaning forward, looked down at his reflection in the pool. By firelight, by moonlight, he stared at himself while emotions

warred within him. He had drunk his fill, yet his mouth was
dry; he had eaten, yet he hungered still. For what? To see
his hatred fulfilled. Or love. He thought his heart could hold
them both. Maybe once, in the mines of Varela, or in the
visions of his wearied sleep. But now? Now he must
choose. He studied his reflection, the worn expression, the
ice-blue eyes peering at him from the flickering surface of
the mirroring pool. Ice-blue eyes with fire imprisoned in
their harsh depths.

Then he laughed aloud, his voice sounding cruel and
mocking. He cut it off and shuddered. Muscles rippled beneath his tattered sleeve. Arm and hand seemed more like
the massive hammer he had swung in the mines of Varela
than flesh and blood. And if that were so, then had his heart
become iron too?

He reached down and muddied the surface, destroying
the reflection of the stranger peering at him from the pool's
surface. Easing backward from the spring, he sat on dry
ground, his arms locked around his drawn-up legs.

"I'm not the man I was," Johnny said, more to himself
as he stared at the ripples in the pool. His voice carried in
the stillness. And caused Pokeberry Tyler's gentle reply.

"Younker, no one ever is."

POP HITNER'S TRADING PO read the sign. The faded black
lettering trailed off at the border of the wood sign. Pop
Hitner hadn't left room for the ST, and rather than begin
again or hammer out a new sign, he stayed with what he
had, figuring that once a person stepped inside they'd know
where they were. The trading post was built of adobe and
rose out of the muddy plain like a squat, ugly little fort.
Timbers jutted from the roofline and shutters hung open.
Dried gourds and corn were hung from the timbers. In the
gray light of dusk, a mongrel hound sprawled in the aban-
doned remnants of a flower plot; any blossoms had long

since succumbed. Lamplight streamed from one of the windows and the smell of tortillas and chili hung on the air. Thunder rumbled out of the north. The hammer of God struck sparks and lit the ominous line of clouds with tendrils of lightning. The ground was moist underfoot. It had rained recently and would soon rain again.

Fifty feet from the post, Johnny cupped a hand to his mouth and shouted. "Hello the house."

"I hear you," a voice answered from within. "Seen you too, since you showed in the valley." A figure appeared in the doorway, keeping himself hidden behind the door, except for his face and his right arm, which brandished a Colt.

Johnny noticed the shotgun poking from the window. "Don't shoot me, Pop. At least not until I've sat down to a bowl of your chili," Johnny called.

The door swung back and a short chubby man in faded overalls stepped out onto the porch. His face was hidden behind a flowing black beard and thick bushy eyebrows. Thunder echoed in the distant hills, rolling over the landscape, rattling the dipper in the *olla* of springwater that was hung from the roof of the porch by a horsehair rope.

"I know that voice," Pop Hitner shouted back. Johnny and Poke walked their horses up to the front porch and dismounted. The mongrel, part coyote and part hound, raised up on its legs and bared its fangs, assuming a menacing crouch.

"Settle down, Hickory," Johnny said.

The dog's hackles fell at the sound of his name and the mongrel trotted up to sniff at the two new arrivals. The animal flinched as Johnny extended his hand, but it began to wag its tail when it recognized the familiar scent.

Johnny Anthem tilted back his sombrero and looked up at Hitner. "You still sticking that shotgun in the window so's folks will think you aren't alone. Hope to God you don't ever need your invisible friend to help out."

"Saints in heaven, it's little Johnny!" Hitner backed away as if he were seeing a ghost. He bumped into the window and knocked the shotgun off the stool he had propped it against. The weapon clattered to the floor inside the trading post.

Johnny climbed to the porch. He towered over the merchant by a good foot.

"I could call you many things, younker, but 'little' ain't one of them." Poke stepped around the younger man and reached out to shake hands with Hitner. The merchant shook hands without even acknowledging Tyler. "Name's Pokeberry Tyler. Most folks call me Poke."

"First I thought you was renegade mescans. We've had a lot of trouble here and abouts with the war and all," Hitner said. "But I'd choose bandits over a ghost any day of the week." He continued to stare at Anthem.

"Well, this ghost could use a cup of hot coffee and a visit to your clothes pile," Johnny said, clapping the merchant on the shoulder, "before anybody else tries to shoot me for a bandit."

He followed Poke Tyler into the post, a low-ceilinged, twenty-by-forty-foot room crowded with barrels and crates, its counters groaning under the weight of pelts and skins, canned goods and bolts of cloth. The room smelled of apples and cinnamon and leather and kinnikinnick, a mixture Pop Hitner favored in his pipe. He liked to brag that his tobacco was a blend taught him by a Choctaw shaman and brought him good luck. Smoke curled upward from a couple of oil lamps and clung to the rafters in ghostly streamers. An iron kettle was hung over the fire in the hearth and a ladle stained with chili and grease dangled from a hook nearby. The table was set for one, but bowls were stacked next to the hearth and tin cups filled a shelf alongside the bowls.

"Help yourself," said the merchant behind them.

The two men needed no prompting. They ladled out steaming portions of dark-red chili. The meat was stringy, the sauce thick as lava and about the same temperature. They gulped down coffee because the scalding liquid seemed to open the pores of the tongue and wash the ferociously hot pepper juices away. Between mouthfuls of food, they told of their escape from Varela's hacienda. Johnny kept Vin's treachery to himself, and when the meal was done, Poke and Johnny eased out of the ladder-backed chairs and warmed themselves by the fire.

"You must be livin' 'cause I can't imagine no ghost puttin' that much vittles away," Hitner said with a wag of his head.

"I'm not dead. Who said I was?" Johnny asked. He was beginning to feel uneasy about the merchant's remarks.

"Vin Cotter. At least so I was told. He saw you die himself, the way Joe Briscoe, Cotter's foreman, told it. Vin himself saw you jabbed full of Mexican lances, like a granny's pincushion."

Johnny glanced over at Poke, then at Pop Hitner. The merchant read something he didn't like in the man's expression. "Looks like Vin was wrong," Pop added.

"Looks like," said Johnny, keeping his tone even, devoid of emotion.

"Everett will sure be happy to see you. Weren't no one more forlorn than him when he heard the news!"

"Just think how it'll cheer him now," said Poke.

Thunder sounded. Hitner glanced at the ceiling as if it were the sky. "Damn rain. We've had enough to last the spring I'll say. You boys better rest up. I'll bring your horses around into the barn and give them each a bait of oats."

Johnny shoved away from the fireplace and walked across the room to a table piled high with shirts and trousers; some were new, others, castoffs left by Lord knew who. The young man chose a couple of plaid shirts and a pair of Levi's that looked to be his size, just barely. He wouldn't have to roll up the cuffs.

"While you're at it, Pop, take a look at my saddle, the one with the silver inlay. See if you'll take it in trade for an outfit. We'll need some food, a change of these duds, and maybe a gun or rifle. What you can't trade maybe you'll take my credit."

"I always have, lad," Pop said. The merchant hurried toward the door, hoping to beat the coming storm. "Take what you need, we'll see how it settles up when I get back. You two stay the night if you've a mind. Plenty of room for a couple of bedrolls near the fire."

"I want to get an early start," Johnny said. "I'm hoping to reach the Bonnet by the day after tomorrow. Ought to make it if I don't stop in San Antonio."

Pop Hitner halted in his tracks and slapped his thigh.

"I'm a darn fool. Good thing you mentioned it. Ride to the Bonnet and you won't find no one there. Everett's brought the whole blame crew and household into San Antonio for the wedding tomorrow. He's throwing a fiesta that the whole blame town's invited to. Really done it up right. I'd go myself, but I got no one to watch the place."

"Who's wedding?"

"Why, Everett's boy, of course. Vin Cotter. Oh, but you couldn't know, I reckon. Vin's got him the prettiest gal this side of the Sabine."

"Rose," Johnny said, the name catching in his throat as the premonition choked the breath from him.

"That's her," said Pop. "Rose McCain."

3

★

Golden was her hair in golden candlelight. And every man in the chapel of San Gabriel Mission envied Vin Cotter as he stood before Father Vicente waiting for Rose McCain, who walked toward him in procession with an entourage of colorfully dressed young *señoritas*.

Everett Cotter, proud patriarch, led his future daughter-in-law, her arm in his. Rose, Everett thought; what a fitting name, such an aptly titled beauty. Her shoulders, revealed by the scooped white silk bodice of her wedding dress, were the color of cream. High cheekbones, a long neck, and yellow-gold hair gathered in thick curls, caught at the nape of her neck by a length of white ribbon; her delicate features framed brown eyes flecked with gold, introspective now but capable of flashing fire. A sheer silk veil covered her head and face to the length of her tall willowy frame (she could look her future husband square in the eye) and trailed in a diaphanous billow to the stone floor. The other *señoritas*, in their gay cotton dresses—ice blues and wild crimson stitchery, yellow flowers and umber—were, for all their loveliness, lesser flowers to this garden's single Texas rose.

A thunderclap shook the stone, startling Cotter's guests.

The aristocracy of San Antonio filled the front pews. Here were merchants and bankers and fellow ranchers, many of Spanish descent, who had traveled more than a day to be at the wedding. Everett Cotter wasn't the kind of man whose invitation one turned down without a first-rate excuse. Cotter didn't look all that imposing. He was short and rather beefy; white hair, close cropped at the collar of his shirt, swept back from his high forehead, bushy sideburns framing his blunt, perspiration-streaked features. He had a barrel chest, short thick arms, and eyes like strong coffee— deep brown and almost lusterless. Even in his finery, a tailored Mexican jacket and trousers of forest-green embroidered with silver thread and high-topped boots of Spanish leather, Everett Cotter seemed more the yeoman with calloused hands and dirt beneath his fingernails than the monarch of his own kingdom. Cotter's ranch, encompassing twenty square miles of prime grazing land, was bordered on the east by the San Antonio River.

If Everett looked about ready to strangle in such formal attire, young Vin appeared wholly at ease, as one cut out for the accoutrements of wealth and station. His clean-cut features had healed from his foray into Mexico. He looked princely in the deep purples of his waistcoat and tight, Spanish trousers sporting swirls of black embroidery. Vin left the physical labor of running the ranch to Joe Briscoe and the ranch hands hired for that purpose. He enjoyed a good hunt; he had learned the importance of paperwork, had mapped the countryside with the idea of adding to the Cotter domain, and, most important of all, had courted Rose McCain. His sharply handsome face, so unlike Everett's, beamed with pleasure as Rose walked toward him from the side of the church.

A Tejas servant moved behind Rose in the shadows, lighting banks of candles to dispel the gloom seeping in through the stained windows of San Gabriel. Rose came to a halt at the altar and stood beside Vin Cotter, Everett on her left side.

In flickering candlelight the priest and his altar servers, Indian children with cherubic nut-brown faces, and the sanctuary itself took on a dreamlike appearance. Rose struggled to listen as the priest instructed them, reading from holy scripture, as he spoke of the sanctity of marriage. Vin knelt and she took that for a cue and knelt also, but her mind refused to hold to one single thought. She was marrying Vin Cotter. This was the most important day of her life . . . of any girl's life. But it wasn't. Most important—yes, more than any other day—was the time Vin returned from war . . . poor haggard Vin all but collapsing into his father's arms, poor brave desperate Vin with his account of Johnny Anthem's heroic death: how Vin and Johnny had faced down the Mexican dragoons and fought their attackers to a standstill, how Johnny, wounded and dying, passed the reins of his black mare to Vin and begged him not to stay behind to be killed, but to ride to Texas, to carry his last words to Everett and Rose.

Rose looked down at her white arm, sensitive fingers clasped in Vin's small, almost feminine hands. His grasp was painfully firm, as if he never intended to let her go. Rose heard the rumble of thunder coming closer still, and prayed the rain might pass them by so as not to ruin the grand fiesta Everett had planned in San Antonio. Ten beeves had been slaughtered and casks of wine and whiskey brought in from Galveston. Tables were to line a section of Military Plaza right in front of Karl Schilken's elegant hotel. The German proprietor had reserved a suite for the newlyweds away from the street, to ensure privacy for their first night.

The first night . . . Rose closed her eyes. She felt no desire for Vin. He had been kind and solicitous and even endearing, and she would make him a good wife in every

way she could, including as bedmate. But her heart held
no passion. In truth, she worried more about Everett's
happiness. He had given her so much. And with Johnny
gone . . . granting Everett's most-sought-after wish seemed
little enough to do. And Everett Cotter seemed happy, despite his obvious desire to be rid of his tight collar. In truth,
he wasn't a man given to riding the hard spine of a church
pew. More than his neck aches, I'll warrant, Rose thought,
and chuckled aloud but caught herself and looked up, embarrassed.

The padre stared at her in a most perplexed manner, his
eyebrows arching with disapproval. Vin glanced aside.
Rose lowered her gaze and concentrated on the ceremony.
Composure regained, she looked up at the crucifix that
hung above the altar. A wedding blessed by God . . . She
didn't take the seriousness of her vows lightly, but her spirit
was a bit wild . . . like Johnny's. A tear formed in the corner of her eye and left a glistening trail on her cheek. Thunder rumbled.

The priest began, "Do you Vin Cotter take this
woman . . ."

And of course, he did.

"Right fine wedding," Joe Briscoe said as he joined Everett
Cotter at the carriage in front of the church. Briscoe had
ridden to Texas with Everett Cotter. He had been sergeant
under Captain Everett Cotter during the Texas Rebellion.
He was Cotter's foreman now, his right-hand man. Segundo, to the ranch hands. Hell unleashed in a brawl, Briscoe was somber and God-fearing the rest of the time. Other
men of the Bonnet filed past them, heading for their
horses—hardworking men for whom ceremony was an important part of their lives.

"See you at the fandango, Mr. Cotter," one of the men
called.

"Right purty doin's," another joined in. The ranch hands laughed and slapped one another on the back and hurried to mount up, eager to reach the fiesta. These were men with the look of range riders about them, hard men in threadbare finery come to honor one they respected. The Bonnet represented home and country to them, and such men rode for the brand. To Everett Cotter they owed supreme loyalty. And since his fingers were as grimed, his palms as callous-hardened as any of theirs, these men might have owed loyalty but they gave him their affection freely.

Everett took time to thank each man for coming and took care to repeat an invitation to each one of his riders to the fiesta in town.

After the wranglers came the more genteel of San Antonio's citizenry. Landowners and grandees, men of business and station with their wives in tow, demure and gracious women dressed in flowing gowns of Spanish cut, lace and veils. Cotter spoke to each and extended his hospitality.

Joe Briscoe waited for the last of the ranch hands to saddle up and head for town. "Don't seem right not to hurrah the newlyweds into town," he mentioned.

"Vin said he'd ride in with her, just the two of them," Cotter said. "They wanted to be alone for the first few minutes."

"Kinda takes the fun out of it," Briscoe muttered. He stood taller than his boss, in worn black breeches. His unruly brown hair was hidden beneath his sombrero. He reached under his black frock coat and took out his bible. Wind gusted in the courtyard of the mission. A couple of Tejas Indian children scurried out from around a jacal near the priest's house, but were brought up sharply as their mother called them back. A heavyset dark-skinned woman wearing a brightly patched skirt filled the doorway to the adobe hut. The children turned a deaf ear to their mother and stood, hand in hand, gawking at the men and women in their finery as they climbed into their carriages to ride away.

"I should like to read a verse over Vin and Rose," Briscoe said. "To sort of bless their marriage like."

"Vin figures Father Vicente did a fine job already," Everett replied.

"It was me learned them their bible lessons," Briscoe said. "Vin and Rose and Johnny." Briscoe looked up at the stone walls of the church. Above, sighting just past roofline, an army of thunderclouds marched in phalanx, encircling the sun. "I may not be a sky pilot no more but that doesn't mean me and the good book ain't got nothing to say."

"Vin said to tell you no," Everett answered gently. His segundo had a way with prayer. It had been the foreman who read the words over Lilly Cotter's grave when the sickness took her.

"If it was Johnny, he would have wanted me to read over them both," Briscoe said, a touch of indignation in his voice.

"Vin isn't Johnny," Everett snapped. He immediately regretted his tone. Briscoe was an old friend.

Cotter had mourned John Anthem's death as much as any man. But he resented the comparisons the men of the Bonnet had begun to make between Vin and Johnny. It wasn't fair. Vin was cut from different cloth.

Briscoe turned and started toward his horse. His boots thudded on the stone walk. His broad shoulders slouched forward as the foreman slipped the bible back inside his coat. He had never won an argument with Everett Cotter in his life; he doubted this day would be any different. Briscoe swung aboard the dun mare he had ridden from the ranch and was surprised to find Everett saddling up right alongside him, easing himself astride a bold-eyed brown gelding.

"Vin doesn't want me to wait either," Everett explained. "He's a peculiar lad, but right or wrong, he is my son. My son. And one day he'll give me grandchildren. And the Bonnet will grow and prosper. I want to see the next generation, to hold it in my arms, to know everything I have worked for will last. Can you understand what I am trying to say, Joe?"

Joe nodded. He understood. More than Cotter suspected. "I gave up trying to be immortal years ago, Mr. Cotter. Maybe it would be different if I had something to pass along. Me . . . I'm just a segundo." He ran a hand over the pereptual stubble that time had sprinkled with ashen gray. "I'm heading back to the Bonnet."

"Nonsense. Come on in to town."

"Someone ought to stay at the ranch. Leland Rides Horse can't run things by himself."

"He should have come on with us."

"No tame Apache in his right mind would be caught dead in San Antone. Not at some fiesta with a bunch of likkerd-up ranch hands for company. I'll head back and keep him company. Vin won't miss me. That I do know, Mr. Cotter." Briscoe pulled on the reins, turning the mare in the direction of the mission gate.

Cotter reached out and caught the mare's bridle. "Joe Briscoe, you are as thin-skinned as a jaybird stallion." Everett grinned.

The light faded as storm clouds marched across the bone-white sun and the wind kicked up, whipping the loose gravel and chips of dried clay against the horses' legs. A dust devil danced in a freshly tilled garden plot a dozen strides to the left. Father Vicente exited from a side door and waved to the two men before continuing on to the carriage shed.

"I'll see you in town, my friends," he shouted.

"Just pray the rain holds off," Everett yelled back.

The padre waved again and, lifting the hem of his brown robes, scampered in a most undignified fashion the remaining distance to the carriage shed as half a dozen large drops of rain fell on the dry earth.

"Damn," muttered Everett Cotter. Almost on command the shower ceased, but the patriarch of the Bonnet breathed no sigh of relief, for the thunder continued to roll its promise of unpleasantness to come, as the great cloud peaks overhead pulsed with electric life.

"See you back at the hacienda," Briscoe said.

"I want you at the fiesta," Everett replied sternly, impatient with the foreman's stubbornness. The two men locked eyes in an unspoken contest. But Everett was too fond of his segundo to break the man's pride. He added, and gently, "Please, my old friend."

Briscoe nodded at last. "In San Antone." Any man who seemed to command the weather was best obeyed.

Cotter and his segundo touched spurs to the flanks of their horses and the animals responded with a brisk trot. The men rode from the mission courtyard out onto the Camino Real. Following the road east, they headed toward the gaily lit sprawl of businesses and homes of brick, wood, and adobe, east toward the cypress- and cottonwood-lined streets and plazas of the century-old city of San Antonio de Bexar.

Vin Cotter watched his father and the segundo turn their horses on to the Camino Real and sighed softly to himself. Alone at last. Then a door behind him opened and he swung around to watch as Rose emerged from a dressing room beyond the bleak chamber.

Rose McCain. His Rose now. Guilt was an ember striving to flare within his heart. For a moment he thought of Johnny, but only for a moment. Life was surviving. To live sometimes meant to act swiftly and surely. Vin had mastered his destiny, he had won a beautiful woman for himself, and what was next?

The Bonnet itself.

Rose finished tying the last bow at her throat. Her wedding dress was hidden beneath the dark-blue folds of her traveling cloak. A matching bonnet shadowed her features.

"Vin . . . I'm ready."

Vin Cotter looked at her, appraising his heart's obsession, his triumph. He regretted nothing. That was the problem with victory. Once a man beheld his prize, the path to his triumph was often allowed to become overgrown and obscured by weeds of necessity. Vin smiled at his own metaphor.

"I wasn't born to be a gardener," he mused aloud. Rose stared at him, perplexed by this sudden revelation. Vin realized his mistake and shrugged, deciding he preferred to be thought of as a man of mystery. He crossed the clay-tile floor, his boots clicking on the fired surface. Then he took Rose in his arms and felt her stiffen as his arms closed around her. She relaxed as he whispered his love for her.

"I'll be a good husband to you, Rose. And we'll have a wonderful life. You'll be my queen, I promise, and you'll want for nothing."

"I want us to be happy, Vin. That's all. Just happy—"

His lips bruised hers, his kiss cutting short her reply. She responded, closing her eyes, her thoughts haunted by other memories, another man's face. Sweet Jesus, help me, a voice cried from within. Vin had been kind and supportive. He was bitter from standing in his father's shadow, but she knew she could help him find his own path. She must learn to love him. All she needed was time. She must learn to love, to hold him in her arms and not hunger for an impossible dream.

Thunder rumbled.

Wind moaned in the chimney.

A cold, spare room with an empty floor, its stone walls unadorned save for a single crucifix, ladder-back chairs hanging from the walls, split timber near the hearth. A small gray mouse stood motionless, watchful in the woodpile. There was nothing to keep them here.

"Come," Vin said, and he took Rose by the arm and led her to the side door into the bleak light of noon. She gasped at the menacing thunderheads rolling out of the north. The sky overhead was a blanket of gunmetal gray pushed downward by the savage-looking storm on the horizon to the north. A distant downpour hung like a shroud across the Camino Real.

"It looks as if we'll get a bath on our way to San Antonio," Rose sighed.

"Then lucky for us we aren't going into town," Vin said, leading her over to his carriage with its pair of roan geldings in harness.

"Aren't going?" Rose drew back, but Vin insisted and helped her up into the carriage. She scooted over and he climbed up beside her.

"That's right," Vin said.

"But the fiesta—"

"I don't intend to have our marriage demeaned by allowing us to be hurrahed by a bunch of drunken ranch hands."

"But your father?"

"My father included," Vin firmly replied. He placed a hand on her arm. "Let them have their celebration. I have arranged our own. Roasted quail, apple pie, and a fancy Bordeaux from father's own stock. And, of course, privacy. We'll have all of the Bonnet, my beloved, to ourselves." He kissed her neck, nuzzled behind her ear, and whispered, "My queen."

Vin took the whip from its brass ring and cracked the tip above the heads of the two roans. Rose started to protest anew but held her tongue. However hurt Everett might be, Vin was her husband now. And his mind was made up. He'd planned this from the beginning. She was his wife and would have to go along.

Vin steered the carriage away from the mission, through the gates, and onto the Camino Real, heading away from San Antonio. Rose glanced over her shoulder, around the edge of the canopy at the veil of rain blocking the way east. Rose needed the fiesta, the gaiety of friends and neighbors, to offset the sudden yet familiar sadness that colored what was supposed to be one of the happiest days in her life. By marrying Vin she had at last buried Johnny—or at least interred the possibility that somehow everyone was wrong: that Johnny Anthem had not died in Mexico, that he would somehow return to her.

The hope for one future was ended. The reality of another had only just begun. But in such a transition there are always tears.

Tears to fall like rain.

4

★

Rose winced as thunder seemed to shake the carriage. She held the cloak in her tight fists as protection from the elements. Rain buffeted the carriage and whipped about the canopy to claw at the newly married couple huddling together for warmth. Vin's wedding attire, purple and black-embroidered jacket and trousers, offered him little insulation against the downpour and the wintry wind.

The road was barely visible in the torrent, the hills obscured beyond the sheets of water unfurled from the foreboding sky. The Camino Real was barely passable; the wheel-rutted path to the ranch would be a mad undertaking. They had traveled, in three exhausting hours, what they should have managed in one. The geldings fought Vin every step of the way, threatening to bolt with each ear-splitting cannonade and every salvo fired by the storm. The air reeked and trees split and crashed to earth, broken by the storm, limbs crushed beneath the weight of the ravaged trunks.

"We'll have to wait this out," Vin shouted above the din.

"Apache Cave isn't too far," Rose shouted back. She and Johnny and Vin had explored the shallow hole in the wall often, in happier times, in the innocent days of youth.

"I remember the way," Vin shouted back. On the slopes around them, juniper, ash, and oak bowed in the wind's embrace. Water coursed through the gulleys and raged like tiny rivers. Vin tried to get his bearing, cursing himself for braving the elements. They should have waited the storm out at the mission. Or headed into San Antonio. Then at least they wouldn't be stuck out here alone in the hill country. The hotel boasted a good sturdy roof. And hot coffee. And warm beds.

A spray of water lashed his naked cheek. Vin swore aloud and wiped his face on the soaked arm of his jacket. Where in hell was the turn-off to Apache Cave? He thought he recognized a trail to the left. It was impossible to tell for sure . . . Yes, he knew it. The fury of the storm eased for a moment, and he managed to identify just exactly how far along the Camino Real he and Rose had traveled. He judged the cave to be another five miles as the crow flies. But without wings, it would take them longer. He recalled some tricky crossings and was resolved to walk the last mile or so. Still, it was a better alternative than continuing on into the storm for the rest of the day, and still winding up ten miles shy of the Bonnet.

Rose's grip tightened on his arm. Vin looked ahead, following her gaze, and saw the figure blocking their path in the road. It was a man astride a weary-looking gray stallion. A large man wrapped in a serape. His head was downcast and rivulets of water poured from the brim of his sombrero. Was this a madman blocking the road? A bandit? Vin realized with a sickening tightness in his gut that he was unarmed. He grabbed the whip from its holder on the side of the carriage and swore he would answer any command to pull up with a lash across the stranger's face.

The figure in the road didn't move. Vin called out to the man and shouted for him to stand to one side of the road, and still the figure did not move. Vin pulled back on the reins a moment.

"Hey, you there. Well? Are you thunderstruck?"

Still no reply.

"Vin, go around him," Rose cautioned, a premonition growing in her mind that the stranger was more than he seemed.

"The ground falls away, it's too steep and the earth is treacherous," Vin snapped. He stood, balancing his foot against the splash board, and brought the whip down smartly across the backsides of his geldings. The animals lunged forward. Vin was thrown back in his seat. The carriage skidded in the mud and, gaining speed, bore down on the figure, who moved at last, but not out of the way. He tilted his head to face the oncoming carriage. A hundred feet, fifty, twenty-five. The rain lost its intensity enough for both occupants in the carriage to recognize the stranger.

"Johnny!" Rose cried out, startled, unable to believe her eyes. It couldn't be! My God, it was. The same face, his face—Johnny Anthem alive! Rose brought her hand to her mouth and gasped, then tried to pull at the reins, but Vin shoved her aside.

Anthem alive? No. Impossible. How? Vin had come to believe his own story; he'd woven a fiction he could live with out of the fantasy of the past. Anthem alive. And come to kill him. He saw the revolver under the serape gripped in his hand.

Vin's courage failed him. He gave the reins a savage yank to the left and the geldings turned off the road and descended the eight-foot embankment at a gallop. Wheels slid, mud gave way, the carriage lurched to the left. Thunder boomed loudly enough to wake the dead. A tongue of lightning lapped a nearby oak and split the trunk in half with a resounding crack. Wood shrieked and splinters flew away and smoke billowed in the rain-logged air. The geldings neighed in terror, lost their footing, and went down. The right wheel shot upward. Rose fell against Vin, and then past him. Vin heard her scream and braced himself as the carriage overturned completely, muffling his own scream.

Rose landed on a clump of muddy grass, rolled on her shoulder, and slammed up against a length of deadwood. She took a nasty blow to the head in the process. Vision fractured into a montage of lowering clouds, cold heavy raindrops pelting her cheek, and Johnny Anthem looking down at her, concern on his features, tenderness in his voice. She heard herself speak his name. "Johnny."

He nodded and knelt at her side. "Wild Yellow Rose," he gently said.

She closed her eyes and he couldn't tell if she had heard him. He stood and walked over to the carriage, drawing his knife. A few seconds later he had cut the roan geldings free of their traces and led them away from the wreckage. Then he returned to the overturned carriage and, lifting the corner, managed to work Vin's unconscious form to safety.

Johnny propped Vin against the side of the gully, drew his revolver, and aimed it at him. But he stood there, in the rain, again a figure of inaction, more statue than man. His hand tightened only so far on the trigger, and no farther. Vin deserved to die but Johnny would not be judge, jury, and executioner. He had lived nine months for this one moment, and now it was lost to him forever. He squeezed the trigger and the revolver bucked in his hand, blowing a hole in the mud above Vin's head. Smoke stung his nostrils and lingered for a moment before the rain washed it away.

Johnny holstered the Colt and walked back toward Rose. She was all that mattered to him now. He checked her breathing, then gathered the sleeping woman in his arms. Her bonnet fell away and golden ringlets spilled over and down across his cradling arm. The lightning-blasted oak burned no fiercer than the fire in his heart as Johnny carried Rose in his arms out of the shallow ravine. And her pulse beat close to his. So close, their hearts might have easily been one.

5

★

Rose McCain Cotter woke with the downpour droning in the night. Gingerly she probed the cut on her forehead, and as her vision cleared, the crude paintings on the cave wall beside her shimmered into stark relief. Three braves were locked in a deadly struggle with what appeared to be a large brown bear. The animal had raised up on its hind legs and threatened the hunters with fang and claw. One hunter brandished bow and arrows, another a war lance twice the length of the man who wielded it. Several arrows already jutted from the defiant beast. Blood dripped from its claws and it towered over a fallen brave whose unnaturally elongated body was torn and broken.

Rose had seen this cave painting countless times as a young girl. And now as a woman. Then the memory of the carriage wreck and what had caused it came rushing back to her. Turning her back to the wall, she realized suddenly, as the serape covering her brushed against her nipples, that she was naked. Her wedding garments hung on makeshift branch racks near a campfire that blazed in the middle of the limestone chamber. She gasped and, facing the campfire, saw Johnny Anthem beyond the flames and trailing smoke drawn back to the rear of the cave and a narrow

cleft in the limestone ceiling overhead. He slouched against
the wall, a slim black cigarillo dangling from his lips, a
pinprick of ruby light glowing at it tip. His long red hair
curled at the base of his neck. His expression was watchful,
rebellious as he studied the storm from the mouth of
Apache Cave.

Flashes of electricity crisscrossed the heavens and outlined a rolling landscape of juniper- and mesquite-covered
hills. A fierce wind sucked the tobacco smoke out into the
dark. A watery cascade plummeted from the lip of the cave
opening like a miniature waterfall. Johnny watched without
expression. His gunbelt and holster were hung from a fist-
sized knob of limestone. He wore no shirt and his sun-
bronzed torso was streaked with jagged furrows of scarred
flesh, the legacy of his imprisonment south of the Rio
Grande.

The horses at the rear of the cave nickered and pawed
at the pitiful helpings of dried grass some previous visitor
had left. Johnny glanced around toward the shadowy shapes
tethered at the rear where the chamber opened into a spacious room whose domed ceiling bristled with stalactites.
He noticed Rose, raised up on her elbows, her features pale
and bloodless-looking. He had provided her a pallet of
blankets and covered her with his shirt and serape after
stripping away her sodden clothes. The breath caught in his
throat even now at the memory of her supine naked body.
The serape fell away and the round white mound of her
breast showed in the firelight. She appeared not to notice,
was only capable of staring at the one love of her life returned from the grave. Johnny crushed the glowing end of
his cigarillo against the rain-drenched rocks framing the
arched opening and tossed the smoking stub into a pool of
rainwater.

"Rose," he said softly.

The ghost spoke—Johnny's voice, just as she remembered in her dreams! I'm mad, lost in madness, she told herself. The dancing light made the floor and walls pulse crazily. She couldn't speak. He was dead. Forever lost to her. He was . . . alive.

Alive.

Johnny walked across the rocky floor, his bare feet padding soundlessly. He stepped around the fire and knelt by her side. He leaned down and kissed the petal-pink crown of her breast, sliding his hand up to cup the full sweet softness of her flesh. He raised his head then and looked deep in her eyes.

Alive.

No specter of the night, no haunter of the dark. John Anthem, alive, her Johnny. Desire propelled her upward to wrap him in a hungry, desperate embrace. Rose clung to him, wanting him more than anything in her life, wanting his flesh inside her, wanting their bodies to meld together in the firelight, to lose herself in the furious seas of ecstasy. His kisses seemed to draw the breath from her body, yet he could be her breath. If her heart raged to the bursting point, no matter—his was enough for them both.

As he moved atop her, brushing the blankets aside and lowering himself until he lay alongside her body, Rose opened her eyes. By the cruelest twist of fate, through tear-blurred vision, she beheld, among her garments drying by the fire, her wedding dress. She tried to look away before cruel reality ruined the moment's magical madness. She hungered for Johnny. Her need was all-consuming. It demanded her surrender. Yet her spirit ruled defiant. And as quickly as Rose had taken Johnny Anthem in her arms, her hands pushed him away and she turned aside from his savage loving kisses, each like a brand of love upon her flesh.

He raised up on his knees again. His flesh smelled of mesquite smoke and tasted of salt sweat. He didn't hide his puzzlement.

"I thought you were dead," Rose said at last. Her head had begun to ache. But the pain was nothing compared to the frustration she felt over this cruel stifling of her passions.

"And now I am alive," Johnny replied.

"But you are alive . . . too late," Rose said, her voice hardly more than a whisper. Her gaze drifted toward the wedding dress by the campfire.

Johnny turned, following her line of sight. He scowled, crawled over to the makeshift rack, and tore the dress from the branches.

"You mean this? It's only fabric. It can burn. Let the fire have it. What, then?"

"The flames cannot destroy my vows." Realization dawned at last as she looked around. A bride and widow in the same day? "Where's Vin?"

"I left him by the carriage." Johnny glanced down at the dress in his hands, then up at Rose. "Don't worry, I'm no widowmaker. But I left a bullet hole in the mud alongside his head, so he will know he owes me his life." He lifted the dress. "But maybe dear old Vin will have the last laugh, after all. Unless you tell me otherwise. Rose, I have come back for you. A dream kept me alive these past months. It brought me here, to you. Come away with me, Rose. We can leave in the morning, if the storm lets up."

Her heart soared at the offer, her mind reeled with the possibility and the joy of being with him. What were words anyway? Vin had told her Johnny was dead. Had he lied to her? She didn't understand. Nothing made sense anymore. Sweet saints, what am I thinking? I'm married. I'm Vin Cotter's wife. Yet only because I thought Johnny was dead. Leave with him, then. But would it kill Everett? She owed him her life. As did Johnny. She had spoken the words, made her vows before almighty God. The fact that she could even consider leaving with Johnny shamed her.

But she couldn't help herself. Lord forgive me.

"Rose, you don't love Vin," Johnny said.

"I'll learn."

"Love isn't riding a horse, it isn't some lesson in a grammar book. You can learn to endure, but not to love." Johnny squatted down and held her hand.

She shook her head, confused. "I don't know. My head . . . hurts. Everything is jumbled. For the love of heaven, Johnny, I can scarcely believe you're here."

"I'll prove it if you let me," he said, desire in his voice. He touched her hair, his fingers brushing her cheek.

She closed her eyes and caught his hand, opened his fingers, and kissed the palm, then closed his hand into a fist. "Johnny, hold me. Just hold me."

He slid alongside her, took her in his arms, her head resting on his chest. "We'll leave tomorrow at the first break in the storm," he said, hugging her close.

Rose stared past the flames toward the sheet of water slanting across the entrance to the cave. The night held no solace, the darkness impenetrable, beyond which tomorrow was only a promise. Tomorrow, he said.

And tomorrow . . . she must tell him.

She closed her eyes and prayed for unending night.

Morning came. The sun broke through the eastern cloudbank and scoured the remaining vestiges of cloud cover from the heavens. A golden warmth flooded the cave entrance and leached the chill from the limestone chamber. Bone-weary from his ride, Johnny Anthem had slept deeply, oblivious to the tension in the woman he held. Now his arms were empty. The sensation alerted his subconscious mind, the sound of hooves glancing off the limestone floor lifted him to wakefulness. He rolled over on his side, was blinded by the light, and squinted to escape the glare.

His vision cleared in time to see Rose McCain leading one of the horses out of the cave.

Johnny rolled to his feet, across the ashes of the campfire, and hurried outside. Rose was a dozen steps away, leading a bay mare down the rocky incline to the trail below. As Johnny emerged from the cave, Rose saw him and started to mount up. Johnny covered the distance at a run. Rose jerked on the reins of her animal. The mare pulled at her grasp, its hooves sliding on the gravel underfoot. Rose's wedding dress hampered her movement as it caught at her legs, and Johnny reached her as she began to swing her leg over the horse. She pulled herself upward, Johnny yanked back, and the two of them tumbled head over heels down the incline to the bank of the flooded creek below. Rose landed on her bottom and Johnny rolled atop her, pinning her shoulders to the ground. Rose didn't struggle, but closed her eyes and sighed. If only she could have stolen away and later convinced herself this had only been a dream . . .

"Johnny, don't make it harder than it already is." It was agony to look at him. Tears welled beneath her lids, but she refused to allow herself to cry. The heat of his body warmed her through the muddied lace and taffeta trimming of her dress.

"What do you think you're doing?" he said.

"Going home. And if Vin isn't there, then I'll have the hands look for him."

"I am your home. And you're mine." He lowered his lips to hers, but this time she twisted her head aside. Johnny drew away. "You said you would wait for me," he added bitterly.

There in the ravine, man and woman were hidden from the morning sun by the swaying branches of the weeping willows that clung to the creek bank. A rich melodious call bubbled down to them and Johnny shaded his eyes and spotted the brilliant-yellow plumage of a meadowlark, its slashed black V streaked across its sunbright breast. The bird serenaded the couple a moment longer, then darted from the branches of the willow and soared off toward the meadow beyond the creek.

Johnny mourned its passing beauty and the bird's lilting song left melancholy in his heart. It dawned on him, then, that he had lost more than the song of the meadowlark. His dream was lost as well. He stood and reached down and helped Rose to her feet. Her hair, unpinned, fell in molten gold curls across her shoulders, covering her bodice, spilling down her back. No, it was impossible to accuse her, or to hate her. His bitterness softened. "Rose. What has happened?"

"I'm married to Vin."

"Why?"

"I waited for you, John Anthem. Yes, I did. Until news came of your death. Even then I waited. And grieved. I wept for you, for both of us. I was like a shattered mirror trying to pull the pieces of my life together. Vin helped me through that terrible time."

"Good ol' Vin," Johnny said, his lips drawn back in a mirthless smile.

"Johnny, he thought you were dead too. Don't hate him for helping me, for caring about me. Johnny, I had to set my life in order."

"Then set it in order. Leave with me."

"I'm Vin's wife." Rose saw how her words stung him, knew they were more painful than the whip that had marked his body. "I prayed for you to return. Now—it's horrible—but I wish you never had, may God forgive me. But that's what I wish."

"I don't believe you," he gently replied. Mrs. Vin Cotter! For a moment Johnny was tempted to tell her of Vin's betrayal. He wanted to let her know just exactly the kind of man she was married to. But he remained silent, unable to bring himself to hurt her. His love ran too deep. He looked over at her, his expression hidden behind emerald shadows. "Stay here," he said. Then he turned and walked back up the slope toward the cave.

A few moments later, he emerged fully clothed buckling a gun belt around his waist. A sombrero dangled from a leather thong around his neck and covered the back of his neck and part of his shoulders. A breeze tugged at the fringes of the serape draped across his left shoulder like a faded rainbow. He led his gray mustang stallion down the slope.

Rose felt her heart leap in her breast at the sight of the young man she had loved, and lost by a single day, a fraction of a life. Her pulse beat like that of a frightened bird. And yet, already she had begun to build an inner wall to hide her love that she might remain true to honor and to the sacred wedding pact she had sealed before almighty God.

"Where will you go?" she asked, misinterpreting his intention.

"For now, with you."

"But I told you, I'm returning to the Bonnet. At least after I backtrack to the carriage to see if Vin is there."

As Rose walked over to the mare, Johnny hurried past her, picked the reins off the ground, and handed them to her. He held out his hand and helped her up onto the mare's bare back. Then he mounted and walked his horse alongside hers, allowing the animal to drink from the creek.

The sky overhead was cloudless and the pure blue of unblemished sapphire. Rose suspected an ulterior motive. But Johnny's gaze hardened, revealing nothing of heart and mind. She glanced down and was chagrined at the disarray of her wedding dress. It was spattered with mud, the lace torn, the hem a veritable shamble of its former delicately stitched glory.

"No. Not with me and not to the Bonnet," Rose said.

"Just to offer my congratulations to the groom. If he's there. After you, Yellow Rose," said Johnny, waving a hand toward the trail. His voice rang hollow in the morning air.

"But if Vin's there, he'll be furious enough at your behavior to greet you with a gun in hand, don't you . . ." Rose gasped, understanding in an instant that was precisely what Johnny Anthem must have in mind. Now she understood. Rose McCain Cotter was to be a bride and a widow in a single day after all.

"No, I refuse to let you accompany me to the Bonnet," Rose blurted out, hoping to avoid a tragedy. Johnny's hatred of Vin was unreasonable. And there was Everett to consider. His temper was as volatile as Johnny's. "Do you understand? You are not riding anywhere near the Bonnet."

"I'm afraid he hasn't much choice, ma'am," a voice called down from the ridge opposite them.

Johnny and Rose glanced up as half a dozen men skylined themselves along the bluff about fifty feet above the floor of the creekbed. They were riders from the Bonnet. Johnny might have made a break if Joe Briscoe hadn't been leading them. The segundo was a crack shot with Walker Colt or percussion rifle, arms with which all of Everett's men were equipped.

"Howdy, Johnny," Briscoe said. "Vin's at the ranch, all right. We found him wandering down the Camino Real during the storm. Told us what happened. Everett took him on to the Bonnet. Ordered me to hunt you up." The foreman glanced at the men to his right. "Bring the horses around, Angstrom."

Motioning for the others to follow him, Briscoe started down the slope, holding his rifle in the crook of his arm. His eyes never left Johnny, who wisely kept his hands in plain sight, palms crossed on his saddle horn. He waited for the foreman to step up alongside the gray. Johnny nodded to the other hands, with all of whom he was acquainted. They didn't return his greeting. He heard the horses up ahead. Their hooves clattering on the stones in the creekbed echoed throughout the ravine and preceded their arrival by a minute.

"I thought you were dead, Johnny," Briscoe said, staring toward the mouth of the ravine as Angstrom led the horses around the bend in the creekbed.

"Seems everyone did," Johnny replied.

"You might wish you were when Everett gets through with you," the segundo added.

"We'll see." Johnny turned in the saddle and looked back at Rose, who lowered her gaze. Her golden hair spilled forward, hiding her features. Johnny returned his attention to the horses up ahead. The Bonnet hands were already mounting up. And it was clear by their silence toward their prisoner they considered Johnny a traitor to the band. He had made himself a stranger to them, by his actions of the night before. And if these men he had once worked with and ridden with were hostile, what would Everett be?

Johnny exhaled slowly through a dry mouth and silently repeated to himself, "We'll see."

6

★

Everett Cotter paced the porch of the ranch house like a wild animal caged behind invisible bars. Afternoon sunlight slanted in through the western edge of the porch, transforming motes of dust into airborne flakes of gold. His eyes, red from lack of sleep, searched the road that connected the Bonnet with the Camino Real beyond a line of hills and the river to the east.

The ranch house was set almost dead center in the rolling landscape that made up the Bonnet ranch. Cattle grazed in the distance: big brawny longhorns as dangerous to work as they were awesome to look at, with horns as wide as a man could reach from tip to tip. Slash B was the brand they wore, the mark of Bonnet cattle and horses.

Everett lifted his gaze toward the outcropping of limestone that had given the ranch its name. It was a chunk of limestone twenty feet high that crowned a hillock and had been shaped by wind and rain into the shape of a woman's bonnet. A grave plot was located at the base of the knoll and a white tombstone shone in the light of afternoon, Lilly's grave.

Everett paused in his pacing, calling out to his wife in

his mind while focusing on the tombstone at the base of the hill.

Lilly, he betrayed me. Johnny Anthem . . . I took him in. I gave him a home. Raised him as my own. And wept at the news of his death. And now this. He betrays me. Attacks my own son, steals his wife. Betrays . . .

"Mr. Cotter, you give the word, the men are ready to ride," Leland Rides Horse Robinson said from the foot of the steps leading down into the muddy yard. Behind him, fifty yards away, a dozen riders for the brand waited in front of the long low-roofed bunkhouse. Three other ranch hands led fresh horses over from the corral to join the rest of the crew, who were rolling smokes and finishing their coffee by the bunkhouse. Leland Rides Horse was a dark-skinned half-breed whose mother, Cordelia Robinson, had been rescued from captivity among the Apaches by a troop of Rangers. They had brought her and her son to the Bonnet, where Cordelia acted as cook and housekeeper. Leland had matured into an expert horseman, but he was a moody young man, always looking for the slight, often finding insult where none was intended.

"Well?" Cotter snapped. " 'Bout time those boys drifted in from San Antone."

The young half-breed tucked his hands into the back pockets of his faded cotton trousers. His boots were scuffed, mud-stained, and scratched at the toes. A Walker Colt was tucked in the red sash circling his waist. He wore a vest cut from serape cloth over his sweat-stained blousy shirt.

"Maybe Briscoe will have some luck," Leland observed softly. "I still think we ought to wait for him, if you want my opinion, Mr. Cotter." Black hair held in place by a strip of calico hung to his shoulders. He was short, slightly bow-legged, long-armed. He nodded to his mother, who appeared in the doorway.

A rotund, pretty woman in her early forties, Cordelia wore her long brown hair gathered in a bun at the back of her head. Her hands were dusted white with flour. The odor of freshly kneaded bread dough clung to her apron and flesh. "I heard horses," she said.

"It's just the last of the men come in from the fiesta," Everett snapped, more angrily than he had intended. He noticed Leland bridle at the tone. The half-breed allowed no one to treat his mother with disrespect. His deep-set eyes narrowed, his jawline hardened.

Everett wasn't afraid of Leland, but he regretted his sharpness. Cordelia meant no harm. During the few years since the death of Everett's wife, Cordelia had become an integral part of the Bonnet ranch. "How's my son, Cordie?" he asked in a softer voice.

Leland relaxed. Cordelia appeared not to have noticed the tension. Her concern for Vin overrode any sense of ego or thin-skinned pride.

"*Madre de Dios*, Vin sleeps like a baby. He still has some fever, though. But I think it will pass." She blessed herself. "How could this thing happen? Poor Vin. And Johnny was such a good boy. Those two were like brothers. Maybe Vin was wrong, it was someone else. Or a ghost." She blessed herself again.

Everett was no longer looking at her. His gaze was riveted on a distant plume of dust trailing upward against the stark blue sky. He walked over to a nearby rocking chair and grabbed a spyglass off the seat, fearing to trust in unaided eyesight. He steadied his hand, balanced the glass on a forearm as he leaned against a wooden post supporting the corner of the porch roof. Half a dozen riders swam into focus as he squinted through the glass. Eight riders in spring light—six were men of the Bonnet crew, and among them, a man and a woman. Cotter recognized Joe Briscoe's bay in the lead. The woman had hair like spun gold.

"How could such a thing happen, Cordelia? We'll find out." Everett lowered the spyglass and looked across at the housekeeper. "Soon." He turned to Leland. "Tell the men Joe Briscoe is coming in. Tell them to stay put, then join me at the corral." He glanced back at the housekeeper. "Better stay inside, Cordie."

Leland trotted off toward the bunkhouse, unable to hide his excitement.

Cordelia's round cherubic face grew serious. "Everett, don't forget . . . Johnny was like a son to you, like you had two boys." She wiped her hands on her apron and took a step toward him.

"Was, Cordie. Was." Everett stepped off the porch. "Do as you're told." He walked across the yard toward the barn. He tugged at the waistband of his woolen trousers and hooked a thumb in his suspenders as he slogged his way over toward the corral.

By the time Everett reached the fencing, Briscoe and his men were less than half a mile away.

The day hung quiet, the sun a bright sphere against a cerulean backdrop. Along the banks of the San Antonio River, a grove of sandbar willows and white oaks trembled in a passing spring breeze that moments later brushed against Everett's stony expression without tempering his unforgiving countenance.

Although he appeared impassive in his vigil, Everett's mind reeled with memories. It was young Johnny who had earned the respect of the Bonnet drovers. While Vin had stayed behind with Lilly, Johnny, all of thirteen years old, had begged Everett to take him along on the cattle drive to New Orleans, where Texas beef was shipped to the East Coast. Everett Cotter still remembered how the youth had worked hard as any drover, how he drove himself without complaint. Like a son, Cordie had said. Yes . . . but not of Cotter blood. Images of long ago were replaced by more recent memories. Of riding down the Camino Real after Vin and Rose had failed to arrive at the fiesta, of finding Vin, rain-soaked and battered and near delirious, stumbling along the road back to the mission. His only son, beaten, and Rose stolen away by a resurrected Johnny Anthem— no doubt insane with jealousy. Whatever joy Everett Cotter might have felt at Johnny's return had been crushed by his behavior. It was a wrong that demanded retribution. Cotter frowned and rubbed a calloused hand across his face. It was hard to cast aside the love and pride of yesterday. But Johnny's act was a betrayal of the past. He had repaid kindness with treachery.

Everett could feel the attention of the men by the bunkhouse, their eyes boring into him. He knew they were wondering just what he would say and do. It was a good question, one for which he had no answer.

7

★

"New bunkhouse," Johnny observed.

"Old one burned down. Struck by lightning about six months ago," Briscoe replied.

A mile distant, in the slanted sunlight of afternoon, the Cotter homestead seemed to beckon in the warmth. Johnny found the welcome suspect. It was apt to be a lot warmer than anticipated. Taking Rose had been a foolish move. But seeing her with Vin, he'd been unable to control himself. He'd been sure she would run away with him. But Johnny had forgotten in the passion of the moment that Rose McCain was a woman of honor as well as beauty. Both were qualities he loved, Johnny thought with bitter amusement.

"New wing on the ranch house," he noted, squinting in the brilliant sunlight. The land slowly dried beneath the warming sky.

"For Vin and me," Rose said softly from behind him. Johnny turned in the saddle, his eyes staring into hers. He slowed his horse in an attempt to bring her up alongside him. Rose felt drawn toward those icy depths. She couldn't deny her love for him. Not yet. But she would learn; she must.

"None of that," Briscoe ordered tersely. He caught the reins of Johnny's gray. The foreman led horse and rider back to the front of the column. Johnny's hand drifted to his waist, but Briscoe had taken the younger man's Walker Colt before they left the Apache Cave area. Anthem's revolver was tucked behind the hand-tooled leather belt circling the foreman's waist.

"There's other changes too," Briscoe remarked. "Mr. Cotter's bought up papers on Duck Craynor's place. There's good grazing there in the riverbottoms. And the cattle have bred well. They ought to bring a pretty penny in New Orleans. Yes, Johnny, plenty of changes. But the good book says, 'To every thing there is a purpose.' So, what's your purpose, Johnny Anthem?"

"I thought I knew, Segundo." He glanced back around at Rose, who lowered her head. "I thought I knew."

Closer now, Johnny recognized the crowd of men gathered around the oaken tables and bench seats set out in the yard in front of the bunkhouse, where the ranch hands took their meals on warm sunny days. Johnny had many good memories spent in the company of such men, trading lies, daydreaming of pretty girls and someday a place of his own, matching drink for drink of hard liquor, watching the fireflies drift and dart like the living jewels of the night. It had been a good life. Once it had even been enough. Now, it never would be. Not until he had Rose with him again.

Someday, he vowed silently.

By abducting Rose, Johnny had ridden against the brand. The men around him were suddenly strangers. And none more so than the one waiting for him in the corral: Everett Cotter. Brawny arms rested on the top rail, white hair gleamed like a patch of snow in sunlight. Everett was a man whose innate kindness and generosity seemed forever at cross purposes with a temperament akin to that of a powder keg in a house fire. Johnny had borne the brunt of more than one explosion in the past, as had Vin and every other rider for the Bonnet. But such confrontations began and ended in a few brief moments. Each flared up, then passed without leaving a trace of rancor in its participants.

Johnny had understood that it was just in Everett's nature to let loose now and then, especially when things weren't going his way. Everett Cotter claimed he had no use for mavericks, men accustomed to doing things their own way instead of his. Hell, Johnny thought, Everett Cotter was the worst maverick on the place.

The column of riders angled through the open gate and filed along the wheel-rutted path toward the corral. The ground was damp and red clay clung to the horses' hooves as Briscoe led his party to where Cotter stood, his elbow hooked over the top rail of fencing.

"You boys go on over and get some coffee. Reckon Chaw has some biscuits and bacon left too." Everett stepped back from the fence and hooked his thumbs in his suspenders as he stepped past Briscoe. He looked up at Rose in her mud-spattered dress.

"Are you all right, daughter?"

"Yes, Papa Rett, but let me explain, I—"

"No need to. I understand. He took you by force. There was nothing you could do. But are you really, uh, all right?"

She read his meaning then. "Yes," she replied firmly.

"Lucky for you," Everett said, fixing his dark stare on Johnny, who refused to be cowed by the intensity of his foster father.

"Please, Papa Rett, you must listen to me. This is all a—"

"Forget it, Rose," Johnny interrupted. "He cannot hear you. He's already decided what happened, and nothing you say or do is going to change his mind." Johnny looked over at her. She was near enough, he could see his reflection in her warm brown eyes, glistening now, on the verge of tears.

"He doesn't want to hear you. Or me. Go on up to the house. Your . . . husband's waiting for you." The words caught in his throat. They came out sounding harsher than he had intended.

Rose flushed, color returning to her cheeks. It was better than seeing her about to break.

"Go on to the house, girl," Everett echoed in a clipped tone.

Rose looked around her, sensing the curious scrutiny of the ranch hands. She knew what they were thinking. The way she looked, muddied and bedraggled, she didn't blame them for suspecting the worst. But what of Vin? At least he trusted her. She didn't have to worry about him.

"You hear me, girl?" Cotter said.

Rose nodded and walked her horse a few steps from the corral gate, then turned her animal to face Everett and Johnny. "No," she said. "I won't. Whatever you intend to do, Papa Rett, you do in front of me."

Everett swung around, face reddening. Then he thought better of it. The girl was as stubborn as he. "Suit yourself." He looked back at Johnny, nodded to Briscoe alongside the young man. "Get down," Everett ordered.

Johnny pursed his lips a moment, considered making a break for the trees beyond the house. He didn't think Briscoe would gun him. As for Everett, he might be angry enough, but Johnny doubted it. Anthem lifted his gaze to see a man climbing up to sit on the top rail of the corral fence.

Leland Rides Horse was another matter entirely. There was no love lost between Johnny and the breed. Johnny's parents had been murdered by Apaches while Leland's father had been killed by whites. The two men stared at each other now, and a smile crawled across Leland's dark face, a smile that held no humor, but a cruel glee at Johnny's predicament. And Johnny knew that if he made a run to the trees, Leland would shoot him down without a moment's hesitation.

"Give him his gun back, Joe," Everett said as Johnny complied with the older man's demand and dismounted. Briscoe looked at the owner in surprise. "Give him his gun back and I'll take yours, Segundo."

"Mr. Cotter, you can't." Briscoe glanced from Everett to Johnny. "This ain't right."

"You do as I say."

"Take my gun, Mr. Cotter," Leland offered in a silken voice.

"I don't want your damn gun, Rides Horse. I gave Briscoe an order," Everett snapped. His features bunched in anger, growing livid as he turned on his foreman. Briscoe took Johnny's gun belt from the saddle horn and handed the holstered weapon over to Anthem. Then Briscoe drew his own revolver and slapped the gun butt-first into Cotter's outstretched hand. He walked past Cotter, removing himself from the line of fire.

"You get over by the barn," Everett ordered. He gestured in the general direction.

"Like hell," Johnny said. "I want no part of this game."

"You bought into it when you attacked my son and stole that girl." Everett held his revolver down at his side. His hair shown silver in the sunlight. His compact powerful physique radiated determination.

"I won't fight you," Johnny said, rooted in place.

"Very well, then," Everett replied, and walked past the younger man. The owner of the Bonnet moved with quick forceful strides. When he reached the shadow of the barn, he turned again and faced Johnny across the corral at a distance of seventy feet. The smell of leather and dry hay and manure filled the older man's nostrils. It was the good smell of work waiting to be done, of another day's labors lying ahead. Of such mundane scents is the aroma of purpose comprised. Without purpose, a man's life is for naught. Everett Cotter had learned that. Johnny was just beginning to.

"We don't have to do this, Pa—Mr. Cotter."

"You shamed my name," Everett called out. "Boy, there are some things a man can't ride around."

"Bullshit. Name one thing. All it takes is a good horse," Johnny retorted.

"Maybe Johnny left his *cojones* back across the border." Leland chuckled from his perch. Johnny pretended to ignore him.

"I'll count to three," said Everett. "One . . ." Johnny held his gun belt out from his body. "Two." He dropped it at his feet. "Three." Everett whipped his revolver up and fired. The weapon bucked in his fist and a slug of leaden death burned Johnny's cheek. He winced and jerked to one side, much to Leland's amusement. Everett bore down on Anthem, the Walker Colt thundering in his grasp. A slug tore part of the gate away, another gouged chunks of moist earth from either side of Johnny's boots. Another tore a hole in his shirt and left his right shoulder streaked with blood where the lead chunk had sliced flesh.

Johnny Anthem stood a head taller than most men. His shoulders were broad from working the silver mines. He made an easy target, yet not one bullet struck home. Everett's gun clicked on an empty cylinder and then again. As he closed on Johnny, he tossed aside the smoking weapon and, lowering his head, charged like a bull with such startling speed Johnny had no time to dodge. Cotter's left shoulder dug into Anthem's stomach, driving the wind out of the bigger man and propelling him backward, where he collided with the fence. Cotter straightened and gave Johnny a savage head butt to the tip of his jaw. The world exploded for a second, becoming splinters of amber and fiery orange. Cotter backed away.

"Then with my bare hands, then. So help me," Cotter roared, closing in.

Still Johnny made no move to fight back. He raised his arms to ward off a blow and just succeeded. Then a second fist countered and caught him alongside the head, while the first returned with a vengeance, bloodying his nose and staggering him. Johnny slid along the fence for support.

"Bust him up, Mr. Cotter. Bust him good," Leland chortled, staring down at the bruised and bleeding figure staggering along the fence toward him. Suddenly Johnny reached out. His left hand caught Leland's trouser leg, the right snared him in an iron grip around the throat. Johnny lifted him high overhead and slammed him down in the middle of the corral. Johnny might not lift a hand against his foster father, but Leland Rides Horse was another matter entirely.

The breed gasped for air, the wind knocked out of him. Johnny lifted him again, this time by the scruff of his collar and the back of his sash, and charged the corral fence, battering through the post oak timbers with his human ram. Leland landed in a crumpled heap at the foot of Rose's horse, which shied away from the unconscious form. Johnny turned and caught a driving right to the jaw that rocked him over on his haunches. Johnny shook his head to clear his senses, spat blood, and lifted his gaze to Everett, who now stood a few feet from him.

"Won't anything make you fight me?" Everett said. Johnny shook his head. Cotter slapped him. Johnny shook his head. Cotter slapped him.

"No," Johnny said aloud. Cotter slapped him. And slapped him. And slapped him. "No!" He raised his hand. A gun roared and a geyser of mud spewed them both. Everett leapt back, startled.

Johnny, tears streaking his muddy cheek where the flesh still stung, glanced around to find Rose standing not more than a dozen feet from them. She held Leland's revolver in her hands.

"Enough!" She thumbed the hammer and steadied the heavy revolver. "So help me God I'll shoot the both of you if I have to." She glared at Johnny. "You won't protect yourself. You care too much and you are too damn proud." She fixed Everett in a fiery stare. "And you cannot kill him. But your pride won't let you quit." She waved the gun barrel from one to the other. "I say it's finished. Do you hear me? Finished."

Rose's lower lip trembled, and Johnny thought she would break apart in a fit of sobbing. But she was made of sterner stuff.

Everett sank to his knees and nodded as he gasped for breath. "Get out of here, Johnny Anthem. And never come back. Never," he said, breathing hard.

Johnny struggled to his feet. He steadied himself against a corral post, then walked unsteadily over to Rose. He took up his gun belt and slung it over his shoulder. He reached toward her. Rose stiffened. He plucked a torn patch of lace from her wedding dress and dabbed the blood from his lip and cut cheek. He tucked the crimson-stained swatch of finery in her sleeve at her wrist.

"So be it," he said. Their eyes met—searching, plumbing each other's depths in an intimacy few people share. Then he moved around her, mounted his gray, and rode away from the Bonnet and out of her life.

8

★

Vin Cotter poured the last of the Madeira down his throat, gulping the wine without savor or enjoyment, more like a man in the grip of thirst whose gullet is a dry, dusty land. Droplets trickled down his chin like blood oozing from the corner of his mouth. Rose had to look away as she started past him. He caught her by the arm and turned her to him.

Vin wore tight vaquero trousers and a blousy shirt open to the waist that revealed a broad white bandage covering a nasty bruise to his rib cage. He stood in his polished black boots near the dark hearth, steadied himself, swallowed, and slammed his fist down upon the wood, almost shattering the glass in his hand in the process. Then he released her. His eyes narrowed. He shuddered as he looked over at Rose and his father.

Everett's knuckles were bruised and bleeding, his silver hair in disarray, giving him a wild look that was hardly in keeping with the patriarch of the Bonnet ranch. In their fury, father and son were indeed alike. Control was the unique difference: one had mastered the art to a far higher degree than the other.

Running a hand through his silver hair, smoothing the strands, Everett stood in the center of the spacious living room. The furnishings were of walnut and maple, chairs and settees and end tables, smooth and lovely, delicately crafted by New England furniture makers. Curved-back mahogany chairs, upholstered and thickly cushioned with fabrics of elegant designs, sworls of branches and leaves, covered back and seat, stood amid cabinets and corner boys and spindly legged end tables, brought all the way from Pennsylvania to grace Everett Cotter's home. On tabletops, in shelves, and crowding mantel could be found pewterware and fine china and long-stemmed crystal goblets and wine-glasses from Venice that had been in the Cotter family for generations.

Amid such opulence, the drama and tragedy of the previous hours took their course, propelled by pride and anger.

Vin lifted his gaze to Rose when she moved toward the hallway leading to the north wing of the house. He followed her down the hall, across the sitting room, to a large bedroom. There, Cordelia waited with a warm bath for the new bride. Rose looked at Vin, her eyes imploring. He stared past her at the empty marriage bed.

"Go on," Vin snapped. "Wash the damn mud away. And have Cordelia burn that cursed dress." Rose winced, hurt by his remarks.

"Vin . . . ?"

"There are some things all the water and soap in the world won't make clean again." Vin swung around and stalked back down the hall and into the living room to confront his father again. "Order out the men. Anthem can't have gotten far."

"No," Everett replied. He walked over to the liquor cabinet, found a bottle of whiskey, and filled a shot glass for himself. Then he changed his mind and took another glass, half-filling a six-inch tumbler.

"I want him dead," Vin roared. His voice sounded shrill, a spoiled child's. As he began to pace the polished wood floor, he espied Rose, who had moved back to the hallway, watching his display of temper. She caught her breath at Vin's demand. She retreated a step as Vin bore down on her. "Are you deaf? Get out of here!"

Rose stiffened, her eyes flashing fire. But she held back, suffering his outrage. She continued down the hall, hoping in her heart Everett's common sense and decency would prevail. How could she blame Vin? He had been humiliated before the ranch hands. And pride and respect were the qualities Vin coveted most. Johnny had stolen both.

She continued down the hall to the new sitting room. It was furnished much like the rest of the house. Only the best for the newlyweds, Everett had insisted. How painful it must be for him now. Cordelia entered from the bedroom and held the door open so that Rose could see the bath, already drawn. A large slant-back iron tub was filled to the brim with steaming hot water.

Cordelia hurried to embrace Rose, padding across the room with all the solicitude of a parent. "Poor dear, poor dear," she cooed in her most motherly tone. The housekeeper hugged Rose close to her ample bosom, rocking her like a babe in arms.

Rose almost broke then—first the shock of seeing Johnny, then the violent return to the ranch and the fear that she might not ever be able to get her life in order, knowing Johnny was alive and losing him again. Too many feelings all in conflict, all colliding, battering her resolve. And now an embrace and comfort from this woman Rose had loved like a mother almost undid her. Just in time, the two women parted and Cordelia stood back to appraise the torn and mud-stained dress as Rose wiped away a tear.

"I can mend it," Cordelia said.

"Burn it," Rose replied, numbness creeping into her voice. Methodically, she stripped the gown away, peeling off the undergarments, a lace-fringed camisole and underskirts. The bridal attire soon dropped to the floor at her feet and she stood naked on the cold stones, stomach flattened, pink-crowned breasts upthrust, hips tight, legs trembling. Cordelia draped a robe over the young woman's shoulders and brought her a pair of slippers.

"You take a nice warm bath. I'll bring some tea and some hot biscuits with my pumpkin butter. That will set things aright," Cordelia said while gathering up the remains of the dress. She looked up, startled, as Rose laughed aloud.

"Tea and biscuits. Oh, if it were only that simple, Cordie. Sweet heaven but I wish it were so." Rose watched a patch of silk flutter to the floor as Cordelia straightened with an armload of clothes for the trash fire out beyond the garden in back of the house. Cordelia managed to stoop down and scoop up the crimson-stained remnant before heading toward the hallway door.

"Wait," Rose said, crossing to the woman. She caught the patch by the corner and pulled it from between Cordelia's fingers. "I'll keep this."

Cordelia gave her a questioning look, shrugged, and opened the heavy door.

Vin and Everett's voices echoed down the corridor and filtered into the room. And quickly died as Rose shut the door and walked into the bedroom. She paused in the doorway, staring at the canopy bed that dominated the room. Throw rugs of deep gold covered the floor on either side of the bed. A royal-blue canopy overhead matched the lushly stitched coverlet and spread. The pillowcases were trimmed in the same manner. She recognized Everett's hand in this. He wanted everything to be so right.

Rose glanced down at the scrap of silk in her hand. It was stained with Johnny's blood. She pressed it to her heart and closed her eyes, remembering his look. He had said it was over. So be it. And yet his own ice-blue gaze had communicated something entirely different. A plea—no, a vow. He would be back. He would return for her.

She crossed to the dressing table with its shiny walnut surface and jappaned legs, unicorns and manticores in stark relief, entwined in wood, creatures of legend in still life. Rose slumped into the vanity chair, her gaze dropping from her weary reflection to a worn leather-bound Bible on the tabletop. She opened it and slipped the bloodstained silk between the pages, then paused to read the words that caught at her heartstrings. For this moment, alone, in the dew of her youth she wept, silently, setting the swatch with Johnny's blood upon the Song of Solomon.

Set me as a seal upon thine heart, as a seal
upon thine arm; for love is strong as death . . .

Jealousy, cruel as the grave, was like a fire in Vin Cotter's blood. Yet it gave him the courage to stand in open defiance of his father.

"You let him spit on our name," he blurted out. "Why? Because you still think of him as your son."

Everett waved the argument aside and slumped in the nearest chair, the one by the hearth. He propped his feet on a matching ottoman and closed his eyes, rubbing his forehead. The wineglass tilted in his hand, sending a meager rivulet the color of a rose trickling down the stem, to form a puddle on the shiny wood floor. It took him a moment to notice, and when he did, he didn't care. There was always more wine and someone to clean up the mess. Everett opened his eyes to his son's hard glare.

"This argument is over, boy. Over. Go on in to your wife."

"Like hell. You never listen to me. Well, this time I'll have my say whether you like it or not." Vin walked around to the wine tray, ignored the finer vintage, and helped himself to his father's bottle of aged whiskey. He filled a shot glass, downed the contents, took a second. After the third he felt like speaking again. "You were the one told me, the land is hard, it doesn't give an inch, and a man has to be the same way if he wants to amount to something . . . if he wants to stay on top. Maybe you're getting soft. Weakening. Losing your hold. And that's why you let the likes of Anthem ride out!"

"And maybe," Everett said, his words coming slow, as if he had to draw them up out of the well of his own worst fears. "Maybe I got to thinking about how you came back from Mexico, riding Johnny's black mare, and telling me how you fought side by side with Johnny and saw him die."

Color came to Vin's cheeks and he looked away, unable to meet his father's gaze. He gulped the last of the whiskey in his hand and reached out for the bottle. An overwhelming desire to escape the room overrode his thirst, and he hurried out of the living room and started toward the front door.

"I'll order the men to run Anthem to the ground and bring him back across his saddle, head down."

"Vin!" Everett's voice brought his son to attention as it cut through the household and stopped the man by the door in his tracks. "The men ride for the Bonnet. I am the Bonnet. Not you, son. Not yet."

Everett turned his back on his son and inspected his own bruised and bleeding knuckles. Everett's hands ached. He was sore and tired. But by heaven he was still boss. He didn't see the malevolent expression that flashed across Vin's countenance and disappeared as quickly as it came. Everett only heard the front door open and quietly close. He shook his head, trying to clear away the suspicions that had plagued him concerning Johnny and Vin. Everett had hoped and prayed Rose McCain would make a man out of Vin, give him some backbone and confidence: qualities a man had to have to lead other men, to hold on to what was his. Johnny was supposedly killed in Mexico. Vin had been there and had seen it. Now Johnny was alive and Vin had no answer.

The animosity between the two young men was impossible to ignore. What the hell had happened in Mexico? And what was happening now? Johnny and Vin were puzzles Everett Cotter could no longer piece together. All Cotter knew was that life at the Bonnet had suddenly changed. Something was irretrievably lost. All his plans for his son and Rose had collapsed like a house of cards.

Everett shoved himself out of the chair. He looked across the room at the hall leading to the north wing he had furnished for Vin and Rose. He shook his head and walked across the room in the opposite direction, toward the hallway leading to his own and a guest bedroom that had been Rose's as a girl. He paused for a second, reaching back into memory, hearing the laughter of children, of Vin and Johnny and Rose at play in the garden out back of the ranch house.

Sighing, he continued on to his own bedroom, reached for the doorknob, and winced. His hand hurt, the memories faded. Hurt . . .

As did his heart.

9

★

Leland Rides Horse worked the handle of the well pump, and metal screeched painfully on metal in the warming air. He cupped his hands beneath the cascade of artesian water and sucked in his breath as he lowered his bruised head into the icy stream.

"*Saaa-vaa-he*," he muttered as the bracing flow laved his wounds. The muscles of his lean frame spasmed. He continued to pump until the cuts and bruises marring his dark features turned numb from the bath. He straightened, shedding a fine spray from his black hair in the process. A shadow fell across the horse trough. Without turning, he recognized the intruder by the smell of rosewater that clung to his skin. Charlie Gibbs had left the fellowship of his compatriots at the bunkhouse and, with a knowing grin to the other ranch hands, had wandered over to bait the half-breed.

"Anthem sure took your measure. Bad luck, Leland," Charlie said, shoving his weather-beaten hat back on his forehead. He spoke with authority, the better for his voice to carry to his friends. His fair skin was red from the sun, and dried flesh curled like old wallpaper along his forehead.

Spilled whiskey stained his plaid shirt and vest, a soiled legacy of the wedding fiesta.

"Seems to me," Charlie continued, "a fella ought not to let his mouth write a draft his fists can't cash." A chorus of laughter rose from the men at table by the bunkhouse and Charlie glanced over his shoulder, flashing a smile that was momentarily returned by his friends. But their laughter faded.

Even his poker buddies, a Mexican named Sánchez and Kim Rideout, a tall potbellied bronc buster, suddenly turned serious. Charlie sensed their warning, heard a click as ominous as a rattler's warning, spun around, and found himself staring down the barrel of a Walker Colt.

Leland extended his arm and with the gun muzzle covered a mole on Charlie's forehead.

"It's a fool who doesn't follow his own advice," the half-breed said softly. His eyes above the gun narrowed, fixing the good-natured cowhand in place. Leland took a step, then another, forcing Charlie to back toward the bunkhouse. The bronc buster quickened his pace and Leland followed suit, matching the man under the gun stride for stride.

"C'mon, *amigo*, he was only funnin' you," the Mexican called.

Leland kept pushing. Charlie continued to retreat toward the men. He lost his balance, the stacked heel of his boot caught on a stone. The cold kiss of blue steel never left his flesh. The ranch hands started to thin out, not wanting any trouble. Only Sánchez stood his ground. And Kim Rideout, who lowered his hand to the percussion pistol tucked in the pocket of his woolen trousers. Leland's eyes darted aside, though his gun remained firmly pressed against Charlie Gibbs' forehead.

"Be still, Kim Rideout. Or you'll die with your friend." Leland shifted his gaze. "You too, Sánchez, *mi compadre*.

I know about the knife you have sheathed at your neck."

The Mexican's arm lowered, away from the hilt at the back of his neck. Kim Rideout froze in place, unable to decide whether or not to try the half-breed. Rideout was a proud man who had no love for Indians and less for half-breeds.

"You don't scare me none, Rides Horse," the tall ranch hand said, sucking in his belly and squaring his shoulders. It wasn't in his nature to back down.

"For Chrissake, Kim," Charlie blurted out. "If you're gonna show some backbone, do it with someone else's head on the line." Charlie took a final back step that brought him hard up against the wall of the bunkhouse. He hit it with a jolt that caused him to gasp in horror as such a collision might have jarred the finger on the trigger of the gun at his head. He could see his friends now, could read the expression on Rideout's face.

Charlie shut his eyes, his mind reaching into memory in a bumbling attempt at recalling a prayer. "Now I lay me down to sleep—"

"What the hell is going on here?" Vin said, rounding the corner of the house. "Why aren't you men out after Anthem's hide?" Vin was brought up sharply at the sight of Charlie Gibbs backed against the wall with a gun at his head. "Leland?"

The half-breed glanced over at Vin Cotter, then shrugged and returned the revolver to his sash. He untied the bandanna from around his throat and used it to pat away the sweat from Charlie's brow. Then Leland grinned as if nothing had happened between them and clapped the other man on the shoulder.

"My friend, you are a very lucky man," Leland said.

Charlie lowered his head and, unable to bear such humiliation, slunk off toward the bunkhouse. As he disappeared inside, Chaw Stuart, the trail cook, stepped through

the doorway and called in a gruff voice for the men to come
and get it before he threw it to the hogs.

Chaw Stuart was a bearded, rotund individual given to
too much drink and too few baths. Fortunately he had begun preparing the meals in the summer kitchen outside, a
few yards from the bunkhouse, and tended to take his meals
there, away from the men at table inside. Today, his an-
nouncement served to break the tension and the ranch hands
headed for the door in groups of twos and threes, lured by
the iron skillet of golden-brown biscuits Chaw gripped in
both hands. He stood aside and the men held their breaths
and filed past him.

Chaw wiped a hand on his grease-stained undershirt and,
after nodding to Vin in the yard, followed the ranch hands,
who had resolved to endure the trail cook's odious prox-
imity until he ran out of biscuits.

Leland walked past Vin back to the pump, where he
continued to wash.

Vin Cotter sauntered over to the man and stood off to
one side. Their shadows crossed. "Looks like Johnny Anthem took your measure this morning," Vin said.

"And yours the day before," Leland replied, straighten-
ing, his deep-set eyes ever watchful beneath his furrowed
brows.

"Yes," Vin admitted, running a hand across his face. His
expression momentarily bunched as if he were in pain.

"Today, your father said 'Let him go,' " Leland stated.
"Everett Cotter's orders. And today, on the Bonnet, his
word is law."

"But not forever," Vin snapped.

Leland nodded, seeing in Vin something he liked, something he could use. "There will be another day for John
Anthem."

"And on the Bonnet, another voice, a different word, a
new law," Vin said, staring off toward Bonnet rock. "My

law." He glanced around as Leland took a step closer.

"And may it come soon," said the half-breed. He touched the brim of his sombrero as a sign of deference and then headed for the bunkhouse, his own mind racing with the possibilities the future held.

Vin watched him leave and made a mental note that the half-breed would make a fine and loyal segundo when the order changed and a new word ruled the Bonnet.

Johnny Anthem crested the hill beyond the winding ribbon of muddy water that was the San Antonio River and, glancing over his shoulder, saw that he was being followed. Joe Briscoe was just spurring his mount up the slope. The segundo had rougher going because he had to manage not only the horse he rode but the one he led as well. Johnny recognized the black mare trailing Briscoe: it was the horse Vin had stolen from him in Mexico. Johnny held his gray in check and waited in the shade of a limestone ledge for the segundo to reach him. Johnny lit a cigarillo and enjoyed a smoke despite the sensation as the tobacco stung his bruised lips.

A vulture circled lazily overhead, looking for a meal. On a nearby rock, a foot-long lizard sunned itself, its sides puffing in and out with each and every rapid breath. By the time Johnny's cigarillo was no more than an inch-long stub to be flicked away among the rocks, Joe Briscoe had made the ascent and drew abreast of Johnny in the shadow of the crest.

"What are you doing, Segundo?" Johnny looked past the man to the black mare bearing a hastily packed carpetbag from its saddle horn. Joe Briscoe scratched at the silver-shot stubble covering his jaw.

"The right thing," he answered. "I ride for the brand, but that doesn't make me a thief. Some things there you left behind. Appears you might have outgrown 'em, though." He held out the tether to the mare. "I watched you raise the black here from a foal. I don't know how Vin come home with it and I don't want to. I stand by Everett, and that means I stand by his son."

"Just as long as you don't stand in my way," Johnny said. He spoke matter-of-factly, with respect for the foreman who had helped raise him.

"I will if you come back," Joe replied. He inhaled a deep breath of warm air, fragrant with sage.

"You taught me a lot, Segundo," Johnny said. "But I have learned on my own as well." The saddle creaked as he shifted his weight.

The segundo appraised him anew, seeing a big sturdy capable young man, purpose in his eyes and a hardness never there before. A man to be wary of—trouble waiting to be unleashed.

"Don't come back. Forget the Bonnet. Your life here is over," Briscoe warned. He leaned forward, his powerful shoulders hunched, one calloused hand braced on the butt of a dragon Colt in its saddle holster. "Understand?"

Johnny Anthem nodded, no sign of intimidation in his features. "I always have understood you, Briscoe. You're as open as the holy book you used to preach at us from." Johnny took the tether and the black mare walked up alongside Anthem and whinnied in recognition. "But I appreciate this, Segundo. Now the Bonnet has only one thing more that's mine."

The two men, once friends, once teacher and student, stared at each other in silence as the shadow of the vulture passed silently between them.

"I'll be seeing you, Joe," Anthem said evenly. The segundo nodded and, without a reply, turned his mount and trotted down the winding trail leading to the meadow and beyond to the river. Johnny leaned forward and scratched the black mare behind the ears.

"If Poke's as good as his word, we still have time to catch him at Pop Hitner's. We'll have to ride hard, though." He wheeled his mount around and led the black mare up the remaining few yards to a grove of cedars crowning the hilltop. Once there, he paused to look back toward the ranch in the heat-shimmering distance. When he had a place to bring her to, he'd come back for Rose.

But now he had dreams to follow, to take hold of and build upon. The seeds of an empire were waiting to be sown. He closed his eyes and pictured Rose, tawny gold and loving him, his yellow rose, seeing her clearly, though separated by distance and cruel fate.

"I love you," he whispered. "I'll come back."

And nothing and no one would stop him.

PART TWO

OCTOBER 1849

10

★

Memo Almendáriz had been a lot of things in his life—a thief, a rustler, and a bandit—but the only role he was really proud of was that of father. In mid-October of 1849, the northers had yet to blast their wintry way into west Texas, had yet to drive the clouds southward across the Rio Grande a hundred miles away. The dry mountain passes were testimony to a gentle autumn. Memo Almendáriz wanted to live. And he wanted his son to live. But he didn't think he could manage both.

A gunshot echoed in the canyon and reverberated along the cliff behind him, to die lost and lonely among the boulders overhead, where patches of spiny pads awaited the misstep of the unwary. Joaquín, whom his father had nicknamed Chapo for a wild little pony with much spirit, hunched down as a lead slug spattered him with slivers of stone. The twelve-year-old winced and gritted his teeth. Black hair crowned his head like a tousled black pelt, sleek and thick. His nut-brown features betrayed his concern, despite his efforts to remain calm.

Memo patted his son and raised up to answer the Apache sniper with gunfire of his own. The .50-caliber percussion rifle bucked against his shoulder and spent its single charge in a flash of fire and black smoke. Memo knew the shot was wasted; the brave had already hidden with his brothers among the boulders on the opposite side of the canyon. However, returning the brave's gunfire bolstered his own spirits and helped his son to feel less vulnerable. Memo knew such feelings were mere illusion, but he kept it to himself. His round face, usually cheerful, settled into a serious frown. Hope was a faint spark in his once merry eyes. He tugged at his long black mustache and tried to deny what he knew to be true. They were trapped.

With pain-dulled eyes, Memo glanced through a crack in his improvised battlements and looked out at the dust-caked valley floor and the two horses sprawled in death, necks arched, teeth bared. Flies gathered in the sunlight, cutting spirals in dry air, circling their feast of blood. Dead horses meant no escape, meant that Memo and his son would have to fight. The bandit closed his eyes and tried to remember, tried to picture ... yes, there were five, at least five braves he had seen in pursuit. Pain clouded the image in his mind, destroyed his count, and left him wondering if the ankle he'd hurt when his horse went down was broken.

"Papa," said Chapo. He hadn't noticed his father favoring his left foot. He'd been lost in his own fearful speculations.

But maybe more than five now, Memo thought as he poured a powder charge down the barrel of his rifle. He tapped ball and patch into place with the ramrod, then patiently fitted an explosive cap over the nipple underneath the rifle's hammer.

"Papa. What are we gonna do?"

Die. Memo turned back toward his son. A rifle thundered down the canyon and a lead slug gouged the stone overhead. The Apaches were wasting a little powder, figuring they'd soon replenish their stock with what Memo and his son were carrying.

"Papa?" Chapo tried to hide his fear. He wanted to be as brave as his father, but it was hard and his voice trembled, making him feel ashamed. He looked down at the percussion pistol in his slender grip. He knew how to fire the single-shot weapon. He could loose a shot and reload in less than a minute, he was proud of that. But he'd never killed before—at least not a man. Small game, yes, but this was no game. And he had hunted but had never been the prey. "Papa?"

"I don't know," Memo snapped. "I don't know! Now be quiet and let me think There has to be a way. Memo Almendáriz has too much life to be killed by stinking Apaches. There are too many fat *norteamericanos* waiting for me to lift their ripe purses of gold and too many sweet *señoritas* waiting to be kissed, eh?"

Memo wiped away the perspiration on his shiny forehead, and his eyes darted upward under the shading brim of his sombrero as he scrutinized the boulder-strewn slope. The canyon rim cut skyline about three hundred feet overhead. The boy just might make such a climb—that is, if the Apaches didn't pick him off from across the canyon. It wouldn't be easy, but if Memo kept the Apache warriors busy, Chapo at least would be safe for a little while and able to put enough distance between the Apaches and himself to keep alive until night. After that Chapo would have to rely on stealth and all the tricks he'd learned from his father and their life together on the bandit trail. The odds were against him even then, but anything was better than waiting here in the draw to be slaughtered like lambs.

Memo pointed to the wall of the canyon. "You will climb it."

Chapo turned around and looked at the rocky surface with its niches and pockets of cover where a man could scramble through, dodging bullets, crawling hand over hand. He looked back at his father. "I won't leave you. And you can't make me, Papa."

"Leave me? Who said such a thing? You go first. When you reach the top, then you can cover me while I climb."

Chapo's eyes narrowed, studying his father's features for signs of parental treachery.

Memo finished with the rifle and checked the load on his pistol. "Well, my son, are you afraid to try it?"

"I am afraid of nothing. Especially such a climb," Chapo indignantly replied.

"Then climb!"

His father's intensity jarred the youth into action, and spinning around, he took the slope of loose gravel in a crab-legged series of leaps and bounds. Gunfire erupted as he scampered from cover. Lead slugs spattered the stones around him, bit deep into the rocky incline, or ricocheted off into daylight. Chapo slid, crawled, pulled and heaved, and fought his way to the safety of the cliff's first barricade of wagon-sized boulders. With a final lunge of effort he reached momentary safety and heard his father's gunfire.

Chapo rested in the shadow, enjoying the coolness and feeling safe behind this boulder, where he had found a niche just his size. No one could touch him here. He wiped the sweat from his eyes, left a smear on his brow, and glanced down at his hands. The knuckles were bloody from his initial endeavors and he had most of the climb still to come. But at least he thought he could pick a trail among the rocks. It might not be any more than a path fit for a mule deer, but he had the confidence of youth. And when he reached the top, he could help his father to safety. He grinned, imagining that they were already safe. A sprinkle of gravel, a fist-shaped stone dislodged and tumbling down the slope dampened his mood. The grin faded, his body stiffened as he grew alert, drawing deeper into the niche.

He wasn't alone on the cliff. Suddenly panic, like a great weight slamming into his chest, left his throat dry and his breath came in ragged gasps. The pressure continued to build until the youth could no longer endure it. He pulled a pistol from his belt, realized he might need both hands free to clamber over boulders blocking his path, and returned the pistol to his belt. A scorpion ventured out into the sunlight, driven from his shadowy world by the frightened intruder. The insect lifted both savage pincers to the sun, its barbed tail poised for a paralyzing strike. The scorpion burrowed beneath a rock near Chapo's worn leather boot and waited for some unsuspecting prey to cross its path. Nature mirrored Chapo's plight. Apaches—whose name means "enemy"—and scorpions, both were hunting this day. Another rock tumbled down the slope. Chapo gritted his teeth and bolted from cover.

Memo propped himself up on the boulder, his boots dragging in the dry wash as clouds of coffee-colored dust swirled upward in a passing breeze. He sighted down the barrel of the rifle and wondered if he had ever come close to wounding any of the braves he had shot at. They were like shadows—no, like ghosts, shifting, sliding in and out of nooks and crevices, silent as dreams, deadly as the worst nightmare. He'd seen their handiwork before, on captured villagers, on *compadres* who had fallen captive to them. Men died slow—oh, mother of mercy—so slow, and screamed for death, for an end to pain while ants feasted on their eyes, while hot coals burned through flesh and muscle and sank into a man's bowels, and all the while, a screaming without end. Memo looked down at his useless left leg. The ankle would barely support his weight and reduced him to a hobble.

"I cannot run, you blood-hungry devils," Memo growled, and spat at the earth beneath his feet. "But you will not take me alive." One bullet, his last, was for himself.

The stone dislodged from above struck dirt a few yards away and Memo turned around, hoping to catch a glimpse of his son darting among boulders. Strange that the braves across the ravine hadn't tried harder to bring Chapo down. The hairs at the back of his neck rose and he shivered despite himself. He tried to pick out the point above from which the stone might have fallen, and just by luck or cruel taunting fate he glimpsed movement. Coppery-brown torso covered by loincloth and breeches, knife gleaming in the sunlight—an Apache brave leapt from behind an ocotillo and landed on a narrow footpath three-quarters of the way up the slope. He appeared but for a second and vanished just as quickly . . . like a ghost . . . like an Apache.

Chapo. His son was no match. Chapo! The bandit started up the slope, scrambled a couple of yards over loose shale, but his leg crumpled beneath him and he went down hard, cracking his jaw against a jagged outthrust ledge. Pain was a skyrocket shooting up from his twisted ankle to explode inside his skull. Memo tumbled and slid back to the floor of the ravine as two Apaches broke cover and rode at a gallop on their tough mountain ponies in a desperate charge, each brave battling to be the first to claim the bandit's scalp. Their war cries rang out, shattering the stillness. The standoff was ended; it was time to kill or die. Memo rolled over on his back and waited for the braves, rifle in hand. He couldn't help his son now. Hell, he couldn't even help himself.

Joaquín Almendáriz, called Chapo for a wild pony of the *barrancas*, climbed with all the strength of his limbs. Panic pumped adrenaline into his wiry arms and legs. He climbed hand over hand, fighting his way through cactus-choked crevices where foot-long coal-black lizards slithered in the shadows and rattlers warned "beware-beware" with the quivering of their tails.

Chapo climbed and left a trail of blood from crimson welts on his hands and knees where the cliff's savage armaments had gouged his flesh. But he scarcely felt the pain for the images of an army of Apache warriors hounding him up the steep incline, their paint-smeared faces like grinning masks of death. Chapo climbed through a labyrinth of tumbled boulders and limestone rubble and tasted the dirt that billowed around him as he scrambled to safety.

The scrape of his boots on stone, the noise of his frantic efforts echoed over the cliff, revealing his location to his pursuers. But he no longer cared—the summit was all that mattered. The summit was safety, or so his frantic thoughts concluded. From the summit he could make his stand and cover his father while Memo worked his way up the path his son had taken.

Chapo lifted himself over a chunk of limestone, found a footpath that led up between two boulders through a fissure wide as a mule deer. He headed for it on instinct, his breathing ragged and his legs grown leaden as he scrambled into shadow. He started to breathe a sigh of momentary relief at this place of respite when part of the shadow moved.

A figure loomed great and terrible, lunging out to catch the twelve-year-old by the scruff of his neck, hauling him out of the fissure and hurling him into the sunlight beyond. Chapo cried out, heard a war cry answer his as he hit the dirt and twisted around to bring his pistol up. A gunshot exploded a few feet away. A tall, powerfully built gringo with hair the color of fire backed out of the fissure. The revolver in his hand trailed black smoke that clung to his smooth, worn buckskin shirt, and in the pocket of darkness between the two boulders, another figure stirred. A red hand emerged out of darkness and clawed at the hard earth as if seeking a handhold to the life that flickered and winked out. The red hand grew still. Fierce and hard was the face of the *norteamericano* with his hard bronze face and scruff of red beard.

Chapo raised the pistol in his hand and cocked the single-shot weapon.

The gringo spun around and batted the gun away as he loomed down over the youth and the gringo's ice-blue eyes were as merciless as a Texas norther as he stared at the twelve-year-old. He pinned the boy with the force of his presence, and Chapo regretted ever brandishing his gun at this giant, regretted even more the fact he hadn't been able to shoot him when he had the chance. And then incredibly so, the gringo's fierce visage was split by a grin that was as surprising to the boy as the appearance of sunlight in the midst of a raging blizzard.

"No need to shoot me in the back, *muchacho*, a simple thank-you will do," said Johnny Anthem. A roar of triumph sounded behind him, and he spun around, raised his Colt on reflex, caught a blur of motion, and fired. The heavy weapon boomed and spat fire and brimstone, and through gunsmoke he glimpsed the charging form of the brave he had just shot—the *compadre* of the dead man among the twin boulders. He saw a flash of cold steel and reached out to block the brave's knife thrust.

Johnny twisted, lifted with his free arm, and brought his shoulder underneath the attacker. There was a stench of gunsmoke, blood, and grease as muscular arms and legs kicked and pummeled. The warrior was dying, but he was still trying to drive the knife home in a killing blow, wanting to take his killer with him. Johnny wasn't about to let him. He straightened and then, lifting with the strength of his arms, allowed the Apache's own momentum to carry him over the battlements of limestone and over the edge of the cliff. The warrior shrieked in horror and his cry trailed off and died as quickly as the man. Gunfire resounded and reverberated through the ravine like the cadence of approaching thunder.

"My father," Chapo said, and scrambled the couple of yards to the edge of the cliff. He looked down in time to see one of the Apache braves double over on horseback. He clung to the animal's mane and rode away from the rock, behind which Memo waited for death. The second brave wheeled his horse as Pokeberry Tyler rose from concealment farther along the ridge and leveled his Walker Colt. He fired three shots in rapid succession. Geysers of dirt erupted inches in front of the mountain pony. The animal reared and pawed the air, and the brave turned and galloped up the dry wash between the cliffs. A third brave broke cover and headed after the others. Chapo jumped, startled, as Johnny loosed a shot. Pokeberry repeated with a shot of his own, but neither scored a hit upon their fleeing foe. Horse and Apache brave rode at a gallop, joining in a smooth sleek motion that defied the efforts of the white men to bring them down. Chapo clambered to his feet and shook his fist at the departing braves. He shouted abuse and then turned, a grin beaming from his face.

"We have beaten them, *señor*. See, they run like rabbits."

"We won today," Johnny replied. "A rabbit today can return a lion tomorrow." He drew a metal flask and began loading his cap-and-ball revolver, measuring black powder into the six-chambered cylinder and tapping home a hefty lead ball in those that were empty. He replaced his spent caps and then holstered the weapon and looked up at the boy, who had suddenly grown serious. Chapo stood precariously close to the sheer drop, his youthful features suddenly old with concern. Johnny stepped up alongside him and stared down at the seemingly lifeless figure of Memo

Almendáriz sprawled on his back, legs and arms splayed out upon the hard-packed earth.

"My father," Chapo said in a voice choked with concern. *"Father!"* His voice resounded along the walls, returning in kind—weakened, faded, so lost and so alone.

11

★

Anthem's land. It was a big country with room enough for a big man's dreams. Johnny had chosen wisely and well. The broad valley, split by a spring-fed creek lined with cottonwood and oak and willow, was a place thick with foliage. It was home to a nameless array of wildlife—birds with bright plumage whose piping melodies added to the symphony of gurgling springwater and the sigh of the wind among the boughs. Steep treeless slopes carpeted with buffalo grass and dotted with cactus and madrona trees rose five hundred feet to east and west, the base of each incline a half-hour's walk from the creek's banks across a fertile valley floor. A mile into the valley, following the creek from where it emptied to the south on the sundrenched plains, set upon a grassy knoll between the ridges east and west, low, newly constructed adobe walls delineated the beginnings of a hacienda. Each sun-baked brick had been cut and placed by hand, by Johnny Anthem.

Anthem stood now upon the three-foot-high wall and watched the clouds play shadow chase with the golden countryside, creating a sea of shifting shapes wherein he found serenity. The creek revealed itself in sunlight as it glimmered through the autumnal foliage like a ribbon of twinkling lights in this familiar display that had given Johnny Anthem the name for his ranch.

"Luminaria," he said to the twelve-year-old boy who sat against the hardened walls so laboriously erected. Luminaria: for the festive paper lanterns of fiesta, a word for beauty and joy, a word fit for dreams.

"This valley?" asked Chapo.

"And beyond," Johnny replied. "Climb these ridges. And as far as you can see, I will make it mine."

Down below, by the creek, a corruscating tendril of smoke drifted up through the trees. Pokeberry starting supper. He hadn't called out to them, so Memo must still be unconscious. Anthem's valley was an hour's ride from the ravine where Memo and his son had made their stand. Johnny allowed his gaze to drift over to the makeshift corral—a wall of oak limbs and underbrush that blocked off the northernmost reaches of the valley, where east ridge and west joined like the curve of a horseshoe to form a natural windbreak against the winter winds out of Canada.

The noise of more than thirty half-wild mustangs drifted back from the corral, their hooves trampling the earth, a neighing call rising from the lengthening shadows. Chapo kicked at the earthen wall. It was solid as stone.

"What will you do for cattle?" he asked. He and his father had been returning from an aborted raid over in the Pecos country. He tried not to appear too interested in what might well be a future market for the men who had ridden with Memo Almendáriz. Suddenly, his very speculations shamed him, and the boy couldn't meet Johnny's gaze. Chapo owed this man his life, but it was difficult to feel grateful.

"Poke and I caught a string of wild mustang. It's taken me this whole month to straighten the kinks out of them so they'll bring a good price with the Rangers. I'll buy a good shorthorn breed bull and cows with the money I get from selling the horses. We can breed them with the wild long-horns we've seen. And we've seen plenty."

Anthem's eyes took on a bright dreamy quality as he envisioned a great herd of prime beef stretching out from the valley and onto the high plains. He could hear them, bellowing and calling to one another across the landscape while the sky deepened in hue and filled with stars; he pictured himself watching over his empire from the balcony of his hacienda. And Rose at his side . . .

"Johnny, get on down here and bring the boy," Poke's outcry drifted up from their camp by the creek. Tyler's voice shattered Johnny's daydream and he burst into action. Slapping the boy on the shoulder, he leapt from the wall. The urgency in Poke's voice had alerted him to trouble. Johnny took his gun from his belt.

Chapo could only think that something was wrong with his father—perhaps his condition had worsened. The boy tried to quell the tide of panic that rose in his breast like a flash flood in the Sierras, irresistible and crushing. He didn't want to be orphaned here in the wilds of Texas. He stumbled and lost his footing and would have rolled the hundred feet downslope but Johnny's arm shot out and steadied him, forcing the boy upright and halting his momentum.

Anthem and the boy cleared the slope and rushed across a few yards of open ground to the cover of red and wild oak and weeping juniper.

"Johnny," Poke shouted. The crashing of twigs underfoot and the snapping of low-hanging branches announced their arrival as Johnny plunged into the clearing by the creek that served as home until the hacienda on the hill stood complete. A cheerfully blazing campfire separated Pokeberry Tyler, his arms raised aloft, from Memo Almendáriz, who sat upright, one arm braced behind him. In his hand was Tyler's own revolver. Memo shifted his aim to cover Johnny.

"Far enough, *señor*. Now, where is my son?"

Chapo stepped around the big young man and hurried over to his father's side. "Papa, you are alive," he said.

Memo sported a nasty bruise on his scalp. It had formed a lump that swelled purple and sickening white on the border of his receding hairline. "*Sí*, alive and worried for you, my son. You are hurt?"

"No, Papa," Chapo said, and he turned around to look at Johnny, who held his own revolver pointed at the bandit.

"Damnedest thing," Pokeberry muttered.

Chapo glanced over at the wiry old man who stood barefoot on the muddy creek bank: he clutched a pair of socks in one hand. His woolen pant legs were rolled up, revealing thin, bony ankles and scrawny feet.

"I was fixing to wash my socks when he commenced to groaning and carrying on. I figured for sure he was a goner, so I went to check on him and blast if he didn't steal the gun right off'n my belt." Tyler tried to make his explanation sound like he hadn't been made fool of, though it galled Poke Tyler no end that he had been taken unaware, and by a stove-up Mexican.

"Drop the gun, big one," Memo said.

"Not hardly," Johnny Anthem dryly replied. Poke recognized the tone of voice. Hell was coming to tea in a matter of seconds, and he tried to decide which way to leap. Embers in the campfire crackled open, exploding from the heat. The smell of burning mesquite mingled with the savory aroma of half a dozen quail, dressed and spitted on a length of iron suspended over the flames.

The tension in the clearing was a palpable force that dimmed the natural music of their surroundings, stilling the voice of every chattering jay, the rustling of squirrels, hum of bee, the cry of a distant hawk, the chorus of the spring-fed creek. The world around them grew still; death was nigh. The animals sensed it—the heartbeat of this small, shaded, hidden corner of the world fluttered fearfully while death left an empty challenge between the two men, guns leveled at each other.

"Papa, no," Chapo blurted out, reaching out to place his hand upon the revolver in his father's hand. "No." He stepped into the silence of impending violence and by his very youth and a sudden simple act of courage, of caring, disarmed death.

"They fought the Apaches and saved our lives."

Memo studied his son; then slowly, ever slowly, he lowered the revolver to his side and sank back upon the bedroll, casting a wary eye toward Johnny, who holstered his own weapon.

"Saved us? These gringos? Why? I have fought your kind in my own country and have seen nothing to cause me to want to save your life."

"I fought too," Johnny said. "And afterward labored in the silver mines of one of your generals." Johnny turned and lifted his shirt to reveal the patchwork of scar tissue that crisscrossed his back. "I can't say I have any love for your kind either."

"Then again I ask, why?" Memo said, his hand inching over to settle on the gun butt. Pokeberry squatted down and began tugging on his socks and boots while Chapo filled a dark-blue enameled cup with strong black coffee and carried it to his father. Johnny sauntered over to the fire and helped himself to a cup as well, before finding a log for a bench and taking a seat.

"Maybe because I've been in a few tight spots myself these past few months. A helping hand sure would have been nice."

"A soft heart in such a big man, eh?" Memo chuckled

and then winced, gingerly probing the area of flesh around the nasty-looking lump.

"Don't judge him too quick, chili-eater," Pokeberry cautioned, sliding past the fire to retrieve his gun. His fingers caught the pistol by its nine-inch barrel and lifted the heavy weapon free of Memo's grasp.

"A nice gun. I have heard of these 're-volvers' from friends who fought the Rangers of Texas." He looked up at Pokeberry, and this time allowed Tyler to take the Colt.

Pokeberry snatched the gun free and cradled it in his arms as if it were an infant. Then Poke frowned and returned to his place by the fire. "Saved his hide . . . hhur-rumph." He snorted and spat off to the side. "And nary a simple thankee but steals a gun and 'put up your hands.'" Poke shook his head and glanced at Johnny. "Whatever become of gratitude?"

"Maybe these aren't thankful times," Johnny replied, turning to the bandit reclining against a saddle. "My name's John Anthem," he added, offering a work-hardened hand. "That's Poke Tyler."

"And this is Johnny's ranch," Chapo added enthusiastically.

Memo glanced around at the humble campsite.

The cleared area had several makeshift barricades of deadwood and a hut made of branches and deerskin that the two Texans used for shelter during rainstorms. Soon it would be time to build something more permanent for winter, but Johnny and Poke had been too busy trapping horses to worry much about any major construction.

"So, you are a great *haciendado*, eh? But you live very close to the earth—in fact, you sleep on it."

"For a pilgrim who just this morning was fixing to be the invited guest at an Apache skull roast you're mighty particular," Poke interjected.

He drew his knife and, lifting the spitted quail from the

fire, began to work a whole roasted bird off the end of the skewer. "I suppose you'll start griping as how we ain't got no seasoning for these here quails." Using the flat of his blade he shoved the first savory morsel of meat off the skewer. It plopped onto the blanket, narrowly missing Memo's lap. The bandit scooted aside just in time to avoid a burned crotch. He picked gingerly at the sizzling bird and managed to pull a drumstick free.

"Two things in this world I do not complain about, *señor*—food or a willing woman. For Memo Almendáriz, hunger is always the best seasoning."

Midnight, and the campfire was a bed of pulsing rubies Johnny stirred to life with a limb of red oak before adding an armful of deadwood for the reborn flames to feed upon. He took in the camp at a glance. Chapo was stretched out alongside his motionless father, and Poke, his backside to the flames, snored with the precision of a drum corps beating out a crisp cadence. The big young Texan grinned and, stepping over Tyler, continued on out of the firelight, then disappeared into the dark. He proceeded cautiously until his eyes adjusted to the night and by the light of a quarter moon he reached the edge of the creek. He squatted down by the water's edge, watching a blizzard of fireflies swirl and dive in electric profusion on the opposite side of the creek. The wild display captured his attention, so that Johnny failed to notice Memo Almendáriz approaching from the camp until the bandit knelt to take a drink of springwater.

"I thought you were sleeping," Johnny said.

"Almost," Memo said, cupping a handful of icy water over his face and another over the back of his neck.

"Ah, that is better." The bandit sat back and patted a cold hand to the lump on his head. He couldn't remember how it came to be there, though it might have happened when he fell. "A beautiful sight," Memo remarked, watching nature's nocturnal celebrations lighting the opposite bank. "I see why you have chosen this place. To put roots down is important, but something I have never been able to do again."

"Again?" Johnny's interest was piqued.

"*Sí*. My boy had a mother. And not some *puta* from the cantinas," Memo said with a wag of his head, his voice softening with remembrance. "I was a man of substance then, a farmer. A small house, a few good acres, nothing *muy grande*, but mine all the same. Roots, yes." He stared toward the dancing fireflies, fell silent a moment, tugging at his mustache. "Long ago. Too long."

"What happened?"

"What always happens in my country. The local *haciendado* decided he wanted my land and the water on it. He sent his men one night, they burned me out. My wife died in the fire, trapped in the ruins of my house. Chapo was only three. I carried him into the *barrancas*. We survived. I became what you see now: a famous *bandido*, feared by all, worth fifty gold dollars . . . dead. I have devoted my entire life to relieving men like Andrés Varela of the burden of so much wealth. It is the least I can do." Memo finished with a chuckle. "The least."

"General Andrés Varela," Johnny repeated.

"You know him?" Memo asked, then he recalled Anthem's scarred back.

"So you have seen the mines of Varela."

"At close range," said Johnny.

"You escaped. But he left the scars on your back to remember him by."

"Yes," said Johnny, reliving his escape—the saber blade slicing down, to hew flesh and bone, and in the ghostly lamplight, a hand lying in the dust. "But I doubt if he'll ever forget me either."

"You. It was you," Memo blurted out. "The gringo who

maimed him. You clipped the wing of the hawk of Chihuahua. Ahh, Señor Anthem, you are responsible for much grief across the Río Bravo. Varela lived and, mad with hatred, scoured the hills for you." Memo fished a cigarillo from his pocket, struck tinder until the tip glowed, then exhaled a silver-blue cloud of smoke. "And when you were not found, he unleashed his anger upon us poor hardworking robbers. It is why I am come here in the first place. *Sí*, chased out of my own homeland by the monster you created." Memo pointed an accusing finger at Johnny. "It is only justice you saved my life, *señor*, for you ruined my livelihood." He shook his head and sighed dramatically.

"Ruined, you say?" Johnny laughed. "Then perhaps I can undo these terrible consequences."

"You have my attention," Memo replied, inhaling deeply and exhaling with relish.

"I came here to stay, to build on a dream, to plant my roots deep in this ground," Johnny replied.

"Such dreams Memo Almendáriz understands," the bandit said with a wave of his hand, nodding in accord.

"Because you dreamed them once?" Johnny said.

"*Sí.*"

"Then dream again." Johnny watched as the bandit turned slowly, fixed him in a wary gaze. "I need a segundo, a man I can trust, a leader of men. The horses will bring in enough to pay you and a crew. But more than that, whatever I build you and Chapo will share in. It'll be hard work, but then so is the outlaw trail."

Johnny Anthem's excitement was infectious. Memo chuckled despite himself and shook his head no, then stood as if to walk away. He paused after a single step, his gaze fixed on the campsite back up in the trees and the huddled shape of his son sleeping by the fire. His mind was filled with speculation. The notion of permanence was a lovely thought—to have roots again, to take hold, to no longer be a tumbleweed borne on the wind, to leave the *barrancas* forever and recapture what had been, long ago, before Varela came to claim the homeland of Memo Almendáriz. Here was the opportunity to begin anew, without a price on his head and safe from Andrés Varela.

"You will either succeed or leave your bones here to be bleached by the sun," Memo predicted, turning back to Anthem.

"One or the other," Johnny agreed. He stood, and for all his youth, his eyes were aged with vision, his expression determined as he towered over the bandit and extended his hand.

And still, Memo had to think, to weigh the life he knew against the prospect of another.

"Papa," Chapo said, emerging from the shadows. His father looked startled. He hadn't noticed the boy crawl out of his bedroll and walk to the creek. "Your voices carried on the night," Memo's son explained. "I listened and could sleep no longer."

"Then let the decision be yours," Memo said.

"I ride by your side, Papa," Chapo replied. The boy stood barefoot, clad in dirty white cotton breeches and blousy shirt, his thick black hair rumpled from sleep. Just a boy of twelve, but standing tall. He deserved more than the lot of a fugitive on the run, forever testing fate among the hard brutal men of the Sierra del Hueso. A boy like Chapo deserved roots. Yes, and permanence and a chance to be more than his father.

Pokeberry appeared, outlined by the campfire behind him. He yawned, stretching out his bony arms. He shuddered as the cool dry air laved his flesh. "Don't anybody sleep around here? *¿Qué pasa?*" He hooked a thumb in the waistband of his buckskins.

"Let me tell you of the surprises a day can bring," Memo answered. "This morning, I was a bandit, a man of little station living by a gun and my wits. Now, see me, I am employed at this great ranch." Memo's hand swept out in a wide arc as he participated in Johnny's visions of a magnificent hacienda and the western empire Anthem intended to create. "Not just employed," Memo continued, clasping the hand Johnny Anthem offered, "but a man of station . . . the segundo of Luminaria!"

Sleep made Johnny vulnerable. His nightmare reduced to a voyeur—a silent, ethereal observer to his mind's worst creations. And unable to help himself, he watched.

Vin Cotter entered the bedroom. The light flickered as he walked, and shadows swirled around him, reaching out to dim the brightness surrounding Rose. She lay upon the bed, her eyes wide and showing . . . nothing. That made it all the more terrible. Eyes warm as God's brown earth, once aglow with the fire of her youth, with the secret passion she shared with Johnny, the passion and love that gave birth to dreams and ended innocence—oh, such eyes as these, so empty now. She was lovely in her sleeping gown, the taut pink crowns of her bosom straining against the soft cotton, her golden hair undone and flowing over her shoulders in a cascade of shining beauty that not even Vin's darkness could extinguish.

Vin knelt upon the bed and, leaning forward, drew her gown to her waist. Unfastening his trousers, he settled between her legs, taking his pleasure with short savage thrusts that Rose endured. She looked away and her gaze bore through Johnny like a red-hot iron. Her gaze seared his soul, the lifelessness in her eyes broke his heart, killing all passion save that holiest of all, gentle mercy. Her body shook from her husband's onslaught. Her husband. Her husband. Husband . . . Vin buried his face in her warm bosom, his hands like talons clawing at her breasts as he suffered sweet release. He looked over his shoulder then and grinned, staring right at his supposedly invisible audience. His body shuddered as it had during climax, only this time laughter, not a cry of ecstasy, was in his voice.

Laughter, mocking Johnny, growing louder as he watched Johnny watching him. Louder still until his voice rang like some discordant bell pealing derision. Louder and louder, filling the dream, filling the mind of the man asleep.

"Ahhh," Johnny yelled out, and bolted upright, the Colt in his hand, hammer thumbed back and heavy barrel aimed directly at the fading image of Vin's face, unraveled by wakefulness. Johnny aimed his revolver at the quartermoon adrift on the night sky. His expression was tortured, filled with anguish and rage—the face of a man ready to kill. But the image was gone and the music of Luminaria creek flowed around him. The warm crackle of the campfire soothed his spirit. The peace of Luminaria healed him, as it always would in his life, again and again.

"Madre mía," Chapo said, blessing himself with the sign of the cross. He had been awakened by Johnny's outburst and looked across the bed of glowing coals at Anthem.

Johnny realized that not only the boy but his father and Poke were also watching him from their bedrolls. Self-conscious, Johnny coughed and looked away, then he rose, tucked his Colt in his waistband, stretched, and sauntered away from the circle of warmth at campsite to relieve himself in the underbrush. He seemed oblivious to what had happened.

"Don't get riled up, Johnny has some bad spells, only when he's sleeping. I reckon there are some burdens a fella just has got to shoulder. And ain't nothing to be done." Pokeberry shrugged, attempted to explain when Johnny was out of hearing range.

"Did you see his face? Such an expression," Memo softly replied from his bedding. "At first I thought Anthem was too young for all his grand plans, but now, well, I would not want him to face me with such an expression." The bandit shook his head, wondering just what sort of individual he had thrown in with. Still, Johnny had saved his life and Chapo's. No, John Anthem could not be evil.

"I seen the look before," said Poke. "At the moment he cut off'n Andrés Varelas' hand." Tyler shivered and scratched at his stubbled cheeks, making a sound as if he were running the tips of his fingers over sandpaper. "Look of the cougar, yessir. And I pity the poor bastard who drives that boy's back up against the wall." The old man settled back on his blankets, yawned, turned over on his side, and a few moments later began to snore.

Johnny returned to camp and stretched back against his own blankets, his sun-bronzed face settled and calm.

"I'll be driving the horses to San Antonio in a day or two. Poke will stick it out here and start chasing mavericks out of the brush. Maybe you could help him as soon as you're able. Until then, just rest up and hold the camp."

Memo studied the younger man for a minute, in silence, then made his judgment. Johnny's troubles were his business, and his alone. He glanced over at Chapo, who seemed disappointed that Johnny had no task for him. It was important to the twelve-year-old boy that he pull his own weight. A rider of the *barranca* was poor in everything but pride.

"Chapo, tell me, have you ever been to San Antonio?" Johnny asked. The boy brightened at the sound of his name. He wasn't to be forgotten after all.

"No, *señor*. But I sure would like to."

"Are you good with horses?"

"I have learned at my father's side, and he is the best horse thief in all the Sierras. I have driven herds with him even over the great dessert to the . . ." Chapo stumbled, suddenly realizing to whom he spoke. Texans had a tendency to hang horse thieves, especially Mexican horse thieves. "My father has taught me well," he finished in a clipped tone.

"Bueno," said Johnny, tilting his sweat-stained hat down over his face as he settled back on his blankets and pillowed his head on his saddle. "The very qualities I need in the man I'll take with me on the drive," Anthem said. "He has to know horses and he must never have been to San Antone." Johnny peeked out from under the brim of his hat, a grin lighting his features. "But he sure would like to."

12

★

Chapo stared in open wonderment at the city across the river. San Antonio—the name itself was magic to him. He couldn't wait to walk the streets of this wonderful place. He looked regretfully at the corrals, outbuildings, and barracks on the bank of the San Antonio River where Company C of the Texas Rangers made their headquarters. Sixty-five men, the toughest lot the State of Texas had to offer, used San Antonio as a base of operations that contained only one directive: carry war to the Commanches and Apaches, hound them to their mountain rancherias, drive them across the Rio Grande, and put an end once and for all to the depredations that plagued the western frontier.

Civilization swelled like a river on the flood, waiting for the dam to burst, waiting to pour out upon the Texas plains, waiting to wrest the state from the domination of the savage who roamed at will, slaughtering innocent settlers and burning their settlements and farms. The politician's urging of manifest destiny was far beyond the understanding of a twelve-year-old, weary from the two-week drive. Three times on the trek east from Luminaria, Johnny and Chapo espied war smoke and ran their feisty herd of mustangs to cover to escape detection. Yet for most of the waking hours neither man nor boy had time to worry about encountering war parties; the half-wild mustangs required the two drovers' total attention. But now the journey was over.

Chapo watched as ragtag lads no older than himself climbed the post oaks lining Commerce Street and lit the gaily painted lanterns hung in the branches. Ropes were strung across the street at various intervals—whenever a tree or porch post would allow—and from each rope line half a dozen lanterns dangled in the breeze. By sundown the city would be ablaze with bright lights, blue and green, amber and scarlet. Wagons were being shooed from Commerce Street. The shops, ladies' parlors, stately hotels, saloons, and theaters were festooned with star-spangled ribbons; each facade was covered with red, white, and blue in a patriotic fervor unmatched save on the Fourth of July.

"Cattle days," Johnny said, walking up to the youth.

A silver-haired, wiry man with features like tooled leather walked alongside Anthem. The older man wore woolen trousers, homespun shirt, and a heavy gray coat with the collar pulled up around his neck and a long scarf tied at his throat and trailing down over his shoulders. A brace of heavy Colt dragoons were belted at his waist. He was clean-shaven and his brown eyes studied Chapo, noting each detail of the boy's face.

"This is Captain Rex Colby of the Texas Rangers," Johnny said by way of introduction. It dawned on him that Memo and his boy might well have run afoul of the Rangers during their forays into Texas. He hoped Colby hadn't ever seen the boy close up.

"What's your name, boy?" Colby said, his Adam's apple bobbing in his throat as he spoke. He tilted the narrow-brimmed hat he wore back on his forehead. "You look familiar to me."

"I am called Chapo by my friends."

"Hmmm. Maybe it's in the face. Who's your pa?"

"I, uh—" Chapo looked at Johnny for help.

"He doesn't know," Johnny blurted out.

Colby glanced at Johnny and then shrugged. "Ain't no shame in it. I'd rather be an honest bastard than a razor-backed son of a bitch," Colby said, grinning as he leaned his elbows on the hitching rail.

Ranger headquarters was a cluster of low-roofed, long adobe barracks bordering a stable and corral on three sides and an armory and flagpole flying the colors of the Union and the Lone Star of Texas. Johnny, Chapo, and Captain Colby watched as a pair of wagons rolled at a crisp pace down the road in front of the Ranger compound and continued onto the river bridge and into San Antonio. The dust of their passing rose in a column of rust-colored swirls that dissipated in the dying light of a molten-gold sun.

"Folks with little ranches hoping to one day be folks with big ranches and able to afford a suite at the Cattleman's Hotel."

"Ranchers with sizable herds cull their stock before winter," Johnny explained to the boy on horseback. "They drive a few head into the pens on the other side of town and sell what they can to the likes of you and me—ranchers just starting out. Some of the stock isn't much, but I think we might find us a breed bull, what with all the ranchers from Austin to Brownsville come into the city."

"If I were you, I'd take the fifteen hundred dollars I paid you for the horses and get a small safe parcel of land down in the valley," Colby said. "That border country you'll find nothing but Injuns and mescan bandits. Hell, Johnny, I can't see you lasting out the year."

"I'll last," Johnny replied.

Colby shrugged and looked out at the river bridge. A couple of Rangers sauntered past; they didn't salute. Nor did Colby expect such deference. He wanted only one thing from his men: the ability to fight, to stay in the saddle night and day if need be, and to shoot straight.

Chapo watched the two Rangers and saw in their purposeful stride and flashing weapons that these were riders of violence. Save for the badges pinned to their vests, those two men could have easily fit into the gangs of cutthroats who rode the *barrancas*.

"Maybe you will, Johnny. Maybe you will."

"Which is the Cattleman's Hotel?"

Colby pointed to a stately three-storied building whose red-tiled roof rose above the lesser buildings surrounding it. "The tab will be too rich for your blood."

"We'll stay at Mama Rosita's," Johnny said. "But the men I need to see will be at the hotel."

"Or the fiesta tonight." Colby winked good-naturedly at the boy on horseback. "You ever been to a fiesta, lad?"

"Not so grand as this, Señor Colby," Chapo answered, eager to be away from so many lawmen. The Texas Rangers were feared as much across the Rio Grande as in Texas itself.

"Well, you're in for a treat. Most of the times pretty women around here are about as scarce as clean socks in a bunkhouse. But during the fiesta . . ." Colby sighed. "One of these days I'm gonna have to give up chasing Apaches."

"When will that be?" Johnny asked, mounting the black mare he had tethered to the hitching rail.

"Oh, when I know better." Colby chuckled. "And speaking of learning from experience, I saw Everett Cotter in town today. He came in with his daughter-in-law. And Briscoe, of course."

Johnny stiffened. He could tell the captain was waiting for him to show some response. Johnny disappointed him. Colby continued with his advice.

"It's none of my business, but maybe you ought to walk easy tonight. Stay clear of that old man. We go back a long way. His health's been poor and I don't want to see him riled."

"You're right, Captain Colby. It's none of your business," Johnny coolly returned. He backstepped the mare away from the hitching rail and motioned for Chapo to follow him.

Colby watched the man and boy ride off toward the river bridge and thought to himself what a fine Ranger Johnny Anthem would have made, one of the very best, if only he'd learned how to follow orders.

Chapo followed Johnny's lead down Commerce Street as they walked their horses on the edge of the gathering crowd. Man and boy allowed the sights and smells and all the merry din of celebration to assail their senses. Every fiesta was different and could be seen anew with the eyes of an innocent. Cattle days lasted an entire weekend, and this Friday's crowd was only a small part of an ever-increasing throng that by midnight Saturday would swell to fill the entire city with celebration.

Fiesta! Even the word was musical. Johnny rode with the flow of the crowd, his sombrero tilted forward to guard against recognition. He didn't want Everett Cotter to learn of his presence in the city until he was ready to confront the rancher on his own terms. The Bonnet had the best breeding stock in the state and John Anthem could see no reason why he shouldn't start with the very best.

Ahead, the stately facade of the Cattleman's Hotel rose imperiously above the photography parlor on one side and Duquesne's Restaurant on the other. The building hadn't existed six months ago, and now stood as ostentatious testimony to the prosperity enjoyed by the local ranch kings. Johnny sensed his Yellow Rose within, but caution cooled his impetuous nature. There would be time to see her. First a bath, shave, and a change to clean clothes. He rode past the hotel. In good time, he told himself, remembering his newly acquired patience only with the greatest effort.

On the corner a Tejas family gathered around a make-shift stove and freshly cooked tortillas, lathering the hot spongy bread with cactus-flower honey gathered in the spring. Johnny tossed the elderly Indian two bits and received a handful of tortillas in return. Johnny leaned to the left and caught up his purchase, then slowed his pace to pass Chapo a share of the food.

A half-dozen black boys in ragged dungarees adorned with red ribbons performed a series of tumbling feats that brought them a smattering of applause and a few coins thrown their way. One *señorita*, her nut-brown face hidden behind a veil of Spanish lace, journeyed through the streets in the company of three hard-faced vaqueros. Firepits blazed in the plaza. Racks of *cabrito*—baby goat—sizzled over the leaping flames, sending a mouth-watering aroma drifting across the square, which was choked with gaily painted merchant's booths. Craftsmen and artisans hawked baskets and pottery, silver buckles and spurs, finely crafted knives whose blades gleamed in the firelight. A gunsmith stood beside his lethal collection of firearms, a jeweler care-fully watched over his stock of pins and rings, and next to him lay a saddle maker, who continued to work beneath the appreciative eye of a couple of range riders, polishing the silver pommel of his latest creation.

Johnny and Chapo paused a moment at the booth and gazed with unabashed envy at such a fine saddle. Johnny could feel the payment for the mustangs delivered to the Rangers burning a hole in his pocket. Chapo considered various ways he might steal the handsome leather saddle during the confusion of the fiesta, and then looked away, embarrassed by his thoughts. Joaquín Almendáriz was a thief no longer, but a rider for Luminaria and someday would be a man of position with a ranch of his own. And maybe he would grow old and fat and very rich, cursing the bandits of the *barrancas* for their terrible ways, for the outlaw trail they rode, the path he and his father had blazed.

"Chapo, c'mon," Johnny called out to him.

As he nudged his heels against the flanks of his horse, Chapo cast a last wistful glance toward the saddle maker's booth, then followed Johnny, who watched him and smiled. Johnny Anthem was only too familiar with such dreams.

They rode past stalls draped with dried peppers, hung with fresh vegetables, stalls where bakers hawked *pan dulce*, the sweet breads dusted with lemon sugar or cinnamon—a favorite stop for all the children in town. At the north end of the plaza, Johnny recognized the two-storied hacienda and saloon belonging to Mama Rosita. Johnny urged the black mare to a brisk trot and rode beneath the stucco archway that protected the main courtyard from the traffic and dust in the plaza. The courtyard was already crowded with tethered horses waiting to be led off to stalls running the length of the north wall. A man in a serape started out from the shadow of the stalls and walked at a crisp pace to intercept the newcomers before they reached the boardinghouse.

"We have no room here, *señor*. You will have to find lodging elsewhere. Of course, if you have come to enjoy your pleasure with Mama's girls, you may enter but only by the door around back. There is a rail there for your horse." Johnny remained and allowed the man in the serape to draw closer. "I said we have no room for you, *mis amigos . . .*"

"Not even for me, Juan Medrano."

The swarthy yard man peered at Johnny. Night had strewn its velvet canopy across the sky. But the yard man carried a torch to light the lamps in the courtyard. He extended the torch toward the big man on horseback as Johnny tilted his sombrero back on his forehead.

"Señor Anthem," Juan exclaimed. He peered past Johnny at Chapo.

"This is my friend, Chapo. He rides for me," Johnny said. "His father is the segundo at my ranch."

"You have a ranch? Good. I am happy for you. But I have not heard of such a place."

"It is far from here, in the mountains to the west, about a three-day ride from the Big Bend."

"*Madre mía,*" Juan said, and blessed himself. "Bad country."

"For some. Not for me," Johnny said as he dismounted, untied his saddlebags, and draped them over his shoulder. Chapo followed suit and the two new arrivals handed the reins of their mounts to Juan Medrano, who Chapo could now see looked older than Pokeberry. Juan nodded to the boy.

"There is always room for Johnny Anthem at Mama Rosita's, and and a place for a friend of his too."

The old man turned to lead the horses away and Chapo espied the hilt of a knife sheathed between the yard man's shoulder blades. Juan was evidently a man not to be taken lightly. He carried his knife like men Chapo had known in the wild country—bandits and cutthroats like his father.

Johnny shoved open the heavy oaken door to the hacienda and entered a broad spacious room filled with hand-hewn tables and benches and lit by wood chandeliers. The walls were draped with Indian blankets and pelts, and a fireplace big enough to camp in dominated one whole wall. Over the cook fire hung two enormous cauldrons, one filled with a hearty stew of potatoes, carrots, onions, snap beans, and beef, and the other with Mama's special chili, thick and steaming and hot enough to send old Lucifer to the water trough. Men were gathered at almost every table, and from their looks they were mostly drovers and range riders.

Johnny recognized a few Texas Rangers he had accompanied to Mexico a lifetime ago. Here were men with honest faces and even tempers, for Rosita had no use for troublemakers—such men did not last long at Mama's. Johnny glimpsed a massive shape bearing down on him to the right, filling his peripheral vision. He turned in time to brace himself as 258 pounds of woman collided in an embrace that knocked his breath away and almost sent him sprawling to the floor.

Johnny gasped for air and struggled to free himself from Rosita's enthusiastic display, but her lips closed over his and her round strong arms locked firmly behind his back as she smothered him with affection. She flattened her huge breasts against his chest, and he was helpless in her grasp. Chapo stared, awestruck at the sight. And when she gave Johnny one last mighty hug, a roar of good-natured approval erupted from the men at table. At thirty-two, Rosita was huge and round and soft in her widow's weeds of black French silk and crinoline. Her massive breasts, twin upheavals of coffee-colored flesh, defied the constraints of her bodice. Her face, beneath a mask of rouge and white powder, beamed a smile, both jubilant and jaded, of independence and wicked invitation.

"Johnny, *mi novio*," she purred, and pinched his cheek. Then she stepped back and the flesh beneath her arm wobbled as she shook her finger in his face and chided him. "I heard you were alive, that you even came back months ago. For shame, you did not visit your Rosita. Instead you get yourself in trouble at Señor Cotter's expense. But I forgive you now. See, everything is all right."

Rosita silenced the men around her with an angry glance. Faces were quickly lowered toward bowls and bread. Returning her attention to Johnny, her eyes widened as she noticed the boy in trail-worn clothes, a revolver belted at his slim waist and hanging heavy on his hip, his sombrero in his hands as he retreated toward the front door. Rosita wouldn't let him escape but snared him by the arm and brought him into the room alongside the big Texan.

"That's Chapo. He rides for me," Johnny explained. "I was hoping you might be able to find a room for us for the fiesta."

"Of course, *novio mío*," Rosita said, leading Johnny and Chapo through the main dining room of her establishment.

Young, dark-skinned Mexican maidens in prim cotton dresses and aprons, their black hair flowing over bare shoulders, moved among the tables in wholesome contrast to their employer. Mama Rosita's black hair was pinned high atop her head in layer upon layer of thick curls. Where the serving girls smelled of coffee and baking bread and blueberry pies, the aroma of a heady perfume extracted from more exotic spices clung to Rosita. She was a mammoth woman, yet sensual and appealing in her own elemental way. The delicate youthful bloom of her once lovely features had been replaced by a wicked look of experience, beneath which radiated a kindly heart. Many a penniless wanderer had found a hot meal and humble board at Mama Rosita's.

Long tables and curious faces and the pungent smell of chili; a room of hard tables and rough men seated in ladder-backed chairs; Indian blankets hung from adobe walls and everywhere the press of bodies and the clamor of men calling out for whiskey, black coffee, warm beer—these were all fragments of Chapo's assessment. He wasn't fooled by the virginal appearance of the young women. No doubt they could be counted on for more than freshly baked bread. A procession of men formed by the hearth, helping themselves to the contents of the caldrons, each man in turn.

Everyone stood aside for Mama, and if Johnny was recognized, no one called out to alert him. They reached the carpeted stairs and started up. The treads of the stairway creaked underfoot beneath the scarlet rug that led them out of the congestion below. Mama started down the hallway to the left, but Johnny pulled her up and turned in the opposite direction.

"We want to rest, Mama. Please find us a room down this side."

"But, Johnny—"

"Please." He slipped his arm around her ample waist.

Mama pursed her ruby lips, pouted in girlish fashion, and then acceded. "Well, I do have a room here. It was reserved for . . . Well, I suppose I shouldn't say. And anyway, he has not shown and you are here, so come with me."

Johnny continued to walk arm in arm with the woman but Chapo slipped free and glanced over his shoulder, curiosity in his expression.

"Mama's girls sleep on this side of the stairs and, uh, work down at that end," Johnny explained. "And I'll not lie awake all night listening to some poor sot in the brief, happy throes of pleasure."

"Such pleasure could be yours," Rosita purred, and leaned into the tall young Texan, her hand exploring his heavily muscled thigh.

"Rosita . . ." Johnny cautioned.

The woman sighed and continued to the end of the hall and opened the last door on the right. It was a bedroom with a four-poster double bed, a table, and ladder-back chairs. The walls were adorned, like those below, with brightly woven blankets. A solid if canted dresser completed the interior. But the floor was swept clean, and neatly folded towels and washcloths were piled on the dresser. Above the dresser hung the most curious object in the room: a breastplate of Spanish armor, the legacy of some poor conquistador handed down from generation to generation. Johnny lifted it off the wall and placed it on the floor alongside his saddlebags. "I have always wanted to own this. I have enough to buy it now."

"No," Rosita said. "You should have told me. I give it to you. And maybe, Johnny, you give me something in return."

"I'll pay cash," Johnny replied.

"I'll have a girl bring your dinner," Rosita said, sighing. She turned to leave, then paused by Chapo. "So young, so sweet," she said, cupping his chin, her musky smell exciting the youth. "A boy now, but maybe Rosita makes a man out of you one day." She leaned forward and planted a moist kiss on his cheek, brushing a single wondrous breast across his face. Then she looked at Johnny. "The water has been heated in the tub next door, in the bathroom. You can show Chapo—what a wonderful name—where it is. *Sí?*"

Johnny nodded without turning around and unbuckled his gun belt. He draped it around the post at the foot of the bed, then went to the window and looked down at the plaza below, bustling and alive with merriment. Chapo sat on the bed. He wanted to go down to the fiesta, but when he lay back on his side of the bed, his tired frame sank into the warm quilt. His body reminded him suddenly of all the aches and bruises and long hours in the saddle he'd endured for the past couple of weeks. Chapo groaned, exhaled slowly, and fell asleep, oblivious to his growling stomach.

Rosita smiled at Chapo, then looked at Johnny, his unwavering gaze fixed on the plaza below. She knew who he was looking for. And Mama Rosita was afraid—not for herself, but for Johnny Anthem.

13

★

Johnny could picture a stand of quaking aspen that grew on the south-facing back slope of Luminaria canyon as he sat in Mama Rosita's courtyard, with the morning sun leaching the night chill from the air. His stomach was full of flapjacks, but he nursed a cup of strong black coffee gripped in his right fist. It was easy to lose the morning in daydream.

Chapo peered at the big man from across his second tall stack of pancakes. "Johnny?"

Anthem ran a hand through his thick red hair, yawned, and lifted the cup of coffee to his lips. He drank deeply, ignoring that the fact that the liquid had yet to cool. Johnny let the momentary pain shock him from his reverie. He hadn't slept well, knowing Rose was close by. Yet to see her again didn't make any sense. He lowered the cup of steaming coffee to the table and wiped his mouth on the back of his hand. "What'd you say?"

"About Señora Rosita?"

Johnny grinned. "It isn't much of a story. I pulled a drunken hide-hunter off her once. He was mean drunk, crazy as hell. He tried to skin her, said he wanted to teach her a lesson."

"What happened?" Chapo pressed.

"I killed him," Johnny replied without emotion. The incident had taken place a long time ago. He had been sixteen years old and had vomited after the killing. That was all he could remember—acting on reflex, the stench of gunsmoke, and the terrible sickness afterward.

"Mama holds her gratitude like most folks a grudge." He reached for his coffee. "Both can be dangerous," he added.

Johnny glanced up to see Juan Medrano start across the courtyard to where they and Rosita's girls were taking their breakfast. The courtyard was a handsome spot, with sparrows and warblers singing in the juniper branches, where vine-covered adobe walls offered shade and respite from the street beyond and wild roses bloomed in the spring. There was no gate or archway leading outside. The courtyard could only be reached by passing through the main house; thus Rosita ensured her privacy and could screen those guests she allowed into the garden.

Juan Medrano led two new arrivals into the courtyard and headed for Anthem's table. The men knew the way, and though their eyes darted toward the attractive *señoritas* at table in the courtyard, their business was with Johnny. One was a short handsome young range rider, cleanshaven, with rosewater perfume clinging to his freshly laundered wool shirt and nankeen trousers. His companion was tall and narrow-chested, a slight paunch creeping over his beltline. Juan had insisted the men leave their guns inside the house. Johnny recognized them both: Charlie Gibbs and Kim Rideout. He eased back in his chair, his hand crawling over his thigh underneath the table to curl around the butt of the Colt thrust in his belt.

"No need for that," Kim said, his sleepy-looking eyes noting Johnny's subtle motion. Rideout was a good deal sharper than men gave him credit for.

"Oh, I don't know, Kim. I think I'll leave things as they are until Sánchez shows himself. I remember he's always backed you fellows up." Johnny smiled and reached for his coffee with his free hand. "So maybe you boys ought to just back off and skedaddle out of here until I see where I stand with Cotter and the men from the Bonnet."

"You'll wait till hell freezes over for Sánchez," Charlie remarked, hooking his thumbs in his belt. "Sánchez is dead."

"Dead?" Johnny glanced at Juan, who was standing behind the men. Medrano nodded in verification.

"Leland Rides Horse killed him. Said that it was a fair fight, that Sánchez picked a fight with him and went for his gun." Charlie wiped his mouth and tucked his long hair back behind his ears, where it hung down over his collar. "The two of them went out to ride the fence line. Leland brung him back facedown over his horse."

"Hell's hinges, Johnny, you know Sánchez weren't gun-handy. He used that Colt of his more for a hammer than anything else. If he wanted to kill a man, he'd have used his knife," Rideout added, his hangdog features growing increasingly morose.

"What did Everett do?"

"Nothing. Leland is Vin's man. And Mr. Cotter's been walking on eggs around his boy," Charlie said. "Leland drew down on me once, too. So me and Kim here said to blazes with 'em all and quit."

"Being out of work'd be a sight more enjoyable if a body weren't out of money as well," Kim added, folding his arms over his bony chest. "Mama staked us to breakfast. We overheard Juan here telling as how you've got a ranch. And we thought you might be needing a couple of good roundup men."

"I do," Johnny said, easing both elbows back on the table. "There's a sight more than Chapo and I can handle."

"Him?" Charlie asked, incredulous. "You robbin' the orphanage for help?"

Chapo shoved away from the table and started to rise, but Johnny placed a hand on the boy and restrained him.

"He'll do to ride the trail with," Johnny said. "And his pa's my segundo."

"A Mex. We'd be taking orders from a Mex?" Kim asked.

"Is that a problem with you two?" Johnny asked.

Gibbs and Rideout glanced at each other, then Kim shrugged. "Not if he knows cattle," Rideout said.

"My father," Chapo proudly exclaimed, "is what you gringos would call 'an authority.'"

Johnny had to look away to keep from snickering.

"Looks like we're ridin' for your brand," Charlie said. "Uh, but what exactly is it anyway?"

Johnny dipped his finger in his coffee and wrote the letter "A" with a slash through it. "The slash is for the creek running through the valley," Johnny explained, then wiped the makeshift brand away. "Luminaria," Johnny said, rising from the chair. "My land." He turned to Chapo. "You still going to the fiesta?"

"Unless you have something for me to do, Señor Johnny?" the boy replied. "I, uh, told Señora Rosita I would help her shop for the hacienda."

"Sure." Johnny glanced up at Gibbs and Rideout, both of whom were hiding their grins. "Just see she doesn't buy more than you can handle."

Anthem handed a twenty-dollar gold piece to Charlie. "Find a good blacksmith and tell him to make up three irons with the Slashed A brand. And take what's left for an advance on your wages."

"You trust us?" Rideout said, wondering if Anthem could really forget the past so easily.

"You ride for my brand now," Johnny said.

"What about you, Johnny? Where will you be?" Chapo asked.

Johnny brushed away a bee that had begun to circle the pancakes in front of Chapo. The insect returned, refusing to be driven off.

"Me? Oh, I think I'll pick a flower and maybe call on the old curly wolf himself."

Rose McCain Cotter studied her reflection in the mirror of her vanity. She saw a pretty woman, only twenty, dressed in a full gown of Spanish taffeta, blue as the Texas sky. She adjusted the white lace trim on a low-cut bodice that barely concealed the fullness of her bosom.

A knocking at the door brought her out of reverie. Joe Briscoe come to bring her down to breakfast. Everett Cotter would be waiting.

She crossed to the door, her dress rustling as she stepped through gleaming motes of dust dancing in the sunlit room.

"Yes. I'm ready . . . Oh!"

Rose McCain brought up sharply as she opened the door and the daylight streaming in through the windows behind her washed over the face of the man looming in the doorway.

"Johnny," she gasped, and retracted a few steps, startled. Then she tried to correct her mistake, but Johnny took the opportunity to enter the room.

He paused to take in the sumptuous furnishings, the velvet-covered wing-backed chairs and handsome tables, a love seat embroidered with herons, walls draped in deep burgundy, framed chromolithographs suspended from silken cords. Crystal decanters of fine bourbon and brandy and their accompanying cut-glass goblets were arranged like fragile soldiers upon a serving tray. Music drifted up from the street. It seemed the mariachi troubadours knew only rollicking, happy tunes.

"A fine room, Rose, fit for a queen. Is that what Vin has made you, queen of San Antonio?" Anthem noticed his reflection in the mirror; with this room as a backdrop he looked out of place, buckskin among lace. He removed his broad-brimmed sombrero, revealing his sun-weathered features and gently taunting eyes.

"You shouldn't be here," Rose said, although her heart leapt at the sight of him. Did he still feel the same way or was this a visit out of hate? Her thoughts were answered dramatically. Johnny hurried across the rug-strewn floor and swept Rose up in his embrace, his lips bruising hers in a kiss of unrestrained passion. She matched his ardor, her own desires newly awakened by the closeness of him—the strength of his arms around her, the crush of her breasts against his hard chest. Her breath merged with his, her wounded heart became whole and was given vibrant life.

He hungered for her and knew she shared his longing. And when he drew away, it took every ounce of his primitive strength.

"Tell me again I shouldn't be here," he said in a whisper, slowly recovering his own composure. "Who has a better right?" She moved to reply but he cut her off. "No, not Vin. You can't love him. Not and still kiss me like that."

"Everett . . ."

"Breakfasting downstairs, or so the desk clerk told me. I'll see him later," Johnny said, tracing a path of kisses down her long ivory neck. "No more excuses. Ask me to leave, Rose, and I'll go. Simple as that. But I've missed you for too many nights to listen to excuses." She watched his eyes and knew he spoke the truth. Lean and hungry, his countenance was as wild and strong as the country he rode. But though he was changed, he was still John Anthem, her beloved Johnny, whom she would always love.

"Everett's room's just across the hall," she said. "No matter if he's downstairs, Joe Briscoe will be coming to escort me to the fiesta this morning while Everett and the other ranchers conduct their business." Rose stepped around Johnny and closed the door to the room. "He's expecting me, and if I don't arrive at his door before long, Joe will come looking for me."

"If not now, when?" Johnny asked. "Rose, I've got to see you. We have to talk."

"Give me until evening. I'll try to slip away in the crowd. I doubt it will be difficult by evening."

"Where shall I meet you? In the street?"

"Too many people know me," Rose said, shaking her head as she walked across the room to the French doors leading out onto the balcony. Blue, gold, and vibrant red lanterns added color to the morning. The Cattleman's Hotel was newly built and stood three stories tall. From such a vantage point in the sprawling city, Rose could make out the somber gray outline of a ruined mission whose crumbling walls remained unmanned—silent, devoid of life. It stood as a stalwart symbol for those qualities the first Texans and all Texans afterward held with highest esteem: freedom, independence, and courage.

"Wait for me at the Alamo," Rose said, already feeling as if she had committed some terrible sin. Still, Vin was to blame—his aloofness toward her and the bitterness that was an unbridgeable chasm between them, making a mockery of the vows each had exchanged only a half-year ago. She opened the French doors and the street music flooded the room.

"Go quickly," she said. "There's a tree at the end of the balcony. You can climb down and no one will be the wiser."

A knock sounded at the door and Rose glanced up in alarm.

Johnny hurried over to her side. "I'll wait," he said, and his hand cupped the back of her neck and drew her into a parting kiss. He grinned and darted out onto the balcony as the hall door opened.

"Rose?" Joe said, his voice all but drowned out by the joyful raucous celebration that filled the suite. She closed the French doors, muffling the din of celebration. The segundo peeked cautiously around the edge of the door.

"I'm dressed," Rose said, seeing the look of relief flash over his burly features. And was that suspicion in his unwavering stare? she wondered. Rather than meet his gaze, Rose busied herself with a shawl and a last-minute check of her golden hair.

"I'm ready now," she said, taking up her parasol.

Joe nodded. "You look mighty pretty, Rose. Mighty pretty," he said. He wore his Sunday best, tight collar and frock coat and pinstripe wool pants tucked into the high black leather tops of his ill-fitting boots. "But you stay close to me, you hear? 'Cause the fiesta brings out the devilment in folks and anything can happen."

Rose nodded dutifully and followed him into the lamplit hall. Oil lamps with fine shades of milky glass were hung from the walls with care so that they burned brightly as necessary with a minimum of smoke. The Cattleman's Hotel employed one man whose job it was to change and trim the wicks.

"I'll be careful," said Rose reassuringly, while his warning echoed in her mind, amid the constrained passion of her heart.

Anything could happen.

Everett was master of all he surveyed: three eggs, firm, not hard; half a pound of bacon, fried crisp; a platter of cracked-wheat toast; a miniature tureen of pear preserves; a china coffeepot and cup that looked fragile in his bear-paw grip. A waiter threaded his way through the linen-covered tables serving men like Cotter the best that the

Cattleman's Hotel had to offer. Cattle barons from the valley, from Waco, from farther north along the Trinity River, and from the east as far away as the Big Thicket with its dense forests and secret byways, sat at the dining tables.

Cotter, though uncomfortable in his formal attire, his frock coat and close-fitting silk shirt, a gray brocaded vest buttoned tight around his ever-increasing girth, was at home among his peers. These were men he knew by first name, and though he considered no land holdings as grand as the Bonnet, still, he conceded that such men were creatures of destiny like himself.

And yet, in the prime of a life blessed with success, sadness and disappointment had begun to color his days. For Everett Cotter, lord of the Bonnet, was master of his breakfast and little more. Vin continued to frustrate him. How much did he have to do for the boy? When would he stand up and be a man?

Everett's son had grown more and more aloof, taken to hanging around with Leland Rides Horse and other wild elements who frequented the isolated taverns and bawdy houses on the outskirts of town. Why? Was it to shame Rose? It wasn't her fault that Johnny had returned. Cotter closed his eyes and ran a hand across his face. No, don't think of Johnny. Everett swallowed his guilt, forced it aside, letting anger reign in its place. He shoved himself away from the table, his appetite gone.

The Cattleman's Restaurant occupied the rear half of the hotel downstairs, leaving the front of a spacious lobby and—hidden behind twin doors of walnut panels and smoked glass—the Cattleman's Saloon, where the more rowdy elements of the town knew better than to intrude. The restaurant was long and a trifle narrow but plushly appointed, with round walnut tables and cushioned armchairs.

As Everett stood, heads turned in his direction and he

nodded to the Todsons, whose holdings adjoined the Bonnet, and to Carlos González, who owned land grants along the Brazos and who had fought alongside Rett Cotter at San Jacinto.

A waiter hurried over to the Cotter table, his fingers fluttering at the sash at his waist as he approached the cattleman. The waiter was reed-thin and shifted nervously as he walked up to the sullen, solid figure who glared with unintentional ferocity down at the untouched food on his table.

"Why, Mr. Cotter, does something displease you? The eggs not to your liking? The bacon too crisp?"

Everett waved the man away. "Nothing is the matter with the food, Ramón. I have suddenly lost my appetite. The setting is fine. A shame to waste it. Lord knows I would have relished such a fine setting back in the bayous when Sam Houston and I were hiding from Santa Anna. Times change a man. Times change."

"Yes, sir," the waiter said. "I understand, sir." But of course he didn't.

"I'll take my coffee and cigar on the veranda out back. Is the cactus garden completed?"

"No, sir, but it is shady and quiet compared to the porch out front."

Everett grunted in agreement and followed the waiter to the rear of the restaurant and out onto a shaded veranda. There, handmade high-backed easy chairs stood like so many thrones arranged in a row along the wall. Next to each "throne" sat a brass spittoon and an end table for a man's chosen drink. Finches in wicker cages chirped, making sweet music in the dry Texas air. And the broad overhanging roof offered delightful respite from the sun's glare. In the courtyard Mexican workmen carefully toiled over cobblestone walkways and delicate trellises, planting wildflowers and ocotillo. And on occasion, one of the workmen would look up to stare wistfully at the wrought-iron gate leading out of the garden. There was an alley beyond the gate and a stable where the guests' carriages were kept. But a man could follow the alley around the hotel and out into the street. At fiesta time pretty *señoritas* were too numerous to count, and so gay and willing that it made the tasks at hand even more arduous. How cruel was life to grunt and sweat for petty wages when a world of soft-limbed doe-eyed maidens waited to be conquered.

Everett smiled, remembering the feeling, the first quick flush of desire. He chose a chair and, comfortably alone, let the memory of bygone days lull him into a daydream that brought temporary peace. His dreams of adventure and carefree youth lasted until Johnny Anthem called his name.

Johnny stood at the bottom of the steps, his sombrero shoved back at a rakish angle high on his forehead, his thumbs hooked in the broad leather belt at his waist. Cotter noted the young man's buckskin coat was clean but worn at the cuffs and elbows, and he had no doubt that the coarse Mexican shirt beneath was threadbare. His boots were worn, too, and scuffed; his buckskin breeches, thin and tight-fitting, were molded to his long-limbed powerful physique. He reminded Everett Cotter of someone he knew long ago, someone strong and sunburned to leather and standing defiant, casting a bold shadow. He reminded Everett Cotter of himself.

"I wondered when you'd grow the nerve to look me up. I figured I might have to brace you at Mama Rosita's," said Cotter, fishing in his coat pocket for a cheroot. He noted the surprised look on the younger man's face and took pleasure in it while he lit his cigar.

Johnny recovered, fitting a piece into a puzzle. "Rex Colby." He stepped up on the veranda as Ramón the waiter arrived, balancing a coffeepot and plate of biscuits on a silver tray. The waiter was brought up sharply at the sight of the intruder. His dark little eyes darted from Johnny to the wrought-iron gate that the workers had left unlatched. No one in Johnny's attire would have been allowed in the dining room. The waiter placed the tray on the end table by Everett's chair.

"Here you are, Mr. Cotter." He turned to Johnny, who sat on the railing of the veranda. "Now as for you, young man . . ." He reached out to catch Johnny by the arm as if to lead off an errant child.

Johnny didn't budge. But he glanced down at the waiter's hand, then looked the man square in the face. "You have two choices," he said in a venomous voice. "One involves losing your fingers."

The waiter released his hold, gasped, and retreated a step, unprepared for such hostility. He hadn't journeyed all the way from New Orleans just to be maimed by such a drunken lout. He continued to back away.

"That was the other choice." Johnny grinned. His smile was a dry slash beneath his fiery-red mustache.

"Thank you, Ramón," Everett Cotter interjected. "My young friend will be leaving in a moment. And I'll personally see the gate is bolted this time."

"As you say, Mr. Cotter," the waiter sniffed indignantly. He fixed Anthem in an angry stare. "And you, sir, are no gentleman."

"And you, sir, are absolutely correct," Johnny answered. He watched the waiter leave, and then, adjusting his revolver, he balanced a leg on the rail. The door to the restaurant swung shut. "Well, if you've talked to Colby, then you know why I'm here."

"Yes. And it has little to do with cattle," Cotter snapped. "You can't fool me, Johnny. I was running bluffs while you were soiling diapers."

"I've come to you for one of your breed bulls, not to

give you grief, Everett. I have the money, you have the best stock around. I ought to know. I worked your range long enough. I ate Bonnet dust by the peck."

"I remember," said Cotter. "Everything." He wiped a hand across his face and frowned, grabbed the cigar from his mouth, and tossed it out into the garden. A laborer shuffled over and picked it up, tapped the ash from its tip, and tucked the cheroot away in his pocket. "Of all the gall," Everett roared. "To do what you did and then to ask me for help."

"I'm not asking for your help. I have the bank drafts, you know they're good. So just think of me as another customer, just another rancher starting out."

"A rancher." Cotter rose from his chair. "A rancher," he repeated, derisively. "You and some boy squatting on a piece of ground in the heart of mescalero country. That isn't a ranch, it's a burial plot!" Cotter grimaced and sank bank in the chair as pain knifed through him. He willed it gone, forced the pain into submission, and it obeyed, this time.

Johnny studied Everett and felt concern, despite the rancher's hostility toward him. This wasn't the same rugged, powerful individual who had carved an empire out of Texas soil, who had bloodied himself in the war for Texas independence, had fought Apaches and Mexican troops, and driven cattle to New Orleans, blazing a trail through a countryside still wild and infested with desperadoes.

Cotter sensed the younger man's scrutiny and his eyes flashed with anger. He shifted in his chair, reached out for his coffee, saw that his calloused hand still trembled, and tucked it back into the pocket of his coat. "Get the hell out of this hotel before I have you thrown out," he growled.

The older man's harsh words failed to light Johnny's

fuse. He only shook his head and asked in a soft voice, "Everett, do you really hate me so much?" Johnny expected a second tirade from the rancher, but surprisingly Cotter weakly reached for his coffee cup and didn't care if his hand trembled. He downed the contents of his cup, set it aside on the end table, and stood then to face Johnny. Though the younger man towered over him, there was in Everett Cotter a raw power size couldn't diminish.

"I don't hate you, Johnny. I just happen to love my son." Everett turned his back on Anthem and sauntered along the veranda until he came to the finches. He placed his hand on the cage. The tiny fluttering little birds, some golden and black and others olive green with black-tipped wings, darted furiously about their prison. "I wish you well, Johnny—yes, a long and prosperous life. But not in Texas." Everett glanced back at him and wagged his finger side to side. "Not in Texas," he said with added emphasis.

"What do you mean by that?"

"Vin hates you. It has destroyed his marriage so far, and perhaps forever. Who can tell? I think he has even tried to find you. But I'm glad he didn't. My son isn't any match for you, Johnny. He never was and never will be. But he is my son. There's nothing I wouldn't do to help him." Cotter watched as Johnny stood and crossed to him. He caught a glimpse of the gun beneath Johnny's coat, holstered at the waist, high on the left, walnut grip forward for his cross-reaching right hand. A lesser man would have heeded the warning in Anthem's eyes.

"I've passed the word to my friends in the hotel. Not a one of them will sell you so much as a milk goat, much less a breed bull. Whatever offer you make, I'll top. There's nothing in San Antonio for you, not in the city—not in all of Texas, if I can manage it. So take your money and light out. Maybe to California, or stake yourself up to the Rockies and maybe you'll strike it rich. Go anywhere, but go. Maybe then I can save my son."

"You don't own everyone. Not every rancher with good stock is your friend," Johnny exclaimed, taken aback by Cotter's declaration.

"No," Cotter agreed. "But not a one wants to be my enemy either."

"You bastard," Johnny muttered, unwilling to admit defeat yet fearful that his plans were ruined.

"Yes, I am," Everett dryly observed. "But you have left me no choice. If I'm to save Vin—"

"Save Vin!" Johnny blurted out. "He left me to die, Everett." Johnny drew close so that his breath fanned the older man's face. He wanted Everett Cotter to hear every word. "I tried to save *his* life and Vin stole my horse and left me to die. Only I ruined everything, Mr. Cotter. I lived. I endured almost a year in a Mexican hellhole. But I lived and escaped and returned, only to find your son had stolen the woman I loved. Save Vin?"

Johnny turned and descended to the garden, where he paused and added, "You may be right about my chances with the other stockmen, Everett, but there's still something for me in San Antonio," Johnny tilted his sombrero forward and tightened the leather string beneath his chin. "So long, Papa Rett."

Cotter darkened, his cheeks beneath his silvery sideburns reddening as he gleaned Johnny's intentions. "You stay clear of her. You listen, John Anthem. Rose is my own daughter-in-law, Vin's wife. Stay clear, I say. Or so help me Jehovah, I'll take a whip to your backside, do you understand, a whip? Johnny? Johnny!"

Johnny continued through the wrought-iron gate and out into the alley. The din of celebration drowned out Cotter's admonitions. Johnny followed the noise of the fiesta to its source, the crowded streets and plazas of the river city. Not once did he look back at the man in the garden, slumped in a chair on the veranda, his right hand clutched at his coat as he tried desperately to massage the pain from his chest, to rub the numbness out of his left arm, striving to retain control of limb and life.

14

★

The Alamo . . .

The banners were gone now, the sounds of battle long since faded around the old mission, replaced by echoes of music and gaiety drifting on the cool breeze. Johnny Anthem climbed one of the rubble-strewn walls and watched the setting sun burnish the sky, changing heaven from blue to vermilion, and clouds become daubs of vibrant pink, like splatters of paint upon nature's palette.

Johnny stood on the crumbled wall and faced into the breeze blowing out of the west, tugging at the fringes of his serape. He hooked a thumb around the gun butt jutting forward in its holster on his left side and tipped his sombrero back on his shoulders, letting it hang by the thong around his neck, the better to feel the west wind on his face. He looked toward the twinkling lights of the city, whose sprawling outskirts had expanded to within a stone's throw of the mission, and thought with a sigh how his foster father had ruined his plans. Johnny had confronted three different ranchers and offered them top money for their breed stock, but each time he had been turned down, his offer refused. Though the excuses were always different, he knew the real reason behind their reluctance to sell to him. Everett Cotter had put the word out not to do business with Anthem and no one wanted to cross the old curly wolf of the Bonnet ranch.

Across the courtyard, soft in the night, Johnny heard Rose call him by name. His eyes ranged the darkness. He scrambled down from the wall and followed the whisper on the wind of the ruins of what had once been the mission chapel. As Anthem walked a courtyard that had once been clamor-filled, where Texan defenders battled their determined foe, he thought, How still now, peaceful. His footsteps reverberated among the broken walls. His pace quickened as an orange glow warmed the entrance to the chapel ruins. Finally, Johnny broke into a run and dashed through the doorway. He was momentarily blinded by the light that Rose held aloft to assure herself it was Johnny she had called to.

"Rose?"

"Yes," she said, and moved away from the pockmarked wall. She set the lantern on a dusty, overturned water barrel. The barrel was empty; several well-placed musket balls had taken care of its contents long ago. The chapel had been stripped of churchly ornaments, but a few pews remained and Rose McCain Cotter covered one with her shawl, baring her shoulders and revealing the décolletage of her Spanish dress.

Johnny smiled, and as his vision adjusted to the light, his pulse quickened. He noticed she was thinner, now that he had more time to study her without fear of Joe Briscoe stumbling through the door. Anthem glanced over his shoulder at the empty courtyard.

"We're alone," Rose said, sitting in the pew. "I cut through the Widow Purcell's dress shop. Joe's probably still out in front, waiting for me to finish trying on the widow's latest creations."

"Briscoe isn't to be taken lightly," Johnny cautioned.

"No," Rose agreed, a playful look in her eye, "but any man can be taken, one way or another."

Johnny stepped over the debris-littered floor and sat beside her on the pew. He removed his sombrero and hung the hat by its leather thong over the corner of the pew. The chapel's roof consisted of a few soot-blackened timbers stretching forth like skeletal limbs from the battered walls. Stars twinkled overhead; heaven itself was the ceiling. Johnny counted three sparrow's nests balanced precariously on the charred remains of roof beams.

"We're like the sparrows, you and I," Johnny said.

Rose looked perplexed; she frowned for a moment, then shook her head. She'd never understand John Anthem, only love him. He reached under his belt and took out a piece of paper, unfolded it, and handed the scrap to Rose. She looked down at a hand-drawn map. A trail led from San Antonio west and a little north and threaded its way across undulating lines for rivers and irregular blotches for mountains with names like Sawtooth Ridge and the Sleeping Lion—names Johnny interpreted from Indian lore or used as common and widely accepted terminology, all leading to the approximate location of Luminaria. "I want you to come there with me. Keep this map. I'll be in town a few more days. Take it, keep it, let the dream work on you."

"Johnny, I can't leave. I'm married to Vin."

"Marriage?" Johnny retored in disdain. "Rosita told me all about your marriage and Vin's loyalty to you. He used to visit Rosita's until a couple of months ago when she kicked him out and refused to ever let him come back because he cut one of her girls in a drunken rage. Blind drunk, and took a knife to her."

"The gossip of a harlot," Rose said, choking back her tears. "Vin hates you, Johnny. And more than that, he's trying to walk out of his father's shadow. And it's so hard for him." Her bound hair spilled forward to shield her delicate features. "But I won't believe such things of him."

"Mama Rosita may be a lot of things, but liar isn't one of them," Johnny said, continuing to attack her resolve. "Where's Vin now? Why didn't he come in for the fiesta?"

"He's hunting. Leland and Vin went hunting," Rose said.

"Leland Rides Horse," Johnny repeated the name, dislike obvious in his voice. "I can imagine what those two are hunting."

"Stop it! Stop it!" Rose leaned forward and covered her face with her hands. Her whole body shook as she tried to contain her weeping. Images flooded through her, fragments from the past added to her confusion. She remembered her wedding night, relived it in sudden mercifully quick flashbacks, of Vin finally coming to her bed and accusing her of sleeping with Johnny Anthem. She had tried to allay his concern, she bridled at his accusations; she was his wife, she tried to show him, more out of pity than desire, but Vin was impotent with her and left her bedside enraged and humiliated. They slept apart now when Vin was home, and more often he was gone at night, out "hunting" with Leland Rides Horse.

"I'm sorry, Rose," Johnny said, ashamed of his actions. Who was he to torment her so? Love had made him cruel. He put his arm around her shoulders and pulled her to him

Rose resisted, stood and walked toward the front of the chapel, out of the ambience of the lantern's glow.

"Once I asked Vin why he stayed married, why he didn't just divorce me." Rose glanced up at the stars. As a child she had thought each one an angel, so long ago. The world had been easier to understand then. "Vin only smiled, nothing else. Smiled."

"What about you? Why not leave?"

"Because of Everett," Rose said. Johnny sighed in disgust. "He's been ill," the woman continued. "And he seems

frail now. He doesn't understand about Vin and me, and if
I tried to tell him, he wouldn't listen. He has such dreams
for us. My leaving would kill him, I know it."

"But you're here with me. Now."

Rose hadn't heard him approach. His hands on her bare
shoulders startled her, and when she turned, it was to lose
herself in his embrace. His mouth closed over hers and she
clasped her arms around his neck, pulled him to her, and
drank the sweetness of his kiss, letting the fire of his need
for her awaken her own, release the desire in her heart. His
hand stole up to cup her breast and she turned to him will-
ingly, loving his caress. Their lips parted as they pressed
cheek to cheek and held each other close and listened as
their hearts beat as one.

"Yes, I'm here. God forgive me. Love me tonight,
Johnny, I cannot promise tomorrow," she whispered. "Tonight is all we have."

"I won't believe that, Yellow Rose," Johnny softly answered, his hand running through her unbound flaxen hair.
He drank in the clean sweet smell of her, like the prairie
after a spring rain, so alive and fresh with the promise of
rebirth. He held her and never wanted to let her go.

"Take me out of here, let's ride out into the countryside
and make love, and sleep upon the good earth and let the
night hide us. And we can pretend that morning will never
come. Just for a little while, Johnny, can't we pretend?"
She felt guilty. It went against everything Rose believed
in—her own sense of honor, of moral right and wrong. And
yet her need was greater than ideas of decency. How could
she hold her life together without at least one night of love,
of completeness to carry her through the shattered days?

"I'll take you," Johnny replied. "But I have no more time
for games." He hoped that once she was free of San Antonio, Rose might be more easily swayed to escape with
him. He didn't care about consequences. Johnny retrieved

his sombrero and let the hat hang down his back. He picked up the shawl and handed it to Rose. "Come," he said, and took her hand.

They walked together up the aisle of the chapel. Rose brought the lantern but paused to extinguish it before stepping outside. As she paused, Johnny stepped ahead of her and out into the courtyard before bursting into action. He swept his serape aside, his right hand darting down and across to close around the grip of his gun riding high on his left.

Joe Briscoe, standing in the center of the yard, never made a move. He stood like a statue, unmoving and, in the feeble moonlight, implacable. Johnny wasn't taking any chances; he pulled the gun free. He heard a distinct crack of leather and the hard nasty tip of a bullwhip snaked around his throat. The big man was jerked aside and stumbled, lost his hold on the revolver, and sprawled on the ground. He staggered to his feet. Rose hurried toward him.

"Stay clear," a familiar voice roared out. Everett Cotter rode out of the shadows and into the pale glow of moon and stars. "I warned you, Johnny. You lured her, tricked her into coming here. Confused her. I told you to stay away."

Johnny stood. Everett wheeled his brown gelding and tugged on the whip, and Johnny grabbed the slack to keep the pressure off his neck as Everett dragged him over rubble and cactus and wagon debris.

"Everett, no," Rose shouted. "No. It was my fault. Mine."

"He turned your head," Cotter shouted back as he spurred his horse into a trot. Johnny groaned as rocks and splinters clawed at his back, but he forced himself to ignore the pain and concentrated on freeing his neck. He kept the slack with his left hand, his right unwrapped the coils from his throat. A moment more of agonizing pain and he was free and rolled to his feet. He caught a glimpse of Joe Briscoe hurrying up beside Rose to restrain her from entering the fray and getting herself injured.

Everett felt the lack of tension in the whip and turned his gelding to bear down on Johnny, who waited, crouching. In a rush of movement, Johnny dodged the charging horse. The bullwhip darted out as Johnny reached to catch it. He missed, heard the distinctive crack, and yelped as a strip of his hide was peeled away. Everett's gelding reared and pawed the air as he viciously yanked the reins. Once again he charged, and Johnny braced himself, pushed himself erect. His hands closed around a section of wooden wheel, part of a rim and spokes. Now, if the wood wasn't rotted through . . . Johnny had only a few seconds to worry. He saw Everett's arm raise up, lost sight of the black coils as Cotter whirled it overhead. And at the last possible moment, Johnny leapt to his feet, holding the shattered wheel before him like a shield.

The bullwhip cracked forward and wrapped itself around the spokes. Johnny braced himself as the gelding charged past and pulled with all his strength as the bullwhip snapped taut and Everett, caught unawares, flipped out of the saddle and landed with a sickening thud in the dust. Johnny tossed the whip aside.

"You crazy old bastard," he shouted, advancing on the man. Cotter rolled over and crawled to his knees. "That's right, get up," Johnny yelled. "You wanted a fight, so be it. I won't hold back this time."

Everett stood, staggered a moment, dropped to his knees, forced himself to stand again, and took a step toward Johnny and collapsed, dropping facedown in the open yard.

Johnnny broke into a run and reached the older man a few seconds before Rose and the segundo.

"Papa Rett!" Rose gasped in horror as Johnny turned his foster father over on his back. Everett's hand was clutching at his chest and his breathing was rapid and shallow. Cotter managed to open his eyes. He saw Johnny.

"I . . . can't let . . . you ruin it . . . can't let . . ." He glanced at Briscoe, who knelt by him then at Rose. "Daughter . . . take me home." He closed his eyes.

Briscoe reached underneath the rancher and lifted Cotter in his arms. "I'll take him to the doctor," Briscoe managed to say in a tight voice. He started toward the gelding.

Johnny walked alongside and, when Briscoe mounted up, lifted Cotter's limp frame up into the segundo's arms.

"I'm going to Doc Breckinridge's," Briscoe said. "You coming?" He looked at Rose. "My horse is tied over yonder by the grain crib." Rose nodded. Briscoe reined the horse toward town and rode at a gallop through the gate.

Johnny's neck and back still burned, but somehow the pain seemed so much less. He retrieved his revolver and hurried to catch up to Rose as she reached Briscoe's horse. Ignoring propriety, she tucked her dress between her legs and swung aboard to sit the saddle like a man.

"Rose . . ." Johnny caught the bridle to keep the woman with him, hoping to ease her shame.

"No. There's nothing to say. I was wrong. Everything was wrong." Rose McCain Cotter closed her eyes and shook her head. "Leave town, Johnny. Go away. Go far away." She stifled a sob and pulled the reins free of his grasp. "Oh, Johnny, what have we done? What have we done?"

15

★

On the day Everett Cotter left San Antonio to return to the Bonnet, a brisk cold wind sprang up out of the north. Joe Briscoe drove a flatbed wagon to the doctor's house and old Doc Breckinridge himself lent a hand carrying Everett Cotter to the wagon, declaring along the way he would never accuse his stricken friend of being a windbag ever again, seeing as how heavy he was.

Chapo, who had kept watch from an alley across the street, saw the early-morning activity and took off at a dead run. He raced like a frightened antelope down the unusually empty streets, across the quiet, sleepy plaza, and up to the iron gates of Mama Rosita's. He ran through the courtyard, took the front steps in a single bound, and hurried inside the warm dining room.

Johnny was seated before the fireplace, his legs stretched out in front of him as he slumped in a high-backed chair by the fire. In the week following Everett's stroke, Johnny had scarcely ventured outside. Twice he had approached Doc Breckinridge's only to be turned away by the doctor himself.

Johnny spent his time brooding. At night he gave himself to troubled sleep. Charlie Gibbs and Kim Rideout were having a game of crack-a-loo when Chapo burst into the room. Each man would toss a coin to the ceiling and let it fall to the floor, and when both had taken a turn, the two men would gauge how close each coin had come to a pre-determined crack in the hardwood surface underfoot. The closest coin took both. Charlie Gibb's supply of coins was rapidly decreasing, but he seemed to be taking his losses in stride. Johnny had begun to tire of the man's good nature, being in a rotten mood himself. So he was relieved to see the look of excitement on Chapo's face and rose from the chair.

Two of the girls working on dinner's caldron of chili glanced up with obvious delight. They were dark-skinned, sweet-looking *señoritas*, still girlish though five years older than Chapo, in whom all of Mama's girls had taken a special interest. Whether or not Chapo had been initiated in the rites of manhood was anyone's guess. The boy of the *barrancas* certainly wasn't telling.

"Johnny, they are leaving. A flatbed wagon and a half a dozen men. I saw the yellow-haired *señora* riding in back with Señor Cotter." The boy's face was flush from running, his eyes sparkled with excitement.

"Thanks," Johnny replied, alive at last. He grabbed his serape and sombrero and started toward the door. "Stay here with Kim and Charlie," he ordered.

"But I ride with you," Chapo protested.

"The hell if we'll stay," Charlie interjected, sweeping his last couple of coins off the table and into his hat. "Pay Mama for the drinks, Kim."

"Why me?" Rideout protested.

" 'Cause you got all my money!"

"Oh."

"Look, there might be trouble. I hope not, but with Vin in town just about anything could happen," Johnny tried to explain. He could see that Mama Rosita, in her dressing gown and night silks, her face unwashed and dusted with powder and her hair unpinned, had walked in from her bedroom downstairs: the door was open and Johnny knew she'd been listening. The huge woman shook her head as if in silent entreaty, pleading with him not to go out in the street.

Johnny unbuckled his gun belt and placed it on a nearby table, tossing the folds of his serape over his shoulder the better to reveal he was unarmed. "You boys, stay. That's an order. If you can't follow orders, then get the hell out of my sight." He spoke in a gruff voice, regretting his harshness but determined that if there was trouble, he alone would pay the price. He turned on his heel and stalked out the door.

The flatbed wagon hit a nasty rut in the street and lurched to the side, and Everett groaned in discomfort. Rose flashed an angry look at the man handling the team. Joe Briscoe glanced over his shoulder, a look of apology on his face. Rose calmed herself.

"Sorry, ma'am," Joe said. "Doing the best I can. Streets been churned up by the fiesta and all. Lots of wagon and livestock come through town."

"I know, Joe. I know." Rose glanced down at Everett's pale, drawn features and felt a resurgence of guilt. "We're all doing the best we can," she sighed.

"If you can't drive that rig, I'll damn well get someone who can," Vin snapped, riding his horse alongside the wagon. His red-streaked eyes flashed with anger. His features were bunched tight, making a mask of hatred out of his handsomeness and fine delicate looks. He had been in town since last evening, having learned of his father's stroke almost a week after it had happened. He refused to say where he and Leland had been.

Everett opened his eyes to reprimand his son but lacked

the energy for anything but a whisper. It was against Doc
Breckinridge's wishes that he leave town, but the rancher
had insisted he be allowed to return home. He'd grown
increasingly upset, which in itself was a danger to the
man's health.

Vin glanced up at the sound of an approaching horse
and watched as Leland Rides Horse galloped up to the
wagon that Joe held to an agonizing slow pace. The ride
to the Bonnet would take two days and possibly part of a
third at the pace the wagon must keep to, so as not to rough
the patient.

Rose strained to listen as the half-breed reined up by
Vin and related his information. She managed to catch a
smattering of their conversation and heard something about
a bridge and John Anthem. Her pulse quickened. She had
prayed Johnny would stay away. The last thing she wanted
was trouble for him or Vin.

Leland finished his report and checked the revolver he
had holstered at his waist. Vin did the same, and ordered
the other four men to check the loads in their percussion
rifles.

The wagon cleared the end of Prospect Street, already
devoid of its banners as shopkeepers and the local citizens
emerged in the early morning to remove the last vestiges
of their celebration. The wagon received the attention of
everyone it passed. Men doffed their hats in respect.
Women in the shops and houses watched in silence, ob-
serving every detail for gossip later. A dog sauntered out
of the blacksmith's, trotted toward the party, and was immediately shooed away by one of the ranch hands. The
wagon rounded the corner smithy shop and the bridge
across the San Antonio River came into view. To her horror, Rose saw a single figure outlined against the horizon,
a single man waiting at the bridge crossing.

"Johnny," she said softly, and looked down, found Everett watching her. She blushed, wishing she hadn't spoken the name aloud.

"We don't want any trouble, Vin," Joe Briscoe called to the young man riding ahead of the wagon.

Vin turned around and fixed him in a furious stare, his eyebrows arched in disdain. "I give orders. I don't take them. It's time you learned that."

"Gunfire will spook this team. They break into a run, it'll kill your father."

"Then they had better not break," Vin retorted.

A covered wagon rolled down the street behind them, closing fast. Vin studied it a moment but found no threat in it. A mere boy was handling the team, obviously some poor Mexican youth driving for his papa, who was probably passed out drunk in the wagon. River Bridge was a main crossing for the people of San Antonio. The boy would have to follow the Bonnet crew across. Just as long as he didn't get in the way, Vin couldn't care less. He returned his attention to the man at the bridge. Soon, now. He looked over at Leland, who nodded. The breed had no fear of Anthem.

Johnny watched them come, his thumbs hooked in his belt, his sombrero hanging behind his head, the cooling breeze ruffling the shock of red hair worthy of a Viking in days of old. As the wagon drew near, Johnny could see the expression on Vin's and Leland's faces and he began to doubt the wisdom of meeting the wagon unarmed. He hoped someone was watching from the Ranger camp. He was counting on the nearness of Colby's men to keep order. From the look of Vin's armed escort, Johnny began to think he had counted wrong.

He took a few steps out of the roadway, espied Rose in the wagon bed, and stared at her, but she averted her eyes. Then Vin and Leland and the other riders fanned out ahead of the flatbed wagon to face Johnny, about fifteen feet in front of him. The ranch hands not only recognized Johnny, they could tell he carried no gun and kept their rifles balanced on their laps. The rifles were cocked, though. They looked uncertain as to what Vin expected of them.

"I was hoping to see you," Vin said.

Leland walked his horse a couple of yards to the side. Johnny watched him, then returned his attention to Vin. The covered wagon with its scrawny Mexican driver pulled up behind the riders for the Bonnet.

"*Señor*, may I pass, *por favor?* I have far to go," the driver called out. Johnny knew the voice at once and shifted his stance; looking between the mounted men, he saw Chapo sitting on the bench seat of a canvas-covered wagon. He was dressed in the soiled ragged clothes of a peon. Johnny scowled. The boy had ridden into real trouble this time.

"I'm unarmed, Vin. I'm not looking for trouble," Anthem said, returning his attention to the problem at hand.

"But you found it all the same," Vin replied. "Unarmed, is it? You damn near kill my father and you want me to worry whether or not you have a gun." Vin turned to one of the ranch hands and reached over and took the man's Colt from his holster and tossed the weapon in the dirt a few feet in front of Johnny. "Now I don't have to worry."

"*Señor*, please let me pass," Chapo called from the covered wagon. His voice was urgent as he interrupted.

"Damn it all, will someone shut the chili-eater up?" Vin roared out.

Chapo gave a tug on the reins and the team started forward and forced a path between the Bonnet ranch hands, and as he did, the canvas siding flipped up to reveal Charlie Gibbs and Kim Rideout. They leveled their rifles at the Bonnet men, along with a half dozen of Mama's *señoritas*, still in their dressing gowns and brandishing an assortment of revolvers, shotguns, and derringers, not to mention an inordinate amount of skantily covered skin.

Completing the crew was Mama Rosita herself. She dominated the center of the wagon, her hair undone and flowing in the wind like Medusa's own serpentine locks. Mama towered over her lovelies, looming like some goddess of wrath as she pointed a monstrous blunderbuss at Vin's riders while struggling to tuck one of her pendulous brown breasts back inside the silken folds of her sleeping gown. Her rouge and face powder were smeared from sleep into a mask that would have made a mescalero envious. Her warning, that she had loaded the blunderbuss with round shot and carpenter's nails, was more overkill. The riders were already backing off. Even Leland knew better than to drop his hand near his gun. He crossed his palms on his saddle horn.

Vin looked around him, shocked speechless by the rapid turn of events. One moment he had the upper hand; the next, he wasn't even in the game. None of the ranch hands wanted to draw down on a bunch of women, and especially women bristling with such nasty-looking weapons.

"I'm gonna count to three," said Mama Rosita. "And any man I see still carrying a gun, Mama Rosita shoot his cock off, *sí*." She smiled sweetly. And started to count. Rifles and revolvers hit the ground at "one."

"You boys cross on over," Johnny said. He looked across the river and saw activity in the Ranger camp. Men were up and awake, a couple of well-armed Rangers already heading for the bridge. Someone no doubt had alerted Colby. "Now," Johnny said.

The ranch hands lost no time in trotting their mounts across, the better to be out of the range of that blunderbuss.

Leland walked his horse up to Johnny. "Another time," he said in an emotionless voice. Then he followed the ranch hands.

Vin glanced over his shoulder at the prostitutes in the wagon with Gibbs and Rideout, then he whipped his horse. The animal reared and pawed the air and Johnny darted out of the way of its slashing hooves. Vin headed across the bridge at a gallop, leaving Johnny to brush the dust from his clothes. The tension broken, he walked up to the wagon and gave Chapo a hard look.

"Señora Rosita wanted to go for a ride," Chapo explained, wide-eyed and innocent.

Johnny shifted his gaze to Charlie and Kim.

"We just come along to protect the girls." Charlie grinned.

"Well, you better protect them right on back to Mama's before the Rangers get over here," Johnny said.

Chapo caught up the reins and obediently touched his whip to the horses.

Rose couldn't help but stare at Mama Rosita, realizing the woman was all her reputation claimed—and more.

Mama noticed the younger woman's attention and tried to look more ladylike, but couldn't figure out how to begin. "Sorry for your troubles, Miss Cotter," she finally said. The canvas-covered wagon bolted forward and Rosita sat with a jolting thud that threatened to break an axle.

Johnny walked up to the flatbed and peered in at Everett, lying quiet and still beneath his mound of quilts. Cotter was awake and watchful, his hard eyes probing. But he didn't speak.

"How is he?" Anthem asked.

"We'll find out," Joe said, reins in hand. "By the time we get to the Bonnet, I reckon we ought to know. If he survives the trip, he ought to live when we reach home."

"Johnny, what do you want now? Haven't we done enough harm?" Rose said, her tone weary.

"I have something to tell him," Johnny said. He glanced down at his hands and gathered his thoughts. Then he leaned on the siding, picked a strand of dried yellow hay from the weathered wood, and tucked it between his lips, chewing on the stalk as he studied the man lying prone on the bedding.

"I'm not leaving Texas, Mr. Cotter." Johnny shook his head, changed his stance, then cleared his throat. "I got a place, something to hold on to, to build on. I had nobody and nothing when you picked me out of my dead mother's arms. I guess now I'm an orphan again. But this time I have a place to go to. And I'll fight to keep it. You ought to understand that." Johnny looked up at Rose, then back to Everett Cotter. "But I'll stay clear of the Bonnet, of you and Vin . . . and Rose. You won't have any more trouble with me. Ever again."

He paused a moment, then gave the siding a pat. Johnny looked up at Briscoe, then at Everett, and at last at Rose. He backed away to let the wagon pass on.

There was nothing more to be said.

PART THREE

★

JANUARY 1850

16

★

The wind in the buffalo grass tugged at the hem of her woolen cloak. The handstitched blue flannel trim of her cowl fluttered as Rose turned the carriage off the Camino Real and into the courtyard of San Gabriel Mission. Rose guided the bay mare to a brick pillar rising out of the hard-packed earth. The pillar was adorned with iron rings set in stone, and she tethered the bay to one. Several horses, half a dozen two-wheel carts, and a couple of flatbed wagons crowded the mission yard. The single cast-bronze bell in the adobe tower pealed forth over the countryside, summoning the last tardy members of the church community to worship.

Rose hurried up the few remaining steps, paused, and looked back the way she had come as Joe Briscoe walked his horse beneath the arched entrance to the mission. He reined in and sat watching her, a hand drifted to the brim of his hat. He nodded in greeting.

Rose had insisted on riding alone from the ranch. He had quietly, politely ignored her every argument. Times had changed; hard-looking men rode for the Bonnet these days. Briscoe had cautioned her more than once about going out unattended. Roisterers and scalawags could be found as easily around the home fire as waiting in ambush along the road.

Rose hesitated to share the segundo's opinions of the men Vin hired to replace the ranch hands who had quit during the past few months. And yet she had to admit the new faces populating the Bonnet bunkhouse belonged to a rough-cut crew. She considered confronting Briscoe but decided against such an act. Rose was moved that Joe Briscoe worried over her, yet wanted to tell him she was a big girl now and could look after herself. But what was the use in trying to make him understand? Joe had a way of becoming selectively deaf.

Rose waved to him and started up the steps to the church, knowing she would find him waiting for her on the way out. Inside the mission chapel, a number of families, of Mexican descent for the most part, filled the hardwood pews. The regular parishoners were not those friends of Everett Cotter who had come to the wedding, those wealthy ranchers and merchants who comprised the first families of San Antonio. Instead, gathered on this Sunday were Tejas Indians and Mexican farmers dressed in their humble Sunday best, their children freshly scrubbed and seated reverently or, like the very youngest, fidgeting restlessly as Father Vicente, with an entourage of four altar boys, entered from the sacristy.

Rose's parents had been Irish Catholic, and Everett had alerted Father Vicente of the orphaned girl's history. The padre had made several trips to the Bonnet ranch to ensure the girl's upbringing had at least some exposure to Catholicism.

The priest and Joe Briscoe were often embroiled in arguments over biblical references and basic theology. Briscoe was much more the fundamentalist, who saw no use for any single denomination. For him, the good book was enough and churchgoing was a waste of time. In the end,

Father Vicente's kindliness and his concern for living the gospel won over Briscoe's arguments for a solitary theology. Rose felt drawn to San Gabriel's community and found comfort here most of the time.

Vicente's melodic voice resonated through the church as he began to pray in a lyrical Latin tongue, the congregation responding in kind.

> Kyrie eleison, Kyrie . . .
> Christe eleison, Christe . . .
> Kyrie eleison, Kyrie . . .

Rose knelt in the shadows of the last pew and watched as images blurred, remembering another woman with yellow-gold hair standing at the altar in another time—no, not even a year ago, the same woman and yet the same no longer. Rose McCain, obedient bride, not completely happy yet at peace. And peace was precious to a young woman, love lost and rising from the ashes of a private tragedy. I can learn to love again, she had said. Love can live again.

But there was the irony. Love had never died, her heart still yearned, still cried for completeness. Love had never died, it walked into Rose's life on her wedding day and carried her away. She had tried to replace John Anthem in her heart. But love dooms loyalty, destroys resolve, won't be denied. Blame Vin, blame his insane jealousy, his hatred of Johnny Anthem, his determination to be more than his father. And no matter how she tried to bridge the chasm Johnny's return had created, Vin wouldn't be appeased. Why? The fact that Rose had gone to Johnny of her own will in San Antonio doomed the marriage. If Vin refused to believe her before, he certainly didn't intend to start trusting her now.

The haunting ended, the specter at the altar disappeared. Rose lowered her head and prayed, not for herself but for

Everett. Prayed that God would heal him and enable him to wrest control of the ranch away from Vin, who with each day became more and more consumed with power. Prayed for Everett? Rose silently wondered, sadly amused; they were prayers for herself, too. As soon as Everett was well, somehow, someway, she intended to leave. Rose glanced up in alarm fearing that God almighty would appear in wrath and glory as one of the carved wooden saints set in the walls, that He would climb down from His humble niche and accuse her of a most grievous sin against those sacred vows she had once taken.

Lord, I thought I knew him. And I tried. Vin has changed and become someone I cannot reach. No, perhaps he hasn't changed, only I can see him more clearly. But then, curse such sight, for it makes my failure all the worse.

The deep-rooted hatred in Vin Cotter burned like a fire no love could extinguish. It destroyed trust and faithfulness, crippled harmony, and left husband and wife strangers in a lonely place, a state Rose McCain could no longer endure.

For now, though, Everett needed her. His recovery had been slow and his faculties remained damaged. But Papa Rett was alive and growing stronger, and Christmas Day had been brightened when he stood up from his wheelchair and took a few steps before sinking into Joe Briscoe's supportive embrace. Rose remembered something else that day: the curious look of emotion on Vin's face, as if he begrudged his father's returning strength. Everett hadn't noticed, but Rose fixed Vin in an accusatory stare.

Rose shifted her weight on the hard wood kneelers and looked up as Father Vicente bowed to the tabernacle beneath the crucifix and led his flock in a novena. Voices soft and fluid, spoken in unison within the cool, shaded confines of the chapel. A Tejas servant added dry timber to a nearby iron stove. Flames leapt about the fresh fuel, greedily consuming every sliver. Rose pulled her cloak about her and shivered, more from her own shameful thought than the dampness. Vin would never divorce her. Not while Johnny was alive. So be it. Rose didn't intend to spend her days as a prize or a prisoner at the Bonnet. Everett needed her now and she chose to remain because it was the only course her conscience allowed. But when he was well . . . Her gaze drifted from the priest to the wooden image upon its cross.

Forgive me, she prayed, her lips silently forming the words. She didn't know where to go—certainly not to Johnny, for trouble was sure to follow her. "Johnny, what have we done?" she once asked of him, there in the Alamo with the guilt of Everett's possible death weighing on her soul, crushing it down into the ruins underfoot. Yet what had Rose and Johnny done? Loved. Then forgive me for love, for loving still.

The words of the Confiteor drifted back to the woman in shadow who silently recited with the priest, *"Mea culpa, mea culpa, mea maxima culpa."* Through my fault, through my fault, through my most grievous fault.

Rose stepped out into the sunlight and shivered as the cold air washed over her features. Joe Briscoe had tethered his horse at the pillar alongside her carriage. He sat on the ground with his back to the pillar and the north wind and puffed on his clay pipe as he watched the clouds whisk across the azure sky. His cheeks were red and he sat with his wolf-pelt-trimmed collar pulled up around his throat.

"You should have come inside."

"I don't like the Mass," he replied, blowing a plume of smoke from between his wind-chapped lips. His legs creaked as he straightened, his knee joints popped, and he winced from the aches that plagued him every winter.

"Not for the Mass, but for the warmth," Rose explained.

"Maybe next time," the segundo replied matter-of-factly, staring past Rose toward the trio of armed men trotting their

horses at a crisp pace beneath the arch. They were men of
average height with the look of hard workers; Joe recognized the youngest even at a distance.

"Young Todson and a couple of the riders from his
papa's spread," Joe said aloud, noticing the alertness with
which the men rode, as if they expected trouble from him.
He sensed their tension; the expressions on their faces only
reaffirmed it. Dust trailed away from the hooves of their
horses as the three men rode up to the pillar and Joe waited
for them to come. He kept his hands in his pockets, well
away from any sort of weapon. He wanted these men to
know he suspected no mischief from them. In truth he considered young Todson a friend.

Dan Todson, though roughly the same age as Vin, was
a newer arrival to the state. Elder Todson had purchased
land grants to the north of the Bonnet and with judicious
effort had developed a thriving ranch half as large as the
Bonnet. The Todsons had been good neighbors and robust
but fair competitors. They had coexisted peacefully with
the Cotter holdings for more than two years.

Dan Todson removed his hat, nodded to Rose, and, with
a brief command to the men with him, turned his round
features to Briscoe. The riders for the Todson brand held
back, allowing the younger man privacy with the Bonnet's
segundo. Rose stepped forward the better to hear. Todson
was freckle-faced, with a plain and open character that had
never mastered subterfuge. He was showing some belly
now but his shoulders were thick with muscle and his
slightly bowed legs were short and solid.

"I got words for Briscoe, Miss Cotter." He glanced
around at his men. "It's ranching business," he added, looking back at her.

"Then, go ahead," Rose said, stepping out of Briscoe's
shadow. "What affects the ranch affects me."

Todson shrugged. He wasn't in any mood to argue. "Me

and the boys were having a celebrate in town. We ran into Vin at a, uh, place." He coughed and shifted his gaze.

"Dan Todson, I'm well aware my husband enjoys the company of whores. It's a habit he doesn't choose to break. On the other hand, you have always struck me as a happily married young man whose wife, I believe, will deliver you a child in a few more months. My husband is no saint, but then, he's no father either."

Dan blushed and shifted in the saddle. "Now look, Rose, you know I ain't the sort of man that . . . Well, don't you be starting any gossip that would reach Mary. I've had enough trouble from you Cotters. Anyway, I just was having a drink of Who Hit John, it was the boys that climbed the stairs with the ladies, weren't it, boys?"

The ranch hands waiting a few paces back nodded in unison; after all, they rode for the brand.

"What other trouble you had from the Bonnet?" Briscoe said, not liking what the young man was implying. "Seems to me this dry winter, the Bonnet has been the best friend you Todsons have had, what with your springs drying up."

"That's what I mean," Dan replied. "Vin told us we had to drive our cattle off Bonnet range. He knows we're using the spring at Comanche Creek. Everett said we could. And that's what I told him."

"Then that should close the matter. You can leave your cattle at the spring."

"And have Vin round 'em up for stock? No, thanks." Dan shrugged. "Aw, who am I kidding? We have to leave them there. Me and the boys ain't had time to dig out the springs that have dried up on our place. But I aim to stay with my cattle. I don't care how many hard cases like Leland Rides Horse and that Washburn Vin brings with him. If he makes trouble, then Vin Cotter better be ready for it too. You tell him that."

"Washburn, Natchez Washburn?" Joe asked, fearing the worst.

"You didn't know? One and the same," Dan Todson answered. "Oh, you Cotters have some right handy men ride for you. Only thing is they ain't cattlemen. Folks are getting edgy, Joe. Real worried."

"Washburn doesn't ride for the Bonnet," Joe said.

"Vin hired him right there in San Antone."

"We'll see about that," Joe grimly muttered.

"You won't find Vin in town. He rode off when we left, after threatening us." The wind increased; a strong gust tried to steal Todson's hat, but he caught the brim in time and cursed beneath his breath. "The hell with this—uh, pardon, Rose—but I'm heading for home." His gelding backstepped and fought the bit a moment before Dan brought the animal under control.

"You tell Everett what I said. Keep away from Todson stock."

"Don't order me, boy," Briscoe scowled. "And ride easy. One bronc on the prod is enough on any range."

"Dan," Rose called out, "I'll speak to Vin. Maybe he'll listen to me. I'll try. And when Everett takes over again, he'll set things right. You know he will. So just be patient, please. I'll bet Mary will say the very same thing."

"Who said Everett will ever be able to run things again?" Dan grimly retorted.

"Who said he won't?" Joe interjected, his tone deepening, anger in his voice.

"Vin Cotter," young Todson said and, gesturing to his men to follow, rode out of the mission courtyard, leaving Rose and the segundo to ponder his revelation in the cold wintry light.

Three hundred miles from San Antonio, Johnny Anthem wondered if he would see another January. Pokeberry Tyler was of like mind and whispered as much to the flame-haired young man. Johnny peered down through a clump of buffalo grass and ocotillo at the solitary figure of the Apache warrior crouched at the edge of a small spring. Hard scrabble countryside stretched out to the horizon, the distance hiding a maze of gulleys and ravines that stretched north to Sentinel Peak and Luminaria.

The ground behind the Apache brave wore a thick cover of scrub oak and mesquite and heavy underbrush of thorn thicket and wild vines. The brave seemed oblivious to the tracks that led up from the water and into the stand of trees.

Johnny, Poke, and Chapo had been tracking the maverick steer for the better part of an hour, having cut sign a couple of miles away. Johnny was certain the steer had come to drink and imagined the Apache's arrival had frightened the animal away. Still, it might only have ventured into concealment to assess the nature of the human intruder. Longhorns grown to maturity in the wild were a capricious and dangerous lot.

Johnny watched the Mescalero Apache cup water to his mouth and sit back on his haunches. The brave was on foot, wore breechclout and leggings and moccasins, and carried a musket with a broken stock that he placed on the moist sand within reach. The bone handle of a knife jutted from the braided leather strap circling his waist. He began to scrutinize the lay of the land.

Johnny and Poke ducked down below the lip of the ravine they were using for cover. Chapo scrambled up the gravel-littered slope toward the two men, who motioned for him to walk with care. He'd gone to retrieve his rifle from the saddle scabbard on his mare. The youth slowed his pace and began to choose his steps more wisely so as not to alert his intended target beyond the rim.

Crawling crab-legged over the loose debris, Johnny managed to intercept Chapo about halfway up the slope.

"What do you think you are doing?" Johnny asked, keeping his voice low.

"I'm ready for a fight," Chapo answered, surprised. He extended his hand holding the rifle out for Johnny to see.

Johnny shoved the gun aside.

"Put it back."

"What?"

"He aims to parlay with the Injun," Poke said, sliding down to join his companions.

"He'd as soon slit Johnny's throat," Chapo said.

"That's what I told him," Poke interjected with a wag of his head. "We got us a chance for one less Apache to worry about, and Anthem gets some fool notion to kill himself."

"I can pick him off from the rim," Chapo explained as if that were the problem. "He won't take two steps."

"Killing is always the easiest way," said John Anthem.

"I'm not going to let him walk out of here. His kind nearly killed Pa and me. I don't forget so easily." Chapo started past the big man, but Johnny caught him by the arm and jerked him around.

"You aren't some bandit from the mountains anymore, Joaquín Almendáriz. You ride for Luminaria and will do as I say," Johnny said, his tone as icy as the wind whipping their serapes. Chapo lowered his head and stared at the ground. "Poke, you and the boy stay here, and if the Mescalero does put me under, then shoot the bastard."

"The only Apache I ever knew that'd hold still long enough to listen to reason had a bullet betwixt his eyes," Poke grumbled.

"There's a first time for everything." Johnny grinned and clapped the older man on the shoulder. He did the same to Chapo and then turned and scrambled up the slope. His plan depended on the Apache at least being able to understand some Spanish, which many of them did. When the men at Luminaria weren't working on the ranch house and rounding up mavericks and wild mustangs, they were having to guard against attack. Johnny had purchased enough Colt revolvers so that every man went about heavily armed. After a single melee out on the open prairie when Memo, Johnny, and Kim Rideout had driven off a Mescalero war party, the Apache warriors had ridden clear of Anthem's valley, fearing these white intruders with their many-times-firing guns. Not that any of the Slash men felt safe; no one rode alone if he could help it. But Johnny hoped to change the situation. If only he could meet with one of the war chiefs, Johnny hoped to win if not acceptance at least tolerance of the white men in the valley. The prospect of peace was worth any gamble, even the one he was about to take: confronting the brave at the spring, unarmed.

He reached down to unbuckle his gun belt and heard the warrior's startled outcry, which was quickly drowned out by a deafening bellow of animalistic rage, pouring from the throat of the steer. Johnny scrambled hand over foot up the gulley and cleared the rim in time to see the longhorn bull crashing out of the thicket. The Apache dived to his right, grabbed his rifle by the barrel, and threw it at the behemoth bearing down on him. The bull stood as tall as a man, its mighty legs trampled the earth as it lowered its great head and flipped the rifle clear with a lunge of its curved horns. The animal bellowed again and set the earth atremble as it charged. The brave dived for the spring, hoping the shallow pond might slow the beast.

Johnny yanked off his serape and whirled it over his head as he raced down the slope. He loosed a high-pitched shriek and thumbed off a shot, then continued to run, fire, and yell for all he was worth. Geysers of water erupted just in front of the startled bull as lead slugs peppered the pond. The animal dug in its hooves at the thunderous crack of the revolver and heaved its bulk around to ward off this latest intruder. But the gunshots startled the young bull, and the big red-bearded figure stumbling headlong down the slope seemed something other than human. The longhorn, choosing discretion over valor, headed for the safety of the timber once more. The steer crashed through brush and thicket, shattered saplings in an effort to put a respectable distance between itself and Anthem.

Johnny reached the edge of the spring. He bent double, catching his breath, his throat dry and hurting. The Colt dangled from his fist, smoke trailed from the barrel and cylinder.

The Apache stared at the white man in amazement and rose shivering from the water. He lifted his gaze to the ridge above as Poke and Chapo cleared the rim with their rifles menacing. The brave strode from the spring and emerged on the opposite side of the waterhole. His darkened features were as inscrutable as a totem, but so had been the white man's actions. The Mescalero studied Johnny, trying to understand. He trusted no one, especially white men.

Imperceptibly at first, his right hand curled around the bone handle of his knife, as if readying himself for this last battle. Softly, he began to sing his death chant. A knife was no match for the rifles and pistol trained on him.

"No," Johnny said, standing. And then with a single motion of his hand, he demonstrated the brave might go in peace. He holstered his revolver. "Back off," Johnny shouted. Chapo and Poke began to grumble among themselves.

The Apache tightened the swath of scarlet cloth that he wore as a headband gathering back his shaggy black mane. Droplets of icy moisture beaded his wiry torso. He shivered from the cold, but remained true to his race and to his way of life. He wouldn't be the first to turn and walk away.

Johnny folded the serape and placed it on the ground.

The brave, shivering even more violently now as the wind picked up, stared nervously at the coarsely woven blanket. Johnny held his hand palm outward and slowly turned his back to the brave and started uphill. Poke whispered to Chapo at his side and both man and boy disappeared down behind the rim. Johnny continued on up the slope, his shoulders tight from the tension. He half-expected to catch the Apache's knife in the back.

He stumbled, fell to his knees, grimaced, and stooped over to brush a half-dozen cactus spines from his left trouser leg. The nankeen was torn over the knee and the loose threads were stained with blood. He wiped the dirt from his jaw and reached the rim. Only then did he chance a peek over his shoulder. As quiet as a cloud, the Mescalero Apache had stolen away. He was gone.

And so was the serape Johnny had left behind.

Poke and Chapo waited for Johnny just out of sight of the spring. Chapo appeared relieved when Johnny showed himself. Poke only scowled and dug in his pocket for a cigarillo.

"Well, younker, you about turned what hair I got left plum silver with that stunt. You think it made any difference?"

Johnny studied the timber, shielded his eyes from the sun, and peered up as a hawk glided out from Sentinel Peak. Something struggled in its grasp. Johnny didn't bother to reply. Here in the mountains, the answer would come soon enough.

17

★

Everett Cotter sat on the front porch and watched Bonnet rock turn to burnt sienna in the dying light. His hands, clenched into fists, were curled around the armrests of his cane-backed wheelchair. His knuckles were poised inches above his still-useless legs. He had feeling in his limbs from time to time. Pain like a red-hot poker thrust into his muscles. Sometimes he groaned aloud from the excruciating spasms, but at least they were a sign his legs were slowly recovering. At the moment, they were numb again. Everett didn't know which was worse: to sit and suffer the actual agony, or to have them numb and have his thoughts darken with fears of being an invalid forever. He kept a dueling pistol in the drawer next to his bed should such a prognosis come to pass. He wouldn't live half a man. Better a whole life or a whole death.

"Never did nothing partway in all my life," he said aloud. His thoughts were interrupted when Cordelia came outside and found him. He blushed in embarrassment as the woman cried out and hurried toward him, her poundage rippling with each ungainly stride.

"Mr. Cotter, you'll catch your death of cold. Don't you feel that north wind? Here it is only the first week of the

New Year and you're already trying to keep yourself from seeing another." She swooped down on him like a mother hen, jamming his hat firmly down on his forehead and energetically tucking his coat behind his back, fussing over the buttons and taking care to check the shawl wrapped around his legs.

"I am not a child," Everett blurted out, "or some article of furniture to be so violently arranged and . . . Stop it!" His hand dropped to the wheels, braking himself before she propelled him inside.

"I never met a man more stubborn," Cordelia exclaimed, adjusting her bodice and fixing her own woolen wrap in place around her shoulders.

"Nor I a woman more persistent," Everett retorted. "I'm going to watch the sunset." He sank back into his chair exhausted from his efforts, his hand slipped off the wheel. Cordelia was tempted to seize the opportunity and whisk Everett Cotter out of the wind, but he seemed so adamant about staying and so childlike in his weakness that she felt she had to let him stay.

"Very well, a few minutes more and then inside. I've set a lovely table and cooked both of the turkeys Mr. Briscoe brought in yesterday."

"Where is Joe?" Everett asked weakly. "I haven't seen him today. Haven't seen him since he rode in with Rose a few days ago." He rubbed a hand across his face. "At least I don't think I have."

Rose stepped out of the house and walked along the porch toward the man in the wheelchair.

As Cordelia turned to watch Rose approach, a momentary look of hostility crossed the housekeeper's features. She no longer tried to hide her displeasure at Rose's presence.

The housekeeper treated Everett as her own private charge, and Rose suspected the woman's motives. She could read more than just familial affection in Cordelia's eyes, but understood enough of human nature to sympathize with her. Rose McCain, once a foundling in the Cotter household, was now the woman of the house, Vin's wife. Love and pride had ruined many a friendship, and Rose hadn't found a way to avoid it happening at the Bonnet.

"It's getting quite chilly," Rose said.

"I was just bringing him in," Cordelia retorted. Then she softened the harshness of her tone. "He just refuses to budge."

"I'm waiting for Joe Briscoe," Everett weakly explained, as if every breath required conscious effort.

"Joe may not be back tonight, or he'll probably be late. He went looking for Vin," Rose said. She knew the segundo intended to confront Vin Cotter about his handling of the ranch. Joe had said as much to Everett over breakfast. But Rose could see her father-in-law had no recollection of breakfast now. Apparently, he'd forgotten Joe's fears concerning the new ranch hands Vin had employed and Vin's confrontation with the Todsons.

"We'll stay outside, then. I'll put the turkey back near the fire," Cordelia sighed, abandoning her efforts to bring the recalcitrant invalid in to dinner. Nodding coldly to Rose, she brushed in front of the younger woman and disappeared inside the house.

Rose watched the housekeeper leave, more perplexed than ever at Cordelia's animosity. Then she glanced over toward the bunkhouse, where a couple of hired hands lounged against the wall out of the wind and shared a drink, passing a brown bottle back and forth, watching the golden-haired woman on the porch and exchanging comments and appraisals. Rose shifted uncomfortably beneath their scrutiny, and when they laughed, their voices hung guttural and ugly on the air. She patted Everett on the arm—she would have kissed him on the forehead but Papa Rett had never been the sort of person one gave parental kisses to—and followed Cordelia inside, away from the audience by the bunkhouse.

Inside, Rose shucked her heavy woolen cloak and made her way through the dining room, where a large, handsome carved walnut table was set for four, toward the back.

In the kitchen, Cordelia knelt by the stone hearth she used for preparing all her food. It was larger than the fireplace in the living room and contained several tiled niches where bread might be set to rise or stews slowly simmered in black iron dutch ovens. In one of these pockets farthest from the flames but near enough to retain warmth, Cordelia placed the roast turkey, which continued to fill the kitchen with a mouth-watering fragrance.

A memory came to mind and Rose laughed softly. Cordelia craned her head around and frowned, mistaking Rose's amusement for derision.

"Once I used to sneak in here, and wait for you to bring something else to the table, a sweet-potato pie or your fresh bread. And while you were gone, I'd open the oven box and strip the turkey skin away. How angry you would get, and you'd chase me from the kitchen." Rose smiled with the memory. It really hadn't been so long ago, only a few years.

Cordelia said nothing, but turned away.

"What is it?" Rose asked. "Oh, Cordie, please don't hate me. What has happened between us?"

The housekeeper stood up and held her hands palm open, raising them waist high. "Tell me what you see."

Rose frowned and stared at the empty hands. "Why, nothing?"

"And that's what Everett sees, after all these years, nothing, he sees nothing, or worse, a woman that has been with an Apache and birthed a mix-blooded whelp."

"That isn't true. You've always had a home here," Rose replied.

Cordelia shook her head no and walked over to the fire to warm herself. "You mean out there," she said, pointing toward the back door. "I know the truth. It took my own son to show me."

"Leland is a—"

"Breed," Cordelia finished, cutting the younger woman off, her tone mocking.

"I was going to say fool," Rose coolly added. "He has filled your head with poisonous thoughts and made you doubt those who really care about you and hate those whom once you loved."

"I had better bring Mr. Rett inside," Cordelia said with stubborn indignation. "Whether he likes it or not." Cordelia brushed past the younger woman and headed out of the kitchen, then paused, her round figure filling the doorway to the dining room. "I don't hate you, my dear. I pity you." Her eyes were piercing bright, tears glistening in the lamplight. "For you and I are alike. Neither of us can have the men we truly love."

The Corner, a low-slung building of stone and timber nestled on the dry side of a limestone ridge about three miles out from San Antonio, was owned and operated by a liquor-crazed former hide-hunter named Shell. Behind the main house were scattered a half-dozen jacales where a man might slake his passion and earn time in purgatory at the expense of one of the Corner's harlots.

Joe Briscoe had no doubt that he'd find Vin inside one of the jacales, and reflected that the sooner begun, the sooner finished. Joe walked his dun mare across a sluggish stream that was no more than a trickle of moisture undulating over the harsh landscape. The wind tugged at him and Joe scrunched deeper into his woolen coat for the meager warmth found there. He shivered and wondered if it was the cold or someone treading on his grave, and pressed on.

Joe recognized several Bonnet horses tethered off to the side of the main house. Muttering a prayer that the saints above guard him from the Corner's iniquities and demons, he guided his dun across the dusty valley floor to the hitching post.

Four men watched him ride up. They rode for the Bonnet brand, but Joe didn't know a one of them by first name. Vin's hirelings were no more than faces, strangers wearing guns and riding Bonnet stock. Joe would have traded every last mother's son of them for one cowhand the likes of young Johnny Anthem. The men by the horses looked ready to ride, bored and impatient to be off. Joe counted seven horses. But only four men.

"Hello, Briscoe," a voice said from behind him. Joe searched the twilight, settling his gaze on the porch of the brothel where two men watched him with keen-eyed interest.

Leland Rides Horse had changed over the past few months. He had cropped his long black hair and discarded the attire of a ranch hand for the finery befitting a man of position. He looked sleek and wiry in his waistcoat and tight-fitting trousers of deep-ashen gray. His sombrero was tilted back on his dark forehead. A Walker Colt rode high on his right hip. A black sash circled his waist, a gold earring gleamed in his right ear. The breed was less moody now that Vin was running the ranch, but Joe preferred the Leland of old: silent, truculent, a loner. Joe knew how to deal with such men. This new Leland was another matter entirely; the breed had discarded belligerence for ambition. It was a dangerous swap, Briscoe thought as he approached the porch.

The figure next to Leland stepped down from the porch

and into the dying light. The stranger was of average height, garbed in moccasins, beaver cap, and greasy buckskins whose stench no amount of lye soap would remove. A beaded necklace, dangling enough scalps to form a lion-like ruff, covered his shoulders and chest. A Walker Colt also hung from the necklace on a loop of leather that reached to his waist. The cigar clenched in his teeth glowed red-hot at the tip and he exhaled a ghostly banner the wind whipped away. Dark-brown hair curled over his forehead. He reached up and tapped a forefinger against his skull, where a thumb-sized lump of calcium stretched the skin.

"Long time, Natchez," Briscoe said, recognizing the man.

"At San Jacinto, you stopped me from killin' a Mex lieutenant. Walloped me up aside of the head with a rifle butt, you did. See, the lump never went down. See." Natchez Washburn grinned, showing a jagged line of broken teeth. It was rumored he had killed five men in Louisiana. Men called him the scourge of Natchez Under the Hill. A rootless, dangerous individual, he drifted from Texas to Louisiana and back, never lingering in one town too long.

"That was fifteen years ago, Natchez," Joe said warily. "And the lieutenant was already dead. I just stopped you from scalping him." His eyes never left Washburn, but it was clear the segundo now addressed Leland. "Where's Vin?"

"He'll be along," Leland replied. "He's busy out back."

"You boys riding back to the ranch?" Joe asked.

"By way of Comanche Creek," Leland answered.

"Nothing there but Todson cattle."

"Bonnet land . . . Bonnet cattle," Leland retorted.

"Says who?"

"Vin."

"And who put that idea into his head? You, Leland?"

Briscoe started forward, ignoring the fact that Washburn was alreading moving to cut him off. Washburn's mean little features bunched, reducing his eyes to mere slits of flesh. Joe's spurs jangled with every step. His face remained impassive as he brought Natchez to a halt with a single stare, then headed for the jacales.

"Vin wanted to be left alone," Leland shouted. Briscoe ignored him. Leland glared at Washburn. "You'll back me up?" he checked.

The man from Louisiana nodded. "But you better make your first move count if it comes to boot ass," said Washburn. "'Cause men the timber of Joe Briscoe don't give you no second chances," he added.

"I thought you hated his guts?"

"I respect him. Got to," said Natchez. "Don't mean I won't kill him if the situation rises."

The smell of woodsmoke clung to the winter's air and mingled with the faint aroma of burning oil lamps and the syrupy-sweet perfumes the harlots used to conceal their own sweaty stench. The Corner's soiled doves weren't noted for their delicacy. Many of them could see the end of their days on the near horizon. They were used up from too many smoky rooms, cheap whiskey, and disease. The Corner was their last stop. They came to survive, not live, to cling to life until they found the courage to let go and die. Their customers were mostly outlaws, men on the run and peons with a few *centavos* to spare, even an occasional Indian, anyone who couldn't safely enter San Antonio.

"Poor wasted souls," Joe muttered to himself. The lost and the broken, the mean and the decadent, all here. And Vin . . . Vin Cotter, who could afford the most expensive courtesan if necessary. Why Vin? To shame himself? Or Rose? Or perhaps his father?

The more Joe thought of Vin, the angrier the segundo became. He could excuse the way the young man was running the ranch, the way Vin was trying to bully the other ranchers in the area to establish himself. But this treatment of Rose . . . it had to stop. It would stop. Now. Someone had to straighten Vin up, to turn him around before he went too far. Everett was sick and weak and in no shape to teach Vin a lesson. That left Briscoe with the task.

"*Señor*, you look for Juana, no?" a woman called from the door of the first jacal. The prostitute was a short, chunky woman who leaned against the doorsill in what she hoped was an attitude of seductive repose. Her dressing gown parted to reveal pendulous breasts lying flaccid against her torso. Her thighs were thick and ringed with tiny wrinkles of dirt. Her long black hair was pinned high on her head to show off a neck that had once been graceful, one of her best features. But the flesh was bruised, there were bite marks and an old scar marring her throat, and her tone of voice was dull with defeat.

"Maybe another time, Chiquita," Briscoe said in a gentle voice. He flipped her a coin. The prostitute caught it in midair. "Vin Cotter, where is he?"

The prostitute pointed toward the jacal next to hers. Even as Joe turned, the door opened and Vin Cotter staggered out into the yard. He was disheveled and struggled to fit his right arm through the sleeve of his fur-trimmed greatcoat. Within the jacal, a woman cried and cursed him in Spanish, her voice a high-pitched cackle on the wind.

"Shut up. You aren't hurt, you miserable slut. Anyway, I paid you for it," Vin yelled at the doorway. "Paid you well." He swung around and hurled a bottle of tequila through the open doorway, where it exploded in a shower of glass. Out of the jacal's gloomy interior, the cries and curses of the prostitute rose anew.

"Shut up, you hellcat. Have a drink and shut up or I'll have my men take a brand to you," Vin shouted, and unable to don his greatcoat, he tore himself free of it and threw it on the ground. As he retreated from the jacal, he noticed the figure blocking his path.

"Who are you?" he managed, slurring his words. He swallowed, tasted stale liquor, and almost vomited. "Washburn? That you? Tell Leland I want the men ready to ride to Comanche Creek." He wavered, then willed himself erect, blinked, and widened his eyes, trying to clear his vision.

"The men aren't riding anywhere," Joe growled.

"Who are you? Not Washburn." Vin coughed, spat phlegm on the hard-packed clay, and staggered forward. "Who?" Vin thought he recognized the voice. He rubbed a forearm across his eyes. His frock coat was spattered with tequila; his lace shirt, soaked with sweat, was open to the waist. Suddenly, his eyes blazed with recognition, and he roared, "You."

Briscoe slapped Vin across the face. His hand struck with a loud crack and enough force to turn the younger man completely around and knock him to the ground. Vin gasped for breath. His jaw stung from the openhanded blow and tears came to his eyes. He growled and spit blood from his swelling lower lip as he climbed to his feet.

Joe drove a right into his stomach. Vin doubled over, vomited, and sank to his knees as he spewed the sour contents of his stomach out onto the cold clay.

"Maybe that will get some of the panther piss out of your system," Joe said, staring down at the heir to the Bonnet ranch. "You're a poor excuse for immortality, Vin, but you're all Everett's got. He loves you too much to knock some sense into that whiskey-soaked head of yours. I ain't got no such holdbacks. Get up, boy. I'm fixing to straighten you out. And maybe one of these days you'll be worthy of your pa." The segundo heard steps behind him and he swung around to face Leland and Washburn. "That's far enough!"

The two men moved apart from each other, becoming figures in shadow, watchful. Wary. But holding back.

"It's Vin's fight," Leland said to Washburn. The breed wanted to see what Cotter would do. He raised his voice and called out to the segundo, "There's no place for you at the Bonnet anymore, Briscoe. We don't need you."

"Words of wisdom. For a wise man." Natchez chuckled. His hand drifted toward the gun hanging from the beaded rawhide.

"It's time the Bonnet had a new segundo," Leland explained. "One loyal to Vin Cotter instead of that sick old man who will never sit a horse again."

"I see," Joe replied, contempt in his voice. "I'm out, to make way for you and the likes of the scum you've brought onto Bonnet range. Like hell!"

A shot rang out. The report startled all four men.

The whore Juana raised a hand to her mouth to silence her own scream. Peering through the crack in her door, she saw the blinding flash and saw Joe Briscoe raise up on his heels, arch his back, and turn toward his killer.

Vin was seated on the earth, the revolver smoking in his fist. He seemed as startled as anyone by the gun in his hand. He wiped a forearm across his tear-streaked, bruised cheek and bloody mouth.

"Damn you," Vin groaned, and then with sickening realization lowered the gun. He watched in horror as Joe Briscoe lifted the flaps of his coat to reveal he was unarmed.

Joe shook his head and his eyes burned, not with anger but with pity for the one who had shot him. Then he stumbled forward with a single step and sprawled on the frozen earth.

"No," Vin gasped. He staggered to his feet as Leland and Washburn approached.

"I done a lot of things, but I never shot an unarmed man

in the back," Washburn said dryly. "They hang folks for that. Even rich rancher's sons."

Vin looked up in alarm.

"Who said he was unarmed?" Leland replied, removing the revolver from his sash and dropping it by Briscoe's body. He reached out to place a hand on Vin's shoulder. "You need a segundo who rides for the brand, a man you can trust."

"I do." Vin nodded, gratefully. He stooped over, grabbed his gun belt, and stepped away from the body as if the dead man might rise even now to accuse him. "I do," he agreed. "From now on, Leland's word is my word on the Bonnet. I'll tell the men." The gun wavered in his hand, his voice trembled as he spoke. He holstered the gun. "Let's get the hell out of here."

Men were already emerging from the Corner to see for themselves what all the commotion was about.

"Bring the body along after a few of the men see it. And make sure they see the gun," Leland said to Natchez Washburn.

"Y-yes," Vin stammered. "We'll bury him at the ranch. Bring him to the ranch." He hurried off toward the rest of his men, who waited by their horses.

Washburn waited for the younger man to move safely out of earshot before speaking. "If I buy into this, what's in it for me?" he said.

"More money than you'll ever see running whores in Natchez Under the Hill," Leland answered.

Washburn eyed the breed carefully. "I got a feeling being segundo is only the first step with you. What the blazes are you after? What's your game?"

"Let's just say the table stakes are high," Leland Rides Horse purred, hooking his thumbs in his sash. "As high as they can get." He nudged Briscoe's body with the toes of his boot. "And Vin Cotter just gave me an ace in the hole."

18

★

Johnny rounded the corner of the bunkhouse and moved to the low outer walls bordering the compound. He kept to the darkness, searching till he saw the pear-shaped silhouette of Kim Rideout huddled out of the wind, a rifle cradled in his arms. Rideout grumbled, cleared his throat, and begun to snore. Johnny sighed in exasperation. A few days without Apache trouble and the men were getting careless. He listened and heard a rustle of underbrush, then the grunting noisy intrusion of a pack of javelinas making a nightly sojourn to the waters of Luminaria. The cry of a hungry calf floated up the canyon, faint and pleading.

Johnny hurried over to Rideout and knelt by the slumbering ranch hand. Drawing from his belt a twelve-inch bowie with a curved tip, Anthem placed its blunt edge against Kim's throat and rasped in a quiet but guttural tone, "Die, white eyes!"

Rideout's eyes snapped open and he choked back a scream at the cold kiss of hard steel at his jugular vein. Johnny clamped a hand over the ranch hand's mouth to cut off any outcry and sawed at the man's throat, but of course the blunt edge did nothing but rub the skin.

"Uh-oh. Me got dull knife," Johnny said. "You wait

here, white man, while I go get sharp knife. You wait, *sí?*"

Kim frowned, realizing he was in the clutches of the strangest Indian he'd ever encountered, then he recognized Johnny's laugh and relaxed. "Damnation, Johnny, you right near scared me plumb to death."

"You're lucky it was me."

"Hell, I knew it weren't no Apache," Kim retorted, trying to salvage a smattering of his pride.

But Johnny wasn't about to let him off the hook. He squatted down across from the cowhand and handed Kim the hat he had knocked off in the process of waking him.

"Tell that to your gray hairs." Johnny chuckled. "Go on. Get some sleep. Might as well. I can't. I'll take your watch."

"You sure?"

Johnny nodded. He stood and climbed over the wall. "Think I'll take a stroll down to the river." He noticed Kim glance toward the bunkhouse, a look of uncertainty on his face. "Go on," Johnny added. "If I see any Indians I'll let you know."

"That's what I'm afraid of," Kim replied, rubbing his throat. He walked off toward the bunkhouse, his long legs moving at an unhurried pace.

Alone in the chill of a February night, Johnny wrapped the folds of his serape around himself. He turned to take a step onto the already-well-worn path to the creek, but stopped dead in his tracks. Fifteen feet away, an Apache brave blocked the trail: short, broad-shouldered, menacing, and silent.

"Oh, shit," Johnny muttered, staring at the brave, who leveled the business end of a buffalo gun directly at Johnny's chest.

The Apache snorted in disgust and gestured with the rifle. "My thunder-stick will not fire. You wait here, I go and get another." The brave chuckled softly to himself and, with his rifle ready, cautiously took a few steps closer to the wall.

Johnny reddened, realizing the Apache had heard the exchange with Rideout and had just repeated the prank. It was Johnny's first experience with the humor of the native American, and he didn't know exactly how to respond.

The young rancher towered over the brave, yet he felt no more overpowering than if the Apache had stared him eye to eye. The small-statured warrior moved with the economical grace of a panther and was no doubt equally as dangerous. Johnny studied the Apache's face in the faint moonlight and in a moment recognized him as the warrior he'd rescued from the wild longhorn. The brave glanced to either side along the wall and, satisfied that the white man was alone, lowered the buffalo gun.

"You are Anthem?" the warrior asked. It was Johnny's second surprise, that the man should know his name. The brave pointed a clay-smeared hand toward the creek. "My warriors captured a *mejicano*. I do not let them kill him. He says he looks for a white man called Anthem . . . a man with hair like fire."

"I am John Anthem. Where is this man?"

"Why did you not kill Aguila when you had the chance? I am much feared by my enemies," the Apache said.

"Your people are like the land, your spirit is strong. But so is mine. I will fight if I must, but what man wishes to fight the land? I have come to live with the land. I will fight you now if you wish it, Aguila. Or I will live in peace. And raise great herds of cattle. And when your people are hungry, there will be stock for you to butcher and meat to carry to your rancherias to fill the bellies of your children. It is for you and your people to decide."

The Apache's face was harsh as the landscape and seemed as ageless to Johnny. The warrior cradled his rifle in the crook of his arm. "Two sons have I lost to the white man."

"Apaches killed my mother and father. But these things are like the night," Anthem said, glancing up at the heavens. Breath streamed from his nostrils, clouding the chill air. "Night must pass before there can be day again." Johnny looked past Aguila toward the blackness of the forested creek bank. "Where is the *mejicano*?"

Aguila turned and whistled softly to two shadows who came to life and hurried up the slope toward them. Then one of the shadows melted away, leaving the other to continue on alone.

Aguila retreated a few paces and looked over his shoulder at the white man standing by the wall. "I will think on your words, John Anthem," the warrior called back in a matter-of-fact tone.

Johnny didn't press the matter. They hadn't killed each other in the night. As for the morning, well, even an uneasy peace was better than an easy war. A voice out of the dark shattered his reflections.

"Señor Johnny, Señor Johnny," an old man cried out in a dry and weary voice. The figure stumbled out of the night and collapsed, exhausted, into Johnny's open arms. It was Juan Medrano, Mama Rosita's man. And he had a story to tell.

Joe Briscoe had been dead more than a month now. Rose sat at the vanity and stared at herself in the mirror, absently figuring the number of days. Finally, she looked away, unable to bear the sorrow that tortured her expression. She opened the drawer of the vanity and there, among the combs and scarves and pins, she found the map drawn in Johnny's hand. She reached down and touched it. Closing her eyes, she imagined she was with him, his hands caressing the dressing gown away from her shoulders, his head lowering to kiss her naked breasts . . . Only paper, only a dream, a taunting fragment of the past, of what might have been.

The door to her room opened and Rose looked up in the mirror. She pulled her nightgown closed and wrapped a shawl around her shoulders. Vin stood in the doorway, his tight Mexican breeches rumpled and looking slept in. A pencil-thin mustache framed his upper lip, his jawline wore a shadow of beard. His ruffled shirt was open to the waist, revealing the hard pink flesh of his torso. He entered the room and staggered for a moment, then steadied himself against the bedroom door, which closed beneath his weight. Coals in the fireplace exploded in a flurry of sparks that startled him. He jumped, then cursed the dancing flames.

Rose inhaled as the smell of brandy piqued her senses. She stiffened and continued to stare accusingly at him. "What are you doing here?" she asked in a tone as devoid of warmth as the night air pressing against the windowpane.

"In my wife's bedroom?" Vin said. "A funny question for a wife to ask her husband."

"Your room is down the hall. Shall I call for Cordelia to help you to bed?" Rose started to rise, allowing her shawl to fall away. The pink crowns of her breasts thrust against the thick cotton bodice, betraying the arousal her fantasy had created. Vin noticed. Rose pulled the shawl back in place.

Vin glanced over at the cedar bathtub in front of the fireplace. Water glistened in a puddle on the hardwood floor. Wet footprints lead to a towel coiled in a heap at the front of the vanity. The ends of Rose's long blond tresses were dark and wet, the color of burnt umber, and her flesh radiated a fresh-scrubbed glow.

"I . . . am too late to dry your back," he sighed. He walked toward her and sat on the edge of the four-poster bed. He lifted his right hand to reveal a bell-shaped glass with a couple of inches of brandy swirling in the bottom. "It might have been fun."

"Is that the first or the last of the bottle?" Rose asked.

"Ah," Vin answered. "Note the contempt. How poorly you hide it. In fact, you make no attempt at all. And it suits you, this holier-than-thou attitude." He raised the brandy snifter in salute and took a sip of its fiery contents; his neck muscles tightened as he swallowed and he exhaled slowly and with a sense of fatigue. "I missed you at dinner," he said, standing, lifting himself erect with a hand on the bed-post. The canopy trembled at his weight.

Rose folded the map and started to return it to the vanity drawer, but Vin was too quick for her and he snatched it from her hand.

"Give that to me," Rose said, reaching for the map, but Vin danced out of her grasp and, losing his balance, tumbled over onto the bed. He grinned at Rose and opened the scrap in his hand. He stared at it without speaking. Rose expected him to tear it to pieces; instead, he folded it and tucked it in his trouser pocket. He rested his head back against the mattress, his darkly handsome features remaining impassive. He checked the snifter and discovered he had spilled the brandy, so he tossed the glass over his head and onto the bed.

"You're drunk," Rose flatly stated.

"My second brandy," Vin lied defensively.

"Drunk with power," Rose explained. "You think you can do anything to anyone, take whatever you want."

"Oh, you mean the map, dear wife? Drawn in Johnny's own hand, dear wife? Something precious, a last sweet memory of lost love. Or is it lost, now that you know where to find him? Now that we both know?"

"Why do you hate him?" Rose said. "Because he's everything you'll never be?" She wanted to hurt Vin. He had killed Joe Briscoe and brought him home, draped over the saddle, like some fresh kill from the hunt. Joe's stern kindliness and devotion to Rose had been her security. He had stood like an indomitable rock in the flood, someone whose strength and guidance wouldn't fail, someone to cling to while illness struck down Rett Cotter and Vin grew increasingly despotic.

"Anthem . . . yes, once. But I'll make him kneel in my shadow one day."

"To prove what?" Rose asked.

"That you didn't love the better man," Vin replied. He stood and walked to the shuttered window. The night chill seeped through shutter and glass, but the curtains helped to hold the cold air against the wall. "You loved him. And never me. Not even at the altar, while you spoke the vows, you loved him."

"Yes," Rose admitted. "But if you had given me time . . . No! I detest everything you have become."

Vin's hand tightened on the curtain. "This map, you'd leave me if you had the chance and go crawling back to him, wouldn't you? Wouldn't you?"

"Yes," Rose blurted out. "I only regret I waited so long. I've stayed for your father, I don't want to hurt him. I owe him too much to hurt him."

"But you don't care if you hurt me?"

"You have to have a heart to be hurt, Vin. And you haven't. You showed us all that when you killed Joe."

"He attacked me. It was his doing. I wanted Leland for my segundo and Joe wouldn't stand for it. I told you what happened. Damn it. My own father hasn't spoken to me in a month. Now, you . . . Joe was my friend too. Do you think I enjoyed killing him?"

"Yes, Vin, I think you did. And now that you've been blooded, who else will you kill?"

"My father wanted something more than what I was. He wanted me to reach out and take like he had. Well, now

I'm a man. I've proved it, and all I get from him is silence. No one crosses Bonnet range, no one grazes their cattle on our property or uses our water. It's mine, every inch of ground, every rock and tree. Bonnet is mine, and so are you, Rose. I'll never let you go. Never!" Vin walked from the window over to the vanity and stood behind her. Rose felt his hands on her shoulders and caught them as they slid down toward her breasts. He leaned over to kiss her neck, then, at her resistance, smiled, straightened, and drew back.

"You're right of course. It is too late for that," he said. Vin patted the trouser pocket that contained the map. "Too late for everyone." He walked to the door, opened it, and left.

Rose stared at her reflection in the mirror, bit her lower lip, shuddered, and fought back grief. On that bitter February night Rose McCain had plans to make; she had no time for tears.

Vin paused at the door to his room and glanced toward the hallway leading off toward his father's quarters. Maybe tonight, he muttered to himself, feeling a need for some kind of reconciliation, feeling more alone than ever before. The living room was alive with shadows lit only by the dancing flames leaping upward in the fireplace. He made his way down the hall and entered the living room. In the lurid light cast by the crackling fire, furnishings once familiar took on a ghostly life. A vase on the table . . . No, a tureen of serpents now, shadows writhed at its mouth. A tray of bottles was transformed into a miniature kingdom of spires and narrow alleyways. The corners of the room itself, as the wind howled without the shuttered windows, took on stygian depths wherein demons might dwell.

A figure huddled against the spectral backdrop moved. Moved! Someone waits and watches and lives. Lives again.

Vin's mind raced with excuses and silent pleas for mercy. I didn't mean to kill you. The gun fired by accident. I was drunk and angry and didn't know what I was doing. You shouldn't have hit me. It wasn't my fault. Leave me alone. Damn you, Joe Briscoe, stay dead and leave me be.

Vin recoiled against the wall as the figure glided toward him, a shrunken shambling shape, inexorably drawing forth out of the lost depths. Gradually losing its mystical properties, it took on form and dimension, vanishing the nightmarish hallucination brought on by liquor and lack of rest, by feverish drive, and, yes, by guilt. For even Vin couldn't escape his conscience.

Everett Cotter rolled himself into the glow cast by the blazing hearth. One of the axles of his straight-backed wheelchair rasped as his hands worked the rims with surprising strength.

Vin gasped and then, recognizing his father, loosed a sigh of relief. The haunting ended, he tried to collect himself and wiped the perspiration off his forehead and swallowed dryly. He sank into a ladder-backed chair placed against the wall and watched his father with a baleful eye, angry at himself for falling prey to childish fears.

"Goddamn it! Why don't you speak to me? I'm your son!" He waited, but Everett said nothing. "What do you want from me? I can't raise the dead. Hell, it was Joe's fault. He called me out. All right, don't speak. It galls you, doesn't it, old man? I'm running things my way. My way!"

Vin leaned his head back against the wall and rubbed his mouth and neck, then looked back at his father. "Say something, damn you."

But Everett continued to stare at him in silence for a long moment that seemed to last forever, and Vin felt the force of his father's presence for the first time since the stroke.

"It's too late for you, old man," Vin managed to say,

backing away. "Your day is done. The morning belongs to me. Isn't that what you wanted? Well?" Vin waited, then shook his head. "Don't speak, then." He started to leave.

"Vin . . . what hast thou done?" In his hand Everett held a bible aimed at Vin like a gun. And as he quoted scripture, Cotter's voice thundered with divine authority. "The voice of thy brother's blood crieth unto me from the ground. And now art thou cursed from the earth, which hath opened her mouth to receive thy brother's blood from thy hand."

Vin retreated from the man in the wheelchair. He didn't even remember running away. In seconds he was standing in his room amid safe and familiar surroundings, a bedroom warm with the friendly ambience of oil lamps, hoping to dispel the gloom of his father's biblical accusations. He was safe. He slid down the wall until he crouched on the floor, his head bowed forward, his face hidden in his forearms. Safe . . .

And he had never felt more alone in his life.

19

★

There was blood on the hard-packed snow. It streamed in puddles and blotched the virgin purity of the blanketed landscape with crimson patches. In the heart of the hard-faced winter, Comanche Creek was a frozen ribbon of ice broken in spots so that the cattle might drink.

Todson cattle.

It was Todson blood on the frozen ground.

Three inches of snow had fallen during the night, adding to the two that had drifted down the day before. Even at midday, the sky was as sober and colorless as a gun barrel.

It had been a brutal month. The cattle, even the hardy longhorn, had to have food and a source of water, and both were available at Comanche Creek. So Dan Todson had driven thirty head of cattle onto land claimed by the Bonnet ranch, against Vin Cotter's warnings. True, the creek was on the fringe of the Cotter holdings, but it had always been open to the Todsons. Always until now.

Young Dan, afoot, Bill Grace, the Todson foreman, right alongside the younger man, and Sheep Willers, on horseback, were near the cattle when the Bonnet men appeared. Directly across the creek from Dan and his father's ranch hands, lined up four abreast, were Natchez Washburn, his dragoon Colt dangling from a necklace of scalps; Leland Rides Horse Robinson, astride a bold roan stallion; and Bert and Nino, two of the new ranch hands Vin had hired.

"You men can leave, the cattle stay," Leland said, unbuttoning the brass fastenings on his long woolen coat to permit free access to the revolver protruding from the sash at his waist.

"That's my father's stock. We just let them ride out the storm here. That's all. When the snow melts, we'll drive them back," Dan shouted back. He remembered how his voice seemed to be swallowed up by the gray sky as he cocked the rifle held in the crook of his arm.

"Leave now," Leland warned.

"Not without my cattle. Look, half-breed, let's see what Mr. Cotter has to say. Everett Cotter! Not that crazy son of his." As Dan turned toward his horse, he saw the look of alarm on old Bill's face.

Across the creek, Natchez Washburn muttered, "Like hell." Then Leland opened fire.

Dan swung around in time to catch Leland's slug on the rifle stock. The slug ricocheted up into his belly along with slivers of shattered stock and bits of iron hammer. Dan fell, groaning, faceforward into the snow. He lay there for a few seconds feeling the cold on his freckled cheek, telling himself if he was aware of cold then he couldn't be dead. There was gunfire booming on both sides of the creek as men opened up on one another.

Nino blasted with his shotgun, and Bert, figuring the distance was too great to be effective, dropped his shotgun and reached for the Walker Colt beneath his greatcoat. Bill Grace and Natchez Washburn exchanged shots, emptying their guns. Natchez had a deep furrow on his cheek that seeped blood and a hole through the flesh of his left arm, but he was roaring with laughter at the pain and his gun hand never wavered. What made him such a dangerous man in a fight was the fact that he could accept pain without flinching and strike back with deadly accuracy.

Dan brushed the snow off his face and watched as Bill Grace rose up on tiptoes and staggered toward the creek, refusing to retreat. He walked into a veritable hailstorm of lead. Sheep Willers, wounded in the arm and knee, had wheeled his horse around and ridden out of the fray, which left Bert and Nino to turn their guns on Grace.

Dan Todson spat a mouthful of bloody spittle and clawed for his gun. Leland steadied his roan and leveled the Walker Colt in his fist and fired. Todson, his hand still caught in his coat pocket, saw the flash from the muzzle but never heard the roar. His head jerked back with a sickening snap that broke the neck and would have killed him if he hadn't already been dead from the flattened lead slug that ripped through his skull.

Leland returned his revolver to the crimson sash at his midriff. He shuddered as the adrenaline continued to surge through his limbs. Bert retrieved his shotgun. Natchez and Nino sauntered over to Leland, reloading as they approached.

Natchez glanced at the two dead men and nodded. "Well, that was worth the powder," he said, chuckling.

"Hey, Segundo," Nino said, knowing Leland enjoyed being addressed by his new title, "you want us to ride the other man down, the one who ran off?"

"Let him go," Leland said. He stared at the tracks in the snow leading away from the riverbank. "It's his word against ours who started this affair." He raised his eyes toward the other three horses grazing with the cattle about a hundred yards away. "Nino, you and your compadre remain here. Old Man Todson will come out for the bodies. Let him have them. But if he crosses the creek, you fire a warning shot and ride hell for leather to me. I want to know."

Leland enjoyed giving orders. He wasn't sure the men liked taking commands from him, but he didn't give a damn, as long as they followed them. "Natchez, you and me will drive these cattle back up toward the ranch. No sense in tempting Old Man Todson."

"Whatever you say, but we're gonna have to fight him sooner or later. That's his son lying over there. His only son," Washburn said.

"No. That's his heart out in the snow. We just shot Old Man Todson through the heart," Leland replied.

Washburn looked at Dan Todson's lifeless body and shrugged.

Leland emerged from the root cellar into the kitchen, clutching a jar of autumn honey and a half a loaf of bread. A smoked brisket already bore the marks of his knife where the pink meat was sliced into inch-thick slabs. A steaming mug of black coffee sat beside the meat platter on the table.

"A long ride," he said to his mother. "Damn near got frostbit." He sat on the bench by the table and split the half-loaf with his thumbs and worked the cuts of meat into the fissure. He saved a portion of the bread for the honey, crumbled the bread into thumb-sized chunks on a stoneware plate, and ladled the thick, dark honey over the bread. Leland was partial to fall honey—he called it black gold and never passed a hollow log in autumn without checking the trunk for a beehive. He attacked his sandwich first, devouring it with singleness of purpose.

Cordelia sat across from him and reached out to his shoulder. For the first time he noticed a slug had creased his upper arm, tearing the sleeve. As the warmth seeped into his body, he began to feel the burning that accompanied the superficial wound. His hand closed around his

mother's and lingered for a brief tender moment, then he
pulled her hand away. "It is nothing."

"You and the coat will need mending."

"Sit down. I am not Everett Cotter for you to keep fussing over."

"You're my son. I worry about you."

"I can take care of myself. And you too, Mama." He
chuckled, took another bite, and washed the mouthful down
with a swallow of coffee. "That's boiled all day," he muttered, shuddering as the warmth creeped into his bones.
Strong enough to paint with, Leland thought, and bitter as
gall. He finished the sandwich and considered making a
second. Killing had given him an appetite.

"Vin is in the study. He wants to see you. I worry about
him," Cordelia said.

Leland shook his head. "Worry about me. I am your
son." He smiled without warmth. "I'll take care of Vin."

Cordelia noticed the hard edge to her son's voice and
tried to read something more into what he had just told her.
She wanted to think Vin Cotter was Leland's friend. And
yet she knew Vin had no friends. She watched with the
satisfaction of every good cook as Leland greedily spooned
in mouthful after mouthful of her fresh bread and honey
and chased dessert down with the last of his coffee.

Easing back in his chair with a sigh of satisfaction,
hooking his thumbs in the sash circling his waist, he said,
"Now I'll see Vin."

As he slid out of the chair and walked around the table
toward the door, Cordelia resisted the urge to rush to his
side and embrace him. She knew he would rebuff such a
display. Apaches considered emotion-filled performances a
sign of weakness. But Cordelia wasn't Apache and she
wanted to hold her son close because she suddenly feared
for him. He was so hard and angry. She worried that the
fire burning within him would destroy him. She wanted to

tell him . . . what? That people would change?

Leland was an outcast, at least that was what he considered himself. He'd never wanted to be rescued from his father's people. From *his* people. And yet she also sensed that he loved her, if he loved anything, if the hurt in him would allow him to love. She shook her head and began to clear the table. Too many thoughts, she said to herself, too much uncertainty. Bread was simpler. She understood the balance of flour and eggs and milk, but life's ingredients she had not mastered.

Vin stared out at the snow-covered ground and tried to imagine another time, another place, an innocent place. He could still smell the blood; his hands reeked of blood and he doubted the stain would ever leave him. But that was the price a man must pay, the price his father had paid. There were more graves on the Bonnet than Joe Briscoe's. Everett had spilled his share of blood, had taken lives in his fight to build the Bonnet. A man must free himself of guilt. A man must do what's necessary to build something lasting, to achieve power.

"You wanted to see me?" Leland said from the doorway.

Vin gasped and spun around, startled by the sound of a voice behind him. "Well, what happened? Was the Todson cattle on our range?"

Leland nodded. "About thirty head. I brought them into our herd not far from here, over in Austin canyon."

"Dan will be furious. He didn't think we'd do it. But I warned him. Wish I knew what he was planning now." Vin licked his lips and began to pace.

"Dan Todson isn't thinking at all." Leland walked to the desk and helped himself to a cigarillo from a humidor that served as a paperweight. He lit the tip with the closest oil lamp and blew a cloud of fragrant gray smoke into the air. "I killed him."

"What?"

"Dead," Leland added. His dark features split in a grin.

Vin sank into the chair, astonishment on his face. He reached for the lip of the desk for support and caught hold as his cheeks paled. He licked his dry lips and managed to stammer, "My God, my God . . ."

Leland continued to enjoy the effects of his revelation, but disguised his pleasure behind a mask of concern as he continued his account of the battle by the river. "Todson tried to stop us from taking the cattle. He was trespassing. He shoved and we shoved back."

"Todson dead?" Vin softly said, his voice low. "What have you done? Now there'll be war! Old Man Todson won't stand for it."

"If he tries anything, he will get the same thing as his son. Anyway, young Dan was his strength. I doubt the old bastard will cause any trouble."

"What about the Rangers?"

"Only one of the Todson men got away. It'll be our word against his." Leland drew close to the desk and leaned forward, his shadow darkening Vin's countenance. He sensed a weakening in Vin's resolve and fixed him in a burning stare. "I did what had to be done. A man must act, not talk." Leland straightened and stepped back from the desk.

"Goddammit, you're right," Vin said, his excitement returning. The hell with men like Todson. The Bonnet was invincible. The power of his desires and wants returned to fuel his ambition and override his fear. "I'll ride down any son of a bitch who gets in my way."

"And I'll be right alongside, *amigo*," Leland said, quietly earnest. His spirit soared anew. He looked around the room, saw the vast land beyond the wall that was the ranch. He had weathered another storm. It might take time, but he was confident that Vin's reach would eventually exceed his grasp, and when the time was ripe, he'd snap. The Bonnet would come tumbling down. And Leland intended to be there to pick up the pieces.

PART FOUR

MARCH 1850

20

★

It was March. Stormy weather. The time of the muddy-face moon, as the plains Indians called it. And with good reason, Rose thought to herself as a rolling cannonade of thunder rattled the windows. Suddenly, she made a decision: she must escape. Everett seemed to be improving every day. And Cordelia watched over him like a mother hen. The time was right for escape, but how to go about it. Vin had seen to it she was always watched, like a prisoner under guard. No matter what her intention, she could count on being under the watchful scrutiny of Nino or Bert or the one called Natchez with his hungry eyes and cruel smile. She felt undressed whenever the Louisianan was about. And he always seemed to be close by, as if he were taking a special interest in her supervision.

What was that noise in the hall? A board creaked under the weight of a footstep. Vin? No. He had left for San Antonio at noon and more than likely was riding out the storm in the company of some harlot. The thought didn't even anger her; in fact, she blamed herself rather than Vin. She was determined to keep him from her bed. Thunder rumbled and Rose allowed herself the pleasure of a sinful reverie. When she finally did find Johnny, she intended to slake her own unrequited thirst. He was in for an energetic tumble, she grinned, picturing in her mind the two of them running toward each other, arms outstretched, a look of astonishment on his face that she'd found him, a cry of joy on lips she longed to kiss.

The vision forged her resolve and gave her the will to continue. But to find Johnny, first she must escape the ranch. Now. Vin was gone, and it was night; better yet, a stormy night. It would help hide her tracks and enable her to sneak away undiscovered. Yes, tonight was perfect, while the storm split the black sky with jagged blades of fire.

She hesitated, then crossed the room to the chifforobe and brought out a soft shirt, brushed woolen trousers, and thick socks, high-top boots, a broad-brimmed felt hat, and rain slicker. She dressed quickly—in the dark, not risking a lamp for fear of calling attention to herself. Gathering her long yellow-gold hair in a single thick strand, she tied it with a leather strap at the nape of her neck. Then she took a saddle pouch from the chifforobe and filled it with a change of clothes.

Draping the pouch over her shoulder, she unlatched the door to her room, cautiously eased it open, and stepped into the hall. The floor underfoot creaked as she made her way down the hall and entered the living room. Lightning flashed; she cringed and waited for the ensuing thunder-crack, which followed a moment later.

"I couldn't sleep either," a voice called out of the darkness.

Lightning flared again and for a brief second lit the room. Everett stood in the center of the room, dressed in a nightshirt that hung below his knees. He leaned on a cane and took a hesitant step toward his easy chair. That step was followed by another, then another, all slowly forced, every inch of floor bought with patience and pain.

"Damned back," he muttered as he worked to the waiting respite of his chair. At last his hand touched the padded armrest and he sank down, uttering a groan of gratitude.

"Papa Rett," Rose exclaimed, and hurried through the darkness to his side and helped him to his chair.

"You've discovered my little secret. Yes, each day it gets a bit better. Why, I think I could even sit astride a horse if I had to." Everett chuckled. "Another month I'll dance a jig, though it'll hurt like hell. But won't it give Vin a nice surprise?" His hand closed over Rose's as he slowly sank into his easy chair, breathing as if he'd walked a mile. "We mustn't let anyone onto my success. It will be our secret, eh?"

"Yes, Papa Rett," Rose said tenderly. "Our secret."

"Blasted storm. Seems like we haven't had a gentle rain in, well, since I can remember. You used to hate rain. I remember when I found you and young Johnny, it was raining. How frightened you were. Poor little girl, just a wisp of a girl and clinging to Johnny every time the thunder roared. When I lifted you out of his arms, you clung to me and I had to comfort you, had to convince you neither thunder nor lightning could harm you in my arms." He laughed softly at the memory.

"Yes, you and Johnny, and how brave he tried to look, but I think he was as scared as you. He hid it well, though, God knows. He hid it well." He patted the young woman's arm and cleared his throat and coughed.

"Shall I help you back to your room, Papa Rett?" Rose asked in a worried tone.

"No, darlin'. Let me rest. I can make my way back. I'll just sit here awhile. I'll start back to bed after you leave." He sensed her stiffen.

Rose glanced down at her attire. She wasn't exactly dressed for sleep. Her intentions were obvious. What now?

He was in no shape to stop her, unless he chose to alarm the men asleep in the bunkhouse.

"You are going to him, aren't you?" Everett gently questioned.

"Yes," Rose said. She loved her foster father too much to lie.

"For the love of God, Rose, how do you expect to find him? West Texas is Apache country and no place for a man or woman to be wandering around lost in."

"I have a map that Johnny left me," Rose said, lying. "I'm sorry, Everett. I only hope one day you can forgive me. I can't stay here. Not a moment longer. I love Johnny. I always have and always will."

"I want you to go," Everett said in a fragile voice as he choked back his emotion. Such feelings made him uncomfortable, weakness was not the way of Everett Cotter, and yet he felt a great sadness. "Vin . . . there is something wrong with Vin. I don't know. Maybe I'm to blame, maybe no one is. He lied about Johnny and tricked you into a marriage that had no chance from the beginning. I made myself blind to the truth because—because I wanted"— And he remembered how Joe Briscoe had chided him long ago—"because I wanted to live forever."

Everett closed his eyes and exhaled and shook his head. "One life wasn't enough. I wanted more, to know that what I had built would last. Joe knew, he warned me but I wouldn't listen to him. And now he is dead and I have lost everything—the Bonnet, my dreams, and my son. Even my son."

"Everett . . ." Rose sank to her knees and placed her head on his arm. A tear spilled from the corner of her eye and soaked into his sleeve.

Everett stroked her hair and then tugged gently on her arm, as if trying to help her stand. "No tears. They shame me. And no pity. I built this ranch and it's mine no matter what Vin thinks. I'll claim what's mine even if I have to fight him for it. In another few weeks I'll get word to Captain Colby, and by heaven, his company of Rangers will chase the riffraff and roisterers off my land. But we mustn't let your life be sacrificed. My dear, you have a right to be happy. It's your life, Rose, and you have the right to live it. So leave, girl. Take what you need and go with my blessing. You find your John Anthem and be happy. And tell him for me, maybe someday . . . someday."

Words failed so he substituted action and gave her a shove toward the front door. "Quickly, girl. Choose a fast horse and ride like hell and don't look back. Don't ever look back."

Rose started to leave, then turned back to Everett and hugged him, unable to say all that was in her heart. She hurried to the front door and threw it open. Lightning flashed and thunder boomed, the world was bathed in silver fire. She flinched but refused to be cowed. She fought her fear, conquered it, and raced out into the night.

21

★

Rain stung Rose's face and lashed her shoulders, until her back was numb by the time she reached the stable doors. A flash of lightning lit the night, as she scrambled into the safety of darkness. She pulled the doors shut but the wind tore them out of her grasp and sent them banging against the outside walls. Rose shuddered at the noise and hurried inside the stable.

She made her way past the carriages and buckboard parked closest to the front doors and followed a path she had memorized over the weeks. She knew that the nearest oil lantern hung from a post near the first stall.

Straw crackled underfoot. The horses in the stalls sniffed the air and whinnied softly, recognizing her scent. Her questing hands closed around the lantern's wire handle and she lifted the vessel off its peg, struck a match, and touched it to the oil-soaked wick. When it burst into flame, she adjusted the wick and lowered the glass chimney in place. She hated using a light but could see no other course of action. She had to be able to see to saddle a horse.

Moving quickly along the stable aisle, she walked toward the rear stall of a big gray gelding that was the fastest mount the Bonnet had to offer. Rose reached in her pocket and took out a piece of sugar candy and offered it to the bay. The horse pressed against the stall gate as it nibbled the sweet out of the palm of her hand. Rose stroked the animal's soft muscular neck and gave it an affectionate pat; then, setting down her saddlebags, she continued on around the stall to the tack-room door. There the smell of oiled leather was overpowering. She searched among bridles and hackamores and after a while chose a bit to suit the bay. Rose carried the bridle back into the lamplight.

Natchez Washburn was waiting for her.

His hair was plastered down over his forehead and skull, his buckskins were drenched and smelled of grease. The scalps on his gun cord were soggy tufts of matted hair and dripped water at his feet. He wiped a forearm across his mouth and grinned at her. He was holding a lantern, which he slowly set aside in the aisle. As he leaned down, Rose darted past to the opposite side of the stall and almost escaped. But he wheeled and managed to catch the hem of her rain slicker. In a single motion, she pulled free of the slicker. She tripped, stumbled, caught her balance, and in a glance saw Natchez had closed the doors to the stable and bolted them from the inside. She changed direction and headed for a ladder that lead to the loft. She leapt to the rungs, grabbed hold, and started up, hand over hand as fast as she could climb. It wasn't fast enough. Hard grimy hands closed around her waist and tore her from the rungs. With a strength that belied his size, Washburn swung her around and carried her to an empty stall. She kicked and flailed in vain at the man, but he only laughed and buried his face in the small of her back to avoid punishment.

"I was watching for you, saw you in the lightning. Yes'm, watchin' all the while. Had to fool Nino and Bert, told 'em I was goin' to check the horses. Dumb bustheads believed me, too. No way I'm gonna share a nice bit like you with them."

Natchez tossed her onto the straw as if she were a sack of grain. Rose crawled to her feet and lunged at him. But Natchez was a street fighter, with a street fighter's quickness, and he backhanded her, stopped her in her tracks. He grabbed for her shirt, hoping to rip it open and see for himself the naked breasts that thrust invitingly against thick cotton.

Rose recovered enough to stagger back. She slapped his hand away, but Natchez struck her again, a quick jab with his rock-hard fist to the side of her head. As she fell to her knees, he reached down and caught a handful of hair and yanked her head back. Rose grimaced in pain and clawed at the straw-littered ground. He leaned down and stared into her face.

"I hear your own husband don't ride you much. Well, little filly, when I break you, you'll thank me for it and come back begging for more." He lifted her by her long gold tresses and brought his lips to hers. He never saw the bottle her fingers had discovered buried in the straw until it was too late to duck. The brown whiskey bottle shattered against his skull, and as Rose straightened, her head clipped his jaw, breaking a couple of his teeth. He loosed his hold on her hair and fell against the railings.

"Bitch!" Natchez shouted, holding a hand to his lacerated cheek to stem the flow of blood. Rose staggered back, then regained her balance and leapt over him. Natchez lifted his left leg to trip her and brought her tumbling to earth. He growled in satisfaction and, grabbing both her ankles, crawled up her body until he was astride her stomach.

"Try to be a gentleman and offer you soft hay to lie upon," Natchez said indignantly. "Well, if it's the rough floor on your backside you want, then so be it." He hurled his hat away, slipped his gun cord off from his neck, and tossed the gun aside, holding her as she struggled. "Be still or I'll add your scalp to these others, and pretty it'll look too."

Rose looked up into his pitiless eyes, his expression heavy with lust, then peered past him as another set of features materialized out of the shadows. She was sure she had gone mad. Had Washburn knocked her senseless? It was Johnny, or her mad mind was taunting her. It was John Anthem. His figure drew near, stepped into the lantern light. Rain dripped from the hem of his slicker. Silently, he bent over and retrieved Washburn's scalp-adorned gun rope. Striking as sudden as a rattler, Anthem looped the scalp rope around the Louisianan's throat.

Natchez half-turned, astonishment wiping clean his look of lust.

Not a figment of her imagination, Rose thought, her senses reeling, but real. He *was* real. Johnny had come for her.

Anthem lifted Natchez from the woman on the stable floor. He tucked Washburn's revolver in a loop of the leather cord, gave the revolver a sharp twist, tightening the hold on the Louisianan's throat.

"Someone forgot to bolt the back door," Johnny said. "I figured I didn't need an invitation."

Natchez clawed at his neck and drove his shoulders into Anthem's chest, pushing the younger man back against a post. Johnny grimaced, exhaled sharply, and tightened the choke rope. Rose heard a crash of glass and saw that Johnny had knocked over one of the lanterns. Oil spread to the straw, and flames greedily followed, consuming the oil only to gorge on the piled hay. Flames leapt up the wooden wall. The horses neighed in terror and pawed at the gates to their stalls. The two men battled in silence.

Natchez was unable to break Johnny's hold, but he continued to twist and hammer and tried to turn, to free himself before he lost consciousness. Rose crawled to her feet and

staggered past the combatants to the doors and shoved the
door bolt out of its iron track. The wind helped her with
the doors as it tore them from her grasp once more and
sent them crashing against the outside walls. Rose turned
and in the orange brilliance of the leaping flames could see
Johnny clearly against the fiery backdrop.

Johnny seemed older to her—no, more mature—and he
stood tall and terrible, like some bronze avenger. Natchez,
for all his brutal experience, was no match for this man.
Johnny loosed a growl of rage and, lifting the scourge of
Natchez Under the Hill completely off the floor by his belt
and scalp rope, charged down the aisle through the middle
of the stable. Johnny swerved a few yards from Rose and
drove the ruffian facefirst into the wooden siding of the
buckboard.

Rose gasped at the sound of splintering wood and
crushed bone. She glimpsed a mask of blood, Washburn's
flattened nose and swollen bruised forehead. Johnny looked
around at the fire as if debating whether to leave the Louisianan in the path of the advancing flames. But Johnny allowed his own innate decency to triumph over revenge. He
heaved the unconscious man out into the rain-pelted mud.

There wasn't time for embraces, for questions, for an-
swers, only their eyes met for the merest second and held.
Then, their minds working as one, Rose and Johnny hurried
down through the stalls and freed the terrified animals.
Flames found fuel in the loft and exploded toward the roof
on mounds of bundled hay. The horses reared and pawed
at the air and, hooves drumming on the packed earth,
charged through the doorway and vanished in the storm.

Johnny and Rose led the bay gelding and a sturdy dun
stallion out of the stable to saddle them.

"My horses are back in the timber by the river," Johnny
shouted above the din of thunder and roaring conflagration.
"Follow me."

"I love you," Rose yelled in reply, and swung aboard the bay. Johnny leapt astride the dun.

"Don't look back. I don't want to lose you again." Johnny grinned.

"Never," Rose called.

Johnny drove his heels into the dun's flanks and the animal broke into a gallop. The dun needed little urging. The bay pawed at the air and raced away from the stable at a pace that left Rose clinging to reins and saddle horn. In seconds, Rose was soaked to the skin and remembering with regret the slicker that was back in the stable. She cursed Natchez Washburn for its loss.

Lightning flashed, illuminating the world in its bone-white glare. Rose saw Johnny a few yards in front; then, off to one side, a trio of figures came skidding to a halt as the riders charged away from the burning stable. Before they could react, Johnny was already clear of them. Rose recognized the one called Bert shouldering a shotgun and sighting at Johnny's departing silhouette. A tug on the reins and the bay altered its headlong dash to bear down on the man with the gun.

Bert turned as he heard the bay's sudden approach and, raising his arms in horror, dove out of harm's way. As he landed facedown in the muck, his shotgun discharged. Rose heard someone shriek in pain, but resisted the temptation to look over her shoulder. She kept her eyes on the dimly seen horse and rider directly ahead.

At last the ranch receded into the driving rain and soon the droning tempest was all they could hear. Lightning stabbed earthward, split the sky overhead as it skewered the road ahead. Rose might have flinched or hid her face or trembled at the thunderous report that followed. But Johnny rode beside her now, and her life from this day forth would be changed. Come what may, her heart no longer trembled.

Her heart sang.

22

★

Vin stared at the ruins of the stable: timbers like charred crucifixes rose from the rubble; twisted iron and shapeless mounds of charcoal were all that remained of his fine carriage and buckboard. Half a year's supply of oats had gone up in smoke, along with tools and equipment. The stench of roasted leather clung to the air and dank smoke still trailed upward from the fire-gutted remains.

And she was gone. Gone. With Johnny Anthem. Anthem again to plague him, to humiliate him. Anthem, always Anthem. His hand darted down to the gun at his side, and he slipped it from his holster as a scream of rage tore from his throat.

"Aaaaahhhhhh," Vin roared in fury and pain and fired the heavy weapon into the blackened earth. The gun boomed, and he screamed anew and fired and screamed and fired and screamed, expelling the rage that welled in his heart. He killed Johnny in his mind over and over, killed Johnny and Rose, too, for all the pain she had caused him, killed them both. In his mind's eye he saw their bodies dance and whirl and fall as the lead slugs tore through their frames; he watched them fall, watched them sink to the ground all bloody and broken and dead. The hammer on

the revolver struck an empty cylinder that trailed an acrid
residue of gunsmoke. When Vin spat in the dust, his
phlegm was stained pink from the outcry, which had torn
his throat. He shoved the Colt back in his holster and
slapped a nearby beam. The support toppled over in a cloud
of ashes that swelled upward when it struck the earth.

Vin turned as Leland Rides Horse strode toward him
from the bunkhouse. Several of the newer ranch hands were
squatting in the shade by the bunkhouse walls taking in
Vin's display with wary amusement. Vin reddened under
their scrutiny and tried to regain some semblance of composure. He drew himself up and walked stiffly out of the
rubble to meet the half-breed in the ranch yard.

"It happened last night," Leland began.

"I know that, dammit." Vin shaded his eyes and glanced
up at the afternoon sun dipping low on the western horizon.
"The son of a bitch took her with him."

"Nino can't tell how it rightly started," Leland continued. "He and Bert were having a game of checkers and
finishing off the beans when they noticed the stable was
afire. They ran out and saw Johnny Anthem and Rose on
horseback and Natchez lying stone-cold in the yard. Bert
was almost rid down by their horses. It was him that shot
Nino. Accidentally fired his shotgun and caught Nino in the
knee. A mess," Leland said. "He'll use crutches all his days.
Natchez came around and managed to bring in a couple of
horses and took out after Rose."

"And Bert?"

"Lit a shuck for who knows where. Chaw figures he was
afraid to face you."

"Too bad Bert didn't use his brains last night. If he'd
kept a better watch, I'd still have a stable . . . and a wife."
Vin wiped a forearm over his eyes and then patted the dust
from his wool coat. His finely chiseled face seemed to age
as he studied the horizon.

Leland read his intentions; it was easy to see the purpose in young Cotter's bleak angry stare. "Let her go, Vin," Leland said soothingly.

"I'll let her go." Vin nodded. "I'll let her go straight to hell, and John Anthem with her." His gaze bore into Leland's with an intensity the man never knew existed in the son of Everett Cotter. "I want the men brought in from the range and down from the line cabins. I want the horses rounded up, saddled, and ready to ride by the day after tomorrow."

"Texas is a big country," Leland muttered, inwardly fuming. What was the woman that Vin should risk the Bonnet for such an obsession? "It is gonna be difficult to find him."

"Not if I know where to look."

"But, Vin, to leave the ranch with only a skeleton crew, at the mercy of our enemies. I mean, you've pushed plenty hard over the past few weeks. There are men who would love the opportunity to push back, especially when there's no one around."

"You'll ride with me, Segundo. And we take every man who can use a gun."

"Vin, this is wrong," Leland protested. "Maybe later, yes, take the time and hunt Anthem down."

"We leave in two days. And you'll be at my side, as my trusted segundo. You'll be there or I'll have to find a new man to take your place, and your title. You can get rid of your fine clothes and go back to being called breed," Vin said.

Leland's expression never changed; he remained as impassive as ever, but if Vin had taken care to notice, if he could have seen within the heart of Leland Rides Horse, Vin Cotter's blood would have frozen at the menace festering there. But Leland almost bowed as he answered in a subservient tone, "I'll see to it."

Leland swung around and beat a hasty retreat toward the bunkhouse, cursing all the fates that had brought Anthem back now when Vin was just beginning his move to increase the Bonnet domain. He had been able to keep Vin under his thumb until now. The sudden change worried him. An independent, self-assured Vin was of no use to him. Maybe I'll get lucky, Leland mused. Natchez might track Anthem down and finish off both him and the girl. Then Vin could return his attention to more important matters. Like the welfare of the Bonnet.

Damn John Anthem. And damn Vin Cotter too. Once the Bonnet had established its boundary claims and subdued any of its neighbors who wanted to complain, Vin Cotter was going to have an accident, or better yet, he and Old Man Cotter might complete their falling-out and wind up doing away with each other. Yes, that would be even better. Then Leland, riding at the head of the men he had hired, planned to take things over, lock, stock, and rain barrel.

The half-breed glanced over his shoulder and saw Vin make his way up the porch and into the house. Leland smiled, finding hope in his plan, though it required patience. The white in him was eager, but the Apache in him was able to wait.

For now, Señor Vin Cotter, Leland silently admonished. You give the orders, for now.

Everett Cotter sipped the last of the coffee Cordelia had left him and enjoyed a second helping of bacon and eggs. Taking another slice of fresh bread, he sopped their liquid yellow yolks with the crust and ladled it into his mouth. He glanced up as Vin appeared in the dining-room doorway, a scowl on his face, veins like bluish worms pulsing and crawling beneath his pale flesh. His eyes were guarded and older-looking. Everett even felt a tinge of sympathy for his son, but that faded quickly. He no longer knew this young man standing before him. He was a stranger. Everett blamed himself, but not wholly, for he also believed a man must make his own way in the world, for better or worse. In hard country only the hard survived. He looked up at Vin and shuddered, seeing something wild and uncontrolled, a glimpse of mad pride and something darker still that defied speculation. Everett didn't want to know.

"They're together now," Vin said, casting a warning glance at Cordelia, giving her a silent order to depart. The housekeeper understood his intentions and returned to the kitchen.

Everett shifted in his wheelchair, wincing as a nerve in the small of his back protested. "Yes," he said, dabbing another morsel of bread at the spreading yolk. He sighed, enjoying the smells of breakfast that mingled with the cool, rain-washed air lifting the curtains behind the table.

"That's all. Our stable burned to the ground, horses scattered, and my wife stolen away, and all you say is yes."

"She wasn't stolen. She left with Johnny of her own choosing."

"How would you know?" Vin snapped, grabbing the pot from the table and filling a blue enamel tin cup with coffee.

"Because I talked to her. I watched her leave from the front room and saw the fire as well. I doubt it was started on purpose."

"Watched her? There are guns in the cabinet. You could've tried to stop her."

"I told her to leave."

Vin's arm paused as he lifted the cup to his lips; he lowered it to the table. "You what?" he said in a quiet voice.

"I told her to leave," Everett said, sliding the plate away and leaning his elbows on the table. "You stole her, son, with your lies. Your marriage was grounded in deceit, and thus no marriage at all. She was never yours. She never will be. It's time for you to learn, Vin, there are some things in this world that you cannot have. It's a lesson you should've learned a long time ago. But now is better than not at all."

Vin hurled the cup of coffee across the room, where it crashed against the wall and left a brown smear dripping to the floor. "You bastard!" Cordelia poked her head in from the kitchen. "Get out!" Vin bellowed. The woman darted back out of sight.

"Let them go. They have quite a head start. And Johnny can ride and not leave a trail. You won't find them. So let it be." Everett hoped his disturbed son would see the sense of such advice, hoped that there was still time for reason to cut through all the jealousy and hatred seething in Vin.

Everett wasn't prepared for Vin's reaction. A slim pale hand shot out with surprising strength and caught Everett by the collar of the shirt. He lifted his father bodily from the wheelchair until the two men stood face to face, Vin's breath fanning his father's cheek.

"I'll find them. She left me a map." Vin laughed aloud and shoved his father back into the wheelchair with enough force to rattle the old man's teeth. "I'll see they stay together too, since you are so concerned, Father. After all, Johnny was always more important to you than me. Well, I wouldn't think of breaking up such a union made in heaven. No. Don't you worry." He bent forward, and lowering his mouth to Everett's ear, Vin added in a whisper, "I'll see they are buried together."

Vin straightened and walked to the door, then hesitated as he was struck by the realization of how much stronger Everett seemed to be. His father was recovering quicker than expected. He fixed Everett in a steely stare. "The Bonnet's mine now. You'd better learn to live with that. Or do me a favor, don't live at all."

Everett watched his son vanish through the doorway, heard his footsteps fade down the hall and a door slam shut. He lowered his face into his hands and tried to pray but could no longer find the words.

"Mr. Cotter, are you all right?" Cordelia asked from the kitchen. She peered around the doorway, her round motherly features etched with concern.

Everett looked up, embarrassed to be caught in such a weak moment. "I'm going to need a friend, Cordie, in the days ahead. Perhaps very soon, I'll need someone I can trust and count on. I need a friend," Everett repeated, and his voice trembled.

Cordie, seeing Everett made suddenly fragile and vulnerable, was moved to pity. She knew then she might have to choose between her son and this man to see that right was done.

"I'm your friend, Everett," she replied, lovingly, moving to his side, her hands touching his shoulder. He reached up and enfolded her hand with his own. "I have always been," she said.

Rose McCain peered past the edge of her pillow and over the brawny forearm of Johnny Anthem asleep beside her in the four-poster bed. She yawned and managed to reconstruct the night's mad events.

The night was a tableau of thunder and fire and hours on horseback that seemed to last forever as they rode their mounts to exhaustion, never stopping to rest. By daylight they had reached the San Antonio River and headed into the city under cover of the continuing downpour. It was early morning and they kept to the alleys and the fringes of the city until they walked their weary horses into Mama Rosita's courtyard. Juan Medrano, who had returned with Johnny, arrived to take their horses as Anthem lifted Rose in his arms and carried her into the cantina. Rose dimly

remembered Mama Rosita hurrying them past the tables
and the few slumbering souls sprawled unconscious on the
benches as she took them upstairs to the bedroom.

Now Rose swung her legs over the edge of the bed and
padded on bare feet to the shuttered window. She cracked
the shutters an inch and looked out at the western sky
blushing crimson and purple on the skyline. They had slept
the day away. Rose stretched and noticed her mud-spattered
attire. She and Johnny had fallen into bed with scarcely a
word of endearment, taking only enough time to kick out
of their boots before drifting into a blissful and recuperative
sleep.

Rose sighed. She and Johnny had spent their first night
together without sharing so much as a kiss. She didn't intend for that to happen again.

Returning to San Antonio was a daring gambit, but
whether or not they had fooled Vin Cotter was another
matter entirely. Rose crossed to the bed and looked down
at Johnny. Sleep softened the hard planes of his face, re-
storing a look of innocence that his cold-fire gaze often hid.
His waist was a bit narrower than she remembered, but his
mud-spattered shirt barely managed to contain his muscular
torso. His fight with Natchez had been sudden and brutal,
and it was a side of Johnny unknown to her until now. But
he was still the man she loved, and if the recent months
had hardened his exterior, she knew within, he was also
capable of great sensitivity and passion. She bent to kiss
him.

"Proper folks call my place a nice little rest stop on the
way to perdition," Mama Rosita said from the doorway.
She was dressed in her usual attire of black silk and crinoline that swathed her ample frame with a gay flourish of
bows and ruffles. A single black feather was woven into
her coiffure. Her ruby lips turned upward in a smile as she
raised a wine bottle and two glasses and walked into the

room. She placed her offering on the nearest table.

"I was hoping to find a place to bathe, to scrub off some of this dirt," Rose said in a low voice so as not to awaken Johnny. Mama Rosita continued past her to a woven curtain that screened an alcove from the rest of the room. She drew the curtain aside to reveal a small bath chamber.

Dominating the room was a huge cast-iron tub; next to it sat a ladder-backed chair. A heavy-looking cedar wash-stand with a mirror and drawers for towels and a stoneware top stood against the back wall. Steam undulated upward from the surface of the tub.

Rose looked questioningly at Mama Rosita, who nodded and said softly, "We have names much alike, you and I." The madam turned to look at Johnny curled on his side in the bed. "But you have the luck, I am thinking." She shrugged and quietly left the room.

It was sunset and John Anthem was alive. He couldn't think of a better way to end a day. He rolled over on his stomach and stared upward at the ceiling and the flickering halo of light cast by the lantern. He hoped the Bonnet ranch hands were killing themselves searching the countryside for him. He couldn't remember anything but rain and weariness. His whole body was stiff from the trek to San Antonio and the rescue and the ride from Luminaria . . . He raised up on his elbows and looked around the room. For one panic-stricken second he wondered if Rose had been stolen away again. Then he heard a splash of water followed by a feminine cry of pure relief and noticed the merest sliver of light beneath the blanketed doorway. He stared at his own mud-caked clothes and flesh and decided Rose had the right idea.

Johnny caught the scent of lilac water and climbed out of bed, tossing the blankets to the floor. He peeled off his clothes until he stood naked in the room. Then he crossed the room to the curtain and, taking a deep breath, swept it aside.

Rose bolted upright in the tub and watched as Johnny padded toward her, his bronzed naked torso rippling with strength and quite obviously aroused. Her tresses splayed outward like a golden bridal veil on the soapy surface of the bathwater. Cloudy white bubbles clung to her waist and shoulders and neck. Her breasts gently rose and fell with each breath, the taut pink crowns hidden by suds. Rose hardly looked alarmed at his intrusion; in fact, judging by the wicked twinkle in her eyes, she appeared to welcome it.

"There's room in here for the two of us," she said teasingly, and swept the bubbles aside as she raised her arms to him.

Johnny gulped a lungful of steamy air and hurried to join her.

23

★

At midnight Johnny and Rose were gathered around a table with Mama Rosita, who had arrived with a couple of her hired hands bearing platters of freshly baked bread, cuts of smoked ham, and bricks of cheese. A pot of black coffee too thick to drink and too thin to plow completed the fare. The couple were dressed in a fresh change of clothes and, despite their hunger, now and then paused to cast surreptitious looks at each other. A grin split Johnny's features and he looked over his shoulder at the bed, its quilt and sheets in complete disarray.

"I must send for one of my girls to mop up the water," Rosita mentioned. The curtain had been accidentally torn loose, and beyond it, the floor of the bathroom was drenched. "I did not mean to fill the tub so full," Mama added in a wry tone of voice, well knowing she had filled the tub only waist-high. Wet footprints traced a path from the tub to the bed.

"The way I see it," Johnny blurted out, changing the subject, "we can wait here. Mama will hide us until Captain Colby and his company of Rangers return from patrol. They've been gone over two weeks and ought to return any day now, at least I hope it's soon. And when he does, I'll bring Juana to him and she can tell Colby what she told me."

"Juana?" Rose asked, puzzled.

"Yes, Juana," Mama Rosita said. "She show up at my door, many days ago, and she is very frightened. I knew her from long ago. We, uh, worked together—I mean, in the same place." The madam leaned forward and tucked a swath of silk in her cleavage and took a sip of coffee. "Juana saw Vin Cotter shoot Señor Briscoe in the back. The segundo was unarmed. It was murder. Vin Cotter was drunk, and maybe he did not know what he was doing. But Señor Briscoe is dead all the same." Mama Rosita blessed herself.

"Oh, my God," Rose muttered. So it hadn't been self-defense.

"Mama sent one of her men to tell me what happened. The girl was afraid to go to the Rangers; after all, Cotter is a powerful name around here. But I've talked to her and she'll go with me to see Colby. Mama Rosita told me what Vin has been up to. I wanted to get you out of that house as soon as possible. That's why I took the chance and rode out to the ranch."

"It was lucky for me you did," Rose said. She stared at the food on her plate, her appetite suddenly gone. Poor Everett. The news of Briscoe's death had been terrible, but to think that Vin killed him in cold blood. It would break the old man's heart.

"The two of you are welcome here," Mama Rosita said. She slid back from the table and stood and patted smooth the wrinkles in the black silk dress that clung to her plump derriere. "If Señor Cotter or any of his stallions come here, my girls will see they leave as geldings."

A soft rapping sounded at the door, followed by someone hoarsely whispering Mama's name. Mama Rosita strode across the room and threw wide the door. Juan Medrano stood in the hallway, hat in hand, a worried look on his face. He backed away as Mama joined him, and he spoke to her in a low but excited voice. Now and then he looked past Mama toward Johnny. Mama Rosita began to berate her hired man, who continued to protest his innocence of any wrongdoing.

Rose placed her hand over Johnny's, feeling the increase of his pulse rate.

"Start getting your things together," Johnny said. "Find your boots. Your clothes and saddlebag are under the bed, bring them along."

"What is it?" Rose asked.

"Do as I say. Hurry," Johnny snapped, unintentionally harsh.

Rose did as he ordered. She was dressed in a cotton blouse and loose-fitting trousers. Sitting on the edge of the bed, she pulled on her woolen socks and hurriedly tugged on high riding boots.

Mama Rosita reentered the room.

"Vin knows we are in San Antonio," Johnny guessed.

"No. But soon he will," Mama Rosita said. "We had no extra grain. Juan sent his son, Pedro, to the livery stable by the river and gave the boy money to buy two bags of oats, plenty for our needs. But Pedro took one of your horses, *señora*. Pedro thought there would be no harm. But at the livery were two men who recognized the horse. One wore scalps like a woman wears beads. He grabbed Pedro and beat him until the boy told him where he got the horse. He tied Pedro up. Then the mean one sent his compadre, who was called Bert, to bring Vin Cotter. Pedro wriggled free and came running back to tell us. He says the mean one had no name."

"He has a name," Johnny said, strapping on his gun belt. "And it's trouble. Have one of your girls pack us some food."

"What are you doing?" Mama said. "I have seen trouble before."

"Not trouble like this. Those men are rough and primed for cutting loose. You and the girls saved me once, but when Vin and Leland Rides Horse come looking for me, they'll be expecting a fight, you won't have any surprise for them."

Mama Rosita drew herself up to her diminutive height, dug her fists into her hips, and soundly declared, "I am not afraid."

"I'm ready," said Rose.

"Good." Johnny turned and searched the room for any of his belongings. Then, satisfied, he faced Mama Rosita again. "As soon as Colby returns, you take Juana to him and see that she tells him what happened to Joe Briscoe. Colby's an honest and fair man. He may be a friend to the Cotters, but that won't keep him from doing what's right."

"But, Johnny, where will you be?" Mama fussed. She liked his plan less and less.

"Luminaria," Johnny replied. "I'll make my stand on my own ground."

"*We'll* make our stand," Rose corrected.

"I have lost you, Johnny," Mama sniffed. "I think forever." Mama Rosita dabbed at an imaginary tear. But a romantic at heart, she shrugged. "Well, there is always the wild little pony, *mi novio*, Chapo is his name. Next time you bring him with you." Her fantasy firmly in place, her spirits restored, she lead the fugitive couple down the hall. She ordered Juan Medrano to bring the horses and Ceci to pack dried meat and fruit and coffee for a journey.

There were few men downstairs at that hour, and though the commotion roused them from sleep, they stared only for a moment in bleary-eyed incomprehension before settling their heads back on the table boards and drifting off to sleep.

Johnny and Rose waited at a table near the fire for their horses.

The front door opened and Juan Medrano, ducking inside, waved to the couple. Mama Rosita lumbered out of the kitchen with a leather bag crammed with bread and bacon, dried fruit, salt pork and beans, a package of coffee, and a small sack of flour. She handed the provisions to Rose and bussed her on the cheek.

"I don't know how we can thank you, Mama Rosita," the young woman said, affection for the notorious madam welling in her breast.

"I have food to spare," Mama replied.

"No," Rose said, and she leaned forward and whispered, "I mean for the bath."

Mama Rosita laughed aloud and hugged the girl as she led her to the door.

Johnny turned red in the face. When women laugh like that, he thought, it's generally at a man's expense. He quickened his steps and hurried outside to where Juan Medrano held the horses Johnny had brought from Luminaria: a blaze-faced sorrel for Rose and the black mare Vin had once stolen.

Juan stepped forward, but Rose ignored his offer of assistance and vaulted into the saddle on her own. Juan's expression changed, took on a new respect for the woman. He had only glimpsed her riding in fine carriages in town, but saw that she was a natural horsewoman.

"*Vaya con Dios,*" the old man said, retreating into the shadows.

Johnny exhibited an impressive show of strength by sweeping Mama off her feet in an embrace. He kissed her on the mouth and gave her a resounding slap on her behind. She squealed with delight and laughed anew. As Johnny set her down, he held her arm, and grew serious.

"I want you to let Vin search the place. I want him to know I've gone."

Mama frowned. "He'll come looking for you—him and the half-breed."

"Let him," Johnny said. "Soon this will be settled. But I'll choose the time and place. *¿Comprende?*"

Mama nodded, and climbing to the porch, she stood next to Juan in darkness.

"Ride like the wind," she said. *"Vaya con Dios."* Go with God.

And they did.

24

★

John Anthem's long red hair was bound by a strip of rawhide, Apache-style, and his sun-darkened torso was shiny with sweat from the arduous morning climb. He shaded his eyes and searched the terrain he and Rose had recently struggled over. It was a hard-scrabble landscape of arid black gravel and clumps of sotol, yucca, and ocotillo. Mesquite trees were few and far between but offered the only hope of shade on the heat-scoured terrain.

The southern route had been a difficult one, but it cut better than three days off the return journey. It was also harder to track a man in desert country. But not impossible, Johnny thought as he studied a wisp of smoke that fluttered against the azure sky, marking the encampment of their pursuer. Unseen but not unknown, Johnny thought, for it had to be Natchez Washburn. Vin wouldn't have had time to send anyone. But Washburn had been in San Antonio. He could have seen Johnny and Rose leave Mama Rosita's and followed them. Washburn certainly wasn't worried about being seen; maybe he wanted Johnny to know the "scourge of Natchez Under the Hill" was only a day's ride behind. Johnny leaned on his rifle, his left hand closed around the bone-handled bowie knife scabbarded high on his left hip. A grim smile played over his features as he reached a decision.

Rose slipped and sent a shower of pebbles to the canyon floor a hundred and fifty feet below. She finished her climb hand over hand and stood atop the hill alongside John Anthem. The aroma of fresh coffee and sizzling bacon permeated the crisp pure air above their camp. Johnny's stomach rumbled.

"I hope that is a good sign," Rose lightheartedly said, and placed a hand over his stomach. She was in good spirits and had grown increasingly so the farther they got from the Bonnet. She studied the horizon. It took longer for her inexperienced eyes to notice the smoke from the distant campfire. Suddenly she stiffened.

"Natchez Washburn, I reckon," Johnny said.

"Maybe it's Apaches?" Rose suggested, as if that were an improvement.

"You don't see Apaches until you're in a fight. Sometimes not even then. It's Washburn. He wants me to know he's here."

"Why?" Rose softly asked.

"I'll ask him," Johnny replied.

"That's suicide," she blurted out. But she read the intent in his voice and the serious set of his features and knew he intended to wait there for Washburn. Nothing she could say would change his mind.

A wind, heard from far off like an onrushing train, bowed the tall grasses and swept upward to wash over the couple on the hill.

Rose breathed deep, reveling in the fragrance of sage and wild rose, rain-washed chino, and the merest hint of pine. So much beauty awaited them in that range of hills and mountains and twisted valleys, surely they could lose the likes of Natchez Washburn. She expressed as much to the man at her side.

"I'll not lead him farther," Johnny replied, peering out
at the trace of smoke. "Let him go back if he wants, but
come ahead . . . no."

"Why?"

"Because," John Anthem told her, "this land is mine."
He left her side then and started down the steep hillside,
following a deer trail to the canyon floor.

"How far are we from Luminaria?" Rose called after
him.

"Another three days," he called back, "depending how
we push the horses."

Rose glanced over her shoulder at the mountains looming to the west. My God, she thought, he's claimed as far
as she could see. How could any one man expect to hold
on to so much? As he moved effortlessly along the deer
trail, she noticed the scar tissue crisscrossing his back, the
legacy of his captivity. "Andrés Varela," she muttered, recalling Johnny's account of his captivity. She hated Varela
for the pain he'd inflicted on the man she loved.

Using an outcropping of stone for a stool, Rose sat facing the mountains. She took pleasure in the way the shadows clung to the valleys and how the land seemed in
motion. Another breeze washed over her and tugged at the
golden tresses as she stared at the sky. Overhead, a lone
hawk drifted on unseen currents cutting lazy circles in the
sweet spring air. A false tranquillity settled in—false because for all its momentary peacefulness and beauty the
red-tailed hawk was a patient bird of prey. It was waiting
to kill. Rose lowered her gaze from the hovering silhouette
on high to the man in the canyon below.

He was waiting too.

Johhny ordered Rose to hide among the rocks. She did as
she was told, trusting his instincts.

"How do you know he'll pick this canyon?" Rose asked.

Natchez Washburn frightened her. Her head was filled with thoughts of the ruffian's prowess with gun and knife.

Johnny patted her arm reassuringly. "He'll find us, I left tracks for him. Don't worry. I can take care of myself." He noticed she didn't seem set at ease by his bravado. But there was nothing else he could say to her. He had to face Washburn and kill him or drive him off. He had to face the man because there was nothing of the sky-liner or back-shooter in John Anthem.

A half an hour passed. Then another ten minutes.

The black mare shifted her stance, thrust her ears forward, and whinnied softly as the echo of an approaching horse reverberated in the canyon. Johnny readied himself and stared at the opening between the hills. One moment the way ahead was clear; the next, Natchez Washburn was heading into the canyon. He saw Johnny but continued on without pause. As he approached, his hand stole upward to the loop around his throat and he pulled the scalp rope up over his head, knocking off his hat.

His features still bore a trace of Johnny's beating. His thick brown hair was matted close to his skull and his face was sweat-streaked and caked with dirt. He held the scalp-adorned gun rope away from his body, purposefully disarming himself as he closed the distance between himself and John Anthem. At last he tugged on the rein and the weary dust-colored gelding he rode stopped.

Rose, peering past the rim of her hiding place, judged the men to be about a horse's length from each other. She was as surprised as Johnny when Natchez dropped the gun to the canyon floor.

"About time you quit running, boy," Natchez said, his voice rang throughout the canyon.

"I wasn't running," Johnny said. "Just going home." The tall young man looked at the revolver in the dust. "Which is what I suggest you do."

"It's a free country," Natchez said, hooking his thumb around the big-bladed knife scabbarded at his side.

"No it isn't," John Anthem said. "You're on my land now." His eyes narrowed. "And it's time you were leaving."

"Looks like one hell of a lot of land for a young pup like you." Natchez grinned, imagining the young man's blood turning to ice water. "Think you can hold on to it?"

"Why don't you try to take it?" Johnny replied, every muscle tense.

Natchez was caught off guard by the challenge; his features grew livid with rage. He nodded to the revolver in the dust. "I will," Washburn said. "I've been thinking on the way you handled me there in the barn. I got to wondering how you'd do if you had to face me head-on. Loosianna style. You have a knife. So do I. Knives are how a man settles his accounts Under the Hill." He dropped a hand toward the hilt of his Arkansas toothpick. "Of course, if you're afraid to go against me . . ."

Johnny took the Colt revolver from its holster and, leaning over, let the serape slide off. He dropped the revolver onto the blanket, straightened in the saddle, and drew his bowie knife as Natchez went for the blade at his side. But when Natchez showed his hand, instead of a knife, his hand held a small-bore percussion pistol with all four of its barrels pointed at Johnny's midsection.

"Pup, it is a bona-fide cinch you ain't ever been to Natchez Under the Hill."

Johnny stared bleakly at the weapon and realized he'd been tricked, and tensed. His muscles coiled, preparing to spring. He wasn't going to sit there and be shot. Natchez Washburn would feel the kiss of fourteen inches of steel or Johnny would die in the process. Washburn's fingers tightened on the trigger.

"No," Rose shouted, and stood up from cover, the rifle

in her hands. She braced herself against the ledge and sighted down the barrel.

Washburn stared at her in astonishment. But his expression relaxed when he saw it was only Rose, holding a rifle that was much too big for her. "You better be careful or you'll hurt someone," he purred.

Rose shot him off the horse. She squeezed the trigger; the rifle thundered and spat flame and black smoke and sent a .50-caliber slug ripping through Washburn's side. The impact lifted Natchez completely off his horse and sent him sprawling in the dirt. The gelding panicked and stirred the dust as it wheeled in terror and raced down the canyon.

Johnny leapt from the black mare as the gelding bolted past and charged into the dust after the wounded man.

Natchez Washburn stagggered to his feet. He roared in pain and anger and fired through the dust at the rocks. He glimpsed Anthem towering over him and tried to bring the belly gun around, but shock dulled his fighting edge. He screamed and cursed the man bearing down on him. He fired again, but missed as Johnny stepped in close and drove the bowie knife up into the wounded man's chest. Fourteen inches of razor-sharp steel went into the heart of Natchez Washburn. The force of the attack lifted the dying man off his feet. He fell on his back in the battle-churned dust and was dead before it settled.

Johnny staggered back, his muscles trembling from the brief struggle. He backed away from the figure splayed out on the ground and turned toward the limestone battlements as Rose climbed out of her hiding place. She leapt to the canyon floor and walked through the lengthening shadows toward the man she loved. Neither spoke; they simply embraced. They clung to each other. And let the pulse of their hearts erase the memory of how close death had come.

25

★

Leland Rides Horse fixed his attention on the rise ahead and the man waiting there, motionless on horseback, a figure of loneliness and obsession. Vin Cotter stared at the westering sun, feeling the blackish desert release its heat to the cloudless sky. Leland could sense the nervousness in the men behind him. They were beginning to have their doubts about hiring on with Vin—such a strange one, a man who couldn't even hold on to his wife.

"What's he lookin' for?" one of the men called out, a hard case by the name of Reasoner. He was a chunky, bearded individual who often spoke out loud to no one in particular, and usually no one answered him. "Never seen a man stare so," Reasoner said. "Ain't natural. I wish to hell I knew what he was lookin' for."

"He's looking for ghosts," Leland said loud enough for the bearded man to hear.

"Somehow that don't make me feel much better," Reasoner growled. He had no use for half-breed Apaches. But as long as he was paid, Jimbo Reasoner would ride for the devil himself. Of course he wanted to live to spend the folded bills lining his pocket.

"I'd hate to be Anthem when Natchez Washburn catches up to him," Bert added.

"I'd hate to be you if we don't," Leland said as he rode away from the men and up the gentle rise toward Vin.

Vin Cotter's shirt was open to the waist. His chest and neck were sunburned, his cheeks blistered. His eyes were red-rimmed, and he wiped a forearm across his features as Leland approached. Vin intended to keep the wreckage of his emotions private.

He reached inside his waistband to remove the map Johnny had drawn for Rose. The encroachment to the Chihuahuan desert was noted on the drawing as a shaded scribble. Underneath Johnny had written: "A good place to ride clear of."

"You still want to head across?" Leland asked, knowing how Vin was suffering. His sun-blistered torso had to be causing Cotter a great deal of pain.

"The desert's the quickest way." Vin shaded his eyes. The distant suggestion of mountains on the horizon seemed as ephemeral as dreams. "We'll angle over toward the pass here"—he pointed to the map—"about halfway across, I judge it. We might go thirsty, but it ought to cut a few days off our travel."

"The men won't like it."

"They like my money. I'm not worried."

"You ought to be worried about what's happening back at the Bonnet," Leland said.

"I am the Bonnet," Vin said, and he fixed his haggard gaze on the breed. "*I am the Bonnet.*" Vin leaned toward Rides Horse. "Don't look so desperate, Segundo, I promise, nothing will happen to me. But your concern is touching." Vin laughed heartily.

Leland willed himself to remain impassive.

"I'm just trying to look after you, my friend," he said.

"My friend . . . Yes, it's good to have friends," Vin repeated, his voice growing distant, a man drowning in his own disgrace. "Tell me, my friend, what do they say about me, the men who ride with us? Do they laugh, do they think me a fool because my wife ran off with Johnny Anthem? God damn him. Why didn't he die? I left him behind for those Mexican soldiers to kill. I'll never trust another chili-eater as long as I live." Vin swore. "He *will* die, this time, I'll make sure. And I'll be rid once and for all of John Anthem. What do you think about that?"

"The sooner the better," Leland answered.

Vin nodded in satisfaction and clapped him on the shoulder. Cotter urged his horse to a brisk trot that carried him down the rise and straight ahead into the desert's bleak embrace.

Leland Rides Horse, a worried man with a heart full of angry dreams, motioned for the men to follow.

Luminaria.

Chapo saw the couple first. He espied the two riders from his perch on the eastern slope of the bordering hills of Luminaria Canyon. He recognized Anthem's mare and saw the tall willowy figure of Rose McCain alongside John. Chapo's gunshots echoed down the long canyon to alert the rest of the men at their campsite. Then the wild young rider ran to his horse and raced at a breakneck gallop down to the valley floor to meet the two arrivals.

The men had been busy in John's absence. Nestled on the slope above the construction was a single-room cabin made of logs with a thatch roof and a stone chimney rising off one side. The men were gathered around the bunkhouse when Anthem arrived. Johnny dismounted and helped Rose climb down. Her features were dust-caked, but she smiled as she took in the valley with its rain-sculpted cliffs and meandering spring-fed stream.

Kim Rideout and Charlie Gibbs greeted her warmly.

Memo Almendáriz bowed and swept the ground with his sombrero, flashing her a bright smile that lit his dark, Latin complexion. Chapo copied his father and then went a step further and kissed Rose's hand.

"We welcome you to Luminaria, *señorita*," the youth said. "Your beauty puts to shame the sunlight on the water, for its loveliness cannot compare with your own."

Bemused, Rose glanced aside at Johnny, who shrugged and wondered to himself just what other courtesies Mama Rosita had taught Chapo.

Poke Tyler held back. Rose turned to face him as Johnny introduced them. The old man shuffled forward and, making a perfunctory nod of welcome, continued on past the new arrivals, muttering that he had to tend the cook fire. Johnny and the other men watched in uncomfortable silence while Rose stared after Tyler, trying to figure out for herself just how she had managed to offend the old-timer.

Johnny broke the awkward tableau by waving a hand toward the cabin. "You boys been playin' carpenter again?"

"Dang near busted a thumb," Kim Rideout replied with mock indignation. "And don't blame me if it leaks and washes you out the first good rain. I do my best work with a rope from horseback."

"It will not leak," Memo interjected. He was the architect of the humble structure. "I did not think you would return to us alone, Señor Johnny, my friend. Although I did not think you would bring such a treasure either."

"I'm not a treasure," Rose asserted gently. "But a partner." She removed her hat and loosed a cascade of golden hair. "I'm here to work," she said, starting up toward the cabin.

Johnny grinned at Memo and whistled beneath his breath. "I think she'll stand her share of night watch too," Johnny said. He'd forgotten just how proud and forceful Rose could be.

"It would not surprise me at all." Memo laughed.

Johnny listened as a peculiar clacking sound carried to them from up the valley. It was the clatter of horns striking one another as unseen steers grazed in their makeshift corral.

"We got about seventy head back in the canyon," Memo said.

Charlie Gibbs kicked at the dirt underfoot and reached in his pocket for a dried, twisted Mexican cigar. He plopped it between his teeth and clamped down without lighting the tobacco. "Them longhorns are about as easy to brand as grizzlies. Man, oh, man, they put the Bonnet stock to shame. These critters been running wild so long they ain't got no idea what quit is. Lucky for me I don't neither."

Charlie sniffed at the aroma of chili that wafted up toward him from Pokeberry's cook fire a dozen yards away. Kim ambled along beside him, his stomach growling. The taciturn ranch hand stared at the cookpot, a look of resignation on his face that Poke failed to note or take offense at.

"I hope you like the cabin, Johnny. I gathered the dried grass for the bed. I sewed the blankets too to make the mattress," Chapo proudly claimed. "I didn't have time to make anything else but the stools and a table out of a split log. But Señorita Rosita told me a good bed is worth more than any chair. She says sittin's for folks who ain't got nothing better to do. But a man and woman can always find a use for a bed. Uh, I mean . . ." The youth blushed in embarrassment and avoided his father's stern gaze. "Think I'll get some of Poke's chili before he dumps it out," Chapo said as he hurried past his father.

"I think I shall have to meet this Mama Rosita one day. She sounds very motherly," Memo said, watching Johnny.

"That she is, *mi amigo,*" Anthem replied. "Motherly." He clapped Memo on the shoulder, then grew serious. "Segundo, tell the men we may have some trouble before long over this." He nodded toward the woman entering the cabin.

"Ahh. An angry father," Memo said.

"No. A husband," John Anthem explained. He continued on up the slope.

Memo shook his head and whistled between his teeth. He hoped Poke had put plenty of peppers in the chili pot because Memo's blood had just turned cold in his veins.

They made love beneath a mantle of night. Their bodies joined in fiery union, became one in the splendor of moonlight. And when the desert chill washed the earth, John Anthem and his Yellow Rose clung to each other beneath the blankets, passion sedated, desire undiminished, but asleep.

Rose woke before dawn, having dreamed of dust and the Springfield rifle in her arms and sighting along the heavy barrel at Natchez Washburn. Rose had never fired a gun in anger at a man. She'd squeezed the trigger, knowing if she hesitated she would never follow through. She didn't regret shooting the ruffian, but had enough conscience not to take such a thing lightly.

She rolled out of bed and quietly stepped into her trousers and shirt and moccasins. Carefully rounding the three-legged stools and split-rail table that were the cabin's only furnishings, she walked outside into the predawn darkness. A sprinkle of stars shimmered cheerfully over the valley. A dove cooed to its mate down near the brook. The music of flowing water was one of nature's loveliest melodies, she thought. Red coals pulsed with fiery life where Poke had prepared the meal and left a coffeepot hung over the coals so that a warm cup of coffee could be had at any hour.

The old man had remained apart from the others at supper, behavior that puzzled Johnny as well as Rose. Deep-seated animosity from any stranger puzzled her. Rose knew only one way to deal with it and was determined to confront the man as soon as possible.

She walked over to the campfire and stirred the ashes, adding a few pieces of dry timber. Coals burst into flame as tongues of fire greedily lapped at the wood. She added another handful of twigs and split wood. She soon had a cheerful blaze going. Rummaging in the stores, she removed a slab of bacon and filled a big iron skillet with several thick strips. She added a handful of fresh grounds to the coffeepot and set it by the fire. She discovered a batch of sourdough batter tucked away in a cloth-lined wooden box and busily covered the bottom of another skillet with freshly patted-out biscuits. She spooned off some of the bacon grease to keep the biscuits from sticking, covered the skillet, and placed it in the coals.

Rose sat back on her haunches, waiting for the biscuits, and her thoughts turned to Johnny. She shuddered, her limbs and flesh remembering his hard length within her. Yet Rose had matched his ardent kisses with her own; she had tamed him. He'd melted in to her and slept in her embrace.

The door to the bunkhouse opened and Charlie Gibbs sauntered out in his longjohns and headed toward the bushes. He had unbuttoned the flap over his rump and it flapped against the back of his thighs like a breechcloth. The ranch hand glanced over and nodded in Rose's direction. He had covered another few yards before he brought himself up sharply and gasped. He was practically undressed in the company of a lady!

"Holy Hannah!" he blurted out, spun in his tracks, and lit out for the bunkhouse. He grabbed off his hat and slapped it over his naked buttocks as he scampered to safety. Charlie leapt through the doorway and vanished from sight, but his departure was marked by a loud crash, a groan, the dull thump of colliding bodies in the dark of the bunkhouse. A yelp of pain, an angry curse, then rapid-fire Spanish resounded throughout the stillness.

Rose heard footsteps behind her and glanced over her shoulder as Johnny came down to the fire. He wore vaquero trousers molded to his lower torso, a loose cotton shirt, and high black boots. He'd strapped a gun belt around his solid hips. A morning breeze tugged at his tousled red hair. As the sun peeked above the horizon, definition returned to the cliffs and trees and the grasslands beyond the mouth of the canyon.

"What happened?" Johnny asked. He towered over the woman at the fire. But the hardened lines that seamed his features were offset by the gentleness in his eyes. He studied the bunkhouse and remained perplexed as the commotion faded.

"Early risers," Rose said matter-of-factly.

"Like you." Johnny grinned and squatted by the fire. "But, then, why should you be tired? I did all the work."

"Oh, you," Rose exclaimed, and threw a piece of charcoal at him.

Johnny dodged and reached for the coffeepot, jerked his hand away, and blew on his palm, muttering a curse. He wrapped his hand in a bandanna and lifted the pot out of the coals to pour cups of coffee for himself and the others.

As the men of the Slash A wandered out of the bunkhouse into the dawn, Johnny noticed Memo had a black eye and Kim was nursing a bruised shin. Charlie had a cut lip that was swollen and as pink as the blush on his cheeks; he kept looking at Rose, who had to fix her attention on the bacon to keep from laughing.

"Good morning, *señorita*," Memo said, squinting at her with his one good eye.

Chapo, still so much a boy, carried a gun like the others

and took his coffee with the rest. Pokeberry Tyler was the last to emerge. He checked the sky and studied the drifting clouds, then proceeded to the campfire.

"Have a cup of bellywash, old man," Johnny said.

Rose heaped a plate full of bacon and biscuits and sopping, which the old-timer sullenly accepted with thanks. He stared at the grub, shrugged, and headed off to the creek, to eat alone in the shade of the cottonwoods. Rose pretended to ignore the man's behavior and concentrated on helping herself to the last of the food.

"Sure is nice to have a woman's touch at breakfast," Kim said, wiping the grease from his plate with the last of his biscuit. He helped himself to another.

"It ain't that Poke can't handle mush; it's just that he growls so darn much when he plops it on your plate," Charlie added.

"Beans or steak, no difference," Chapo said. "Since you been gone, Big John, every meal has been seasoned with Poke's bad temper."

Johnny glanced at the trail leading down to the creek. He pursed his lips a moment, trying to figure out what had put the burr in the old man's blanket. Setting his plate aside, he rose to his full height. Chapo, Kim, and the other men sensed Johnny wanted their undivided attention.

"Boys, there's trouble ahead. Vin Cotter and those hard cases he hired on are on their way here. I don't know when or how long we have. But I know Vin Cotter, and that's enough for me to warn you: if you're lead-shy, best you take to the hills and wait out the storm. I'll pay you what I can and not think the worse of you. Fact is, I'll reckon you're showing uncommon wisdom."

"*Mi amigo*," said Memo Almendáriz. "Please, do not waste a pretty speech on us. We talked it out last night. Every man here rides for the brand. Luminaria is our home too, and we will not be driven off." The segundo waved to the others and tossed aside his plate. "You boys work for this outfit or are you just here for the *frijoles*?"

Charlie and Kim wolfed down their remaining morsels of food.

"Fetch the irons, Rideout," Charlie said good-naturedly. "Today's as good as any day to get gored."

Kim laughed dryly and nodded at Rose.

"Thank-ee for the grub," the cowhand said to Rose. He started off toward the horses tethered beside the low wall surrounding the courtyard.

"I would be honored to show you around the place," Chapo said, hurrying to stack the tin plates. "Let me tell you, *señora*, no one knows the best lookouts like me."

"Thank you, Joaquín, I think your offer is most gracious," Rose replied.

The boy swelled with pride. Nothing he had done had ever been called "most gracious" before.

"Chapo," John Anthem called out, "I have a job for you first. You can steal my woman afterward." Johnny grinned, enjoying Chapo's obvious discomfort as he blushed and tried to stammer out a defense.

Johnny left his arm around the youth and walked him away from the fire, not wanting to alarm Rose. "Listen to me now. What I have to tell you is very important." Johnny pointed toward a dust-covered wooden door that opened onto a chamber dug out of the earth.

"I want you to take one of the small kegs of black powder and bury it in the back of the canyon, above the corral where the steers are kept. Cut a fuse for a minute. As fast as you are, a minute ought to give you time to get out of the way. If I ever give you the word or if strangers ride into valley and try to take us, I want you to hightail it back there and set off that charge. You understand me?"

"*Sí*. The steers will stampede and God help any men who are caught in the path of such animals."

John Anthem stared down at the canyon floor, his features in a thoughtful expression as he envisioned the carnage wreaked by seventy or so head of wild longhorns barreling down between the cliffs. Tons of wild untamed meat on the hoof on the rampage; gunmen impaled on sharp-pointed horns six feet from tip to cruel tip. Vin would come, no doubt at the head of his little army, riding for vengeance, to settle an old account once and for all.

John Anthem worked his way down the deer trail to Luminaria Creek. He waited in the shade of the post oaks and watched a couple of gray squirrels at play along the creek bank a dozen feet away. The squirrels paused to drink, and Johnny remained motionless, allowing them to finish.

Anthem espied Pokeberry Tyler leaning against a decaying log, his bony legs outstretched and crossed at the ankles. Anthem approached, taking his time. He stepped over a patch of watercress, taking care not to crush the tiny white flowers or edible green leaves spreading from the springwater up onto the bank. He straddled the log as if it were a horse to be ridden, and nudged the empty plate by the old man's side.

"I see you weren't too proud to eat her cooking," Johnny remarked.

Poke yawned and sipped coffee black as his teeth and shooed a fly away from his bald head. "Younker, if I'd 'a been a proud man, I'd been sprouting daisies in some boneyard long ago." Poke drew in the earth with a stick. "There's a passage in the Bible: a time for war a time for peace, a time to make camp and a time to light a shuck, a time to throw your gun aside and a time to keep your powder dry, and always time aplenty to get yourself killed. A time to play a fool too, which is about the same thing."

"And I'm a fool?" Johnny said. "Maybe. Every man's a fool for something: money, power, a game of faro, or a bottle of Who Hit John. I'm a fool for my dream." Johnny shrugged.

"I showed you this here country for a purpose, boy," Pokeberry said. He drew a Slash A brand in the moist dirt. "I reckon you come as close to a son as I'm ever liable to get. I figured to make my stand here one day, to see what I'm leaving behind when I saddle up for the last ride. Maybe have some kids around me, kind of like kinfolk. Ain't none of that gonna happen if you go and get yourself shot full of holes by this Vin Cotter."

"The day hasn't dawned when Vin Cotter can take me. So don't you worry, Poke; you'll have that rocking chair and a passel of grandchildren too. More than you can handle. It's Vin who ought to be worried."

"What are you gonna do, dammit? Kill Vin Cotter? *Her* husband? That's a fine way to take a wife. More'n likely you'll get the drop on him and freeze up and Vin Cotter will shoot your lights out."

Poke heard a gasp behind him and looked over his shoulder at Rose, who had come down to wash the cups and plates in the creek. It was plain she recognized his predicament.

Poke spat, walked past Johnny, and started up the slope. He paused by Rose. "You're pretty as your namesake, and I can't blame Johnny for what he feels and why he's done what he done. You got spunk, Yellow Rose, and I admire you for it. But that don't make me happy you come here." Poke continued on along the path, leaving the couple by the creek.

Johnny looked at the woman above him on the bank. He sensed the fear in her and wanted to console her, to offer reassurance once again. But words failed him. Come to a fight, Vin Cotter had an edge. And there was no way around it. No way at all.

26

★

John Anthem watched a couple of distant eagles cut lazy spirals in the air over Sleeping Lion Mountain. From his vantage point on the bluffs overlooking Luminaria Canyon he could see for miles across the rolling prairie spreading out to the south in a sea of chino grass and yucca plants, a wind-ruffled green plain dotted with desert dandelion and tall-stemmed chicory soon to take on its purple blooms.

Johnny sat on a wind-eroded throne of gray-black volcanic rock and tilted his face to the sun, letting the warmth bathe his features. He enjoyed the peacefulness of an April afternoon despite what waited out behind the hills.

He heard the distant drum of hoofbeats and craned forward a moment to watch as Memo and his son rode out of Luminaria Canyon and headed straight for the draws around a jagged edge and summit he called Blue Top. There were several springs at the base of the mountain and arroyos as numerous as the spines on an ocotillo. He'd been back in camp almost a week now and still no sign of trouble. He'd begun to believe that Vin Cotter had written him off. He hoped so, for Anthem didn't relish having to confront the son of Everett Cotter.

Rose was climbing the last few yards up the trail when

she heard the frenzied warning of a rattlesnake. She paused until she had placed the snake by the sound of its rattling tail, then gave a sawtoothed ledge a wide margin and hurried along the trail to Johnny's side.

She dabbed at her forehead and neck with a bandanna and stepped past Anthem to stand at the farthest point along the cliff. Clouds scudded across an azure sky and cast their shadows on the prairie below, making a patchwork design in ever-shifting patterns of darkness and light.

"It's beautiful. Luminaria is a beautiful dream," Rose said. Johnny stood behind her, placing his hands on her shoulders. She covered them with her own.

"A dream that will come true, now that you're by my side," Johnny said. "Or do you have your doubts now?"

"I just don't want anything to happen to you," Rose said. "Maybe if I talked to Vin . . ."

"You had a year to try to talk to Vin. Joe Briscoe tried to talk to Vin," Johnny bitterly replied. He tightened his hold on her, his fingers dug into her shoulders. "Do you really think I would let you go back to him?"

Rose shook her head no in response. "It has been coming to this all along, hasn't it?"

"From the moment Vin left me to die in Mexico and tricked you into marrying him. I could have forgiven the first, but not losing you. Some men want what they can't have, and when it doesn't work out, they grow crazy."

"I feel sorry for him," Rose said. She lowered her head and tried to sort through all the confusion. Sympathy for Vin even while she feared him.

"So do I," Johnny said. And he held her close, the warmth from his body feeding her own and vanquishing the chill of her fears. "Vin could lose everything, and have nothing. I could lose everything and still be rich because of you, Yellow Rose. Because of you."

She turned in his embrace. Her lips hungrily sought his.

They were alone with the wind and the sky. What better
time for love. Upon the serape-covered ledge their bodies
joined in the hunger of the moment, their lovemaking fiery
and desperate as if for the first time.

Or the last.

Chapo climbed down from his brown gelding and reached
beneath the animal's belly to check the saddle rigging.
Memo dismounted, too, stretched, and rubbed the small of
his back. They had been working the brush-filled arroyos
for the better part of the afternoon. Blue Top Mountian
stretched skyward, blocking them from distant Luminaria
Canyon a good, hard six hours' ride away. Chapo tightened
the cinch on his saddle and stepped around the horse to
watch as Memo cleared a campsite at the base of a broad-
branched juniper. Chapo studied the fading light and realized he might as well unsaddle his horse, after all.

"Come here," the older man paused to call out and
beckon his son. Chapo led his gelding to a cedar and
ground-tethered his horse alongside Memo's. Chapo wiped
the sweat and grit from his eyes with his bandanna. Here
on the western slope of Blue Top the sun's rays came slanting down with an intensity that only night could vanquish.
Memo put his arm around his son's shoulders and walked
with him away from the trees and descended to the rolling
plain that circled Blue Top like an apron of chino grass.

"Good land," Memo commented.

Chapo tucked his thumbs in his belt and nodded. He
breathed in deeply and experienced a rush of spring-sweet
air fill his lungs. Memo watched him, standing tall and lean
and terribly grown-up for his thirteen years. Hard work had
put muscle on his shoulders and thighs. All of a sudden the
thirteen-year-old boy had become a man. How had such a
thing come to be, so quickly? One moment a boy riding
behind his father through the long nights when they had

taken to the wild *barrancas*. And now, a man, doing a man's work.

Memo loved his son more in that moment than he thought humanly possible. No heart could hold such love.

Memo reached up and unfastened a battered gold locket from around his throat and handed it to Chapo. The boy fingered the locket, worked the catch, and unfastened it. Inside he found a tuft of soft black hair, a flower petal, and a pinch of dust.

"When you were born, ah, you had a head full of black curls, *muchacho*, and I clipped one for keeping," said Memo. "The white petal is from the wild rose your mother placed in your crib for you to look at. She pricked herself cleaning away the thorns that the stem might be smooth and safe. The dirt is the earth of your homeland, the home of our family before men like Andrés Varela stole it and drove us into the *barrancas*. The earth is from the place of your birth. While you wear this locket, you are never alone, your mother and I will always be with you."

"Why do you give it to me now?" Chapo asked in a worried tone, putting the locket around his neck.

"Because a man ought to know his beginnings and today I see for myself you are a man." Memo chuckled and clapped him on the shoulder. "But do not worry, you still have much growing to do and many things to learn before you are as smart as your father."

Memo turned him and pointed to the slope rising to a crosswork of ledges and deep crevices and layers of stone that marked the passing of the years in hues of red and gray and brown.

"From this side of the mountain down across the meadow"—he turned and pointed out across the prairie to a hill that rose in the distance out of the plain—"to the hilltop yonder. This will be ours. A place of our own right in the heart of the Slash A Ranch. We will run our cattle, they will drink from the springs. We will build our own place and have a share in John Anthem's dream. And maybe one day you will bring a *señorita* of your own and make her your wife and give me many grandchildren."

"Papa, I think you have been listening to Pokeberry too much. I am only thirteen years and you talk of *señoritas* and love. I may be a man today but I am much too young. Let's build a fire and cook the rabbits I killed this afternoon." Chapo hurried over to his gelding and took a pair of freshly killed rabbits out of the saddlebag.

Memo threw up his hands in a gesture of frustration. "Too young to talk of *señoritas* and love? Why, all that you ever talk of is San Antonio and the girls you met at Mama Rosita's."

"But Papa," Chapo said, the very soul of patience, "that was not love. It was an education." Chapo turned his back on his father, squatted and sat back on his haunches, and busied himself with skinning the rabbits.

"This is my punishment," Memo said aloud, his voice ringing out to the hills, returning on the wind that ruffled the grassy plain. "A boy who has no respect is my punishment for raising him among bandits."

Chapo tossed a handful of bloody fur aside and glanced up at his father. "These rabbits won't cook without a fire."

Memo sighed, shrugged, and departed in resignation. "My punishment," he muttered aloud as he amusing the ground for wood, relishing the amusing exchange with his son.

Even as he saw the armed men riding into camp, Memo's last thoughts were on the richness of life. Then a loud slug knocked the hat from his head as the crack of a rifle resounded off the lonely mountainside. Memo spun around, tearing his threadbare waistcoat in the process, and stumbled toward his son. Chapo, his hands red from the blood of the rabbits, caught his father as Memo fell into his arms.

"Run," Memo managed to say. "Run," he shouted, and sprayed Chapo with his life's blood. One side of his skull was crushed from the impact of the bullet, yet the man clung to life. Chapo looked up in shock and horror as horsemen spread out along the slopes of Blue Top. A man in the lead, a dark-skinned man wearing the trail-worn finery of a vaquero, walked his horse toward the campsite.

"Just hold it there, boy, and no harm will come to you," Leland shouted. He repeated the command in Spanish.

Chapo recognized the half-breed. The boy clawed at the revolver shoved in the belt of his waist. Memo caught his hand.

"Warn Johnny . . . warn . . . war . . ." Memo's blood-smeared eyes rolled back in his head and the tension left his short wiry frame as death rattled deep in his throat.

Chapo shrieked in horror and tore loose of his father's dying grasp. He scrambled to his feet and broke into a run toward his horse. He leapt into the saddle as Leland shouted again for him to stop. The other men scattered out behind the breed began peppering the hillside, black smoke and orange flame blossomed from their hand guns and long rifles, but the distance was too great. Only Leland had a shot. He leveled his Springfield.

Chapo waited for the muzzle flash, and when it flared, he threw himself to the far side of his horse. The slug cut through his saddle space. Chapo raised up, emptied his revolver at the breed, and set the ambusher's horse dancing out of harm's way. Then Chapo wheeled his mount and, sobbing, rode for Luminaria.

Vin Cotter stood on the edge of camp and listened as Leland reported that the boy had eluded pursuit. Darkness draped the land and hid Vin's brooding features, which grew even more introspective as Leland finished.

"Did you have to kill the man?" Vin asked.

"I thought the boy would freeze and we could question him about the map and John Anthem," Leland replied. "Those two had us spotted and would have run off to warn Anthem anyway. Now we have one less man to deal with."

The Bonnet hirelings had tethered their horses out on the prairie. Jimbo Reasoner had already claimed Chapo's rabbits and was busy cooking them over his own campfire.

"You think he'll warn Anthem?" Vin nervously asked. He was a firm believer in the element of surprise.

"As sure as night follows day," Leland replied. He sensed a weakening in Vin Cotter's resolve. Leland intended to assert himself once more. He wanted Vin Cotter dependent on his judgment. It was important for the future. "But Anthem probably heard the gunfire too. I'll bet he's plenty worried."

Vin nodded, his humor returning. He enjoyed the notion of John Anthem worried, of his spending a sleepless night, waiting—waiting and wondering . . . when.

When?

Vin ambled over to Reasoner's cook fire and, slipping out a knife, carved a leg of roasted rabbit from the gunman's intended dinner.

"Hey!" Reasoner growled, and started to rise. But Leland stepped in behind Vin, who appeared to take no notice of the man by the fire.

Vin continued on to his own bedroll and stretched out beneath the branches of the juniper. He lost himself in his own turbulent thoughts. He loved Rose and yet he hated her. He accused her of every infidelity in his mind, selectively blanketing out the deceptions he had weaved to trap her like a spider its prey, only instead of a silken web he had used lies and the bonds of matrimony.

He stripped off the last morsel of meat and tossed the

bone as far as he could throw it down the hillside beyond the juniper. His men had rolled the body of Memo Almendáriz down the same incline. The body had come to rest in a narrow gulley about fifty feet away. Vin shook his head in disappointment. He'd have liked to question the man about how many men Anthem had working for him. If the dead man and the boy were any indication, John Anthem was desperate for help. Why, he might even be alone. No, not alone. Rose was by his side. Vin drove her from his mind. A twig snapped nearby and Leland Rides Horse loomed over him. The dark-skinned breed blotted out the branches and the stars.

"You need anything, *patrón*?" the half-breed said.

Vin shook his head in response; there was nothing he needed now, except to rid himself of the doubts that had dogged his every step for the last couple of days. The nearer he came to Anthem's land, the weaker his resolve, as if the cursed earth itself were sapping his will and making a coward of Vin Cotter.

But Vin was determined to fight it. He watched his segundo make the rounds of the camp, post guards, and assign other men to relieve the first pair.

Why couldn't I be more like Rides Horse? The men respect him. Because he knows what to do. They are even a little afraid of him. Vin recalled how Leland had casually shot the Mexican, in a completely offhand way. The man might have just been a drifter with his son in tow. He might not have even been one of John Anthem's men. Leland had simply murdered the man in cold blood. Vin's own damning conduct had at least occurred at night and in a drunken stupor. And Vin had felt remorse for Briscoe's death, though he tried to deny it. But Leland had killed and it no more bothered him than if he'd swatted a fly. This man, whose lack of feelings had been ably demonstrated this afternoon, had sworn loyalty and devotion to Vin Cotter.

Vin resolved to watch his back in the future. He found some comfort in the fact that Leland and John Anthem had locked horns before.

Johnny espied the dead horse sprawled at the mouth of the canyon. And he recognized Chapo standing by the horse and staring back the way he'd ridden. Johnny glanced around as Rose arrived at his side, the expression on her face just daring him to complain that she hadn't remained behind at the camp. She gasped at the sight of Chapo and slid off the mare as John Anthem dismounted. They walked together toward the boy.

John stared at the gelding lying on its side and would have berated the youth for such cruel mistreatment, but the expression on Chapo's face stilled any protest. He realized the boy must have ridden the horse till it died of exhaustion. He put his hand on the thirteen-year-old's shoulder and stared toward Blue Top Mountain in the distance.

"The one you wait for has come," said Chapo.

Johnny shaded his eyes and studied the pale-blue morning sky, glimpsed a thin wisp of smoke drift upward behind the hills. In a way, Johnny was relieved that at least the waiting was ended and that perhaps before the day was done something would at least be resolved. Realization struck him, talons of ice gripped Johnny's heart as he remembered Chapo hadn't ridden out alone.

"Where's Memo? Where's your father, Chapo?" Johnny softly asked.

"They kill him," Chapo said. "Bastards!" He drew his revolver and checked the loads. "But I will make them pay. Blood for blood." Chapo turned to Johnny. The thirteen-year-old had aged with sorrow, and his features were a mask of mature resolve. "I swear it."

Johnny had seen such a look before, in his own eyes once. Rose, who had watched her own father die with an

Apache arrow in his back, reached out to touch Chapo's shoulder, not to console, for there was no consolation with his father's blood staining his hands. She reached out to share.

Johnny nodded and repeated in a sharp menacing tone, "Blood for blood."

27

★

Sixteen men, counting Vin Cotter, and John Anthem made sure to count the young ruler of the Bonnet . . . Sixteen men paused and formed a circle around Chapo's dead horse. If they needed a sign pointing the way to Luminaria Canyon, the carcass on the prairie was as good as any. Johnny adjusted the spyglass and the familiar face of Vin Cotter filled the eyepiece.

"Is he there?" Rose asked, shielding her eyes from the afternoon glare as she peered up at Johnny. He stood atop the three-foot-high adobe wall that circled the beginnings of the hacienda.

"Oh, yes, it's Vin, all right." Johnny twisted slightly and the tension in him increased. "And Leland Rides Horse, too. The others, well, I don't think I'd invite them to tea. But they're more than welcome to the party we've got planned."

Johnny lowered the spyglass until he could make out the line of trees near the creek. He hoped Poke Tyler and Chapo were well hidden. Johnny grimaced in disapproval. Young Chapo was in plain sight, adjusting a snag in the rope net that trailed along the ground where the foliage was the thinnest. It was important the net remain undiscovered.

Chapo scattered an armful of twigs and branches over the part of the rope and covered the other bare spots with dirt. He'd insisted on taking his father's place at the net and wouldn't be denied. That left Charlie Gibbs to set off the charge back up the canyon. Kim Rideout was hidden up on the eastern slope.

Johnny swung the scope around and located the ranch hand nestled down among the rocks about halfway up the canyon wall. Johnny thought the place had the look of a rattlesnake den, but Kim appeared not to mind. Rideout was a crack shot with a rifle and had brought three Springfields with him from the camp. He had given his spare revolver to Chapo. Rideout caught a glint of sunlight off the spyglass and waved, signaling his readiness.

John Anthem returned his gaze to the mouth of the canyon. The riders from the Bonnet had entered and were warily approaching the walled courtyard. No doubt they had already seen Johnny.

"Don't you think you ought to take cover?"

"Soon as they start the music," Johnny replied. "Anyway, I want to bring them in close."

"Like a worm on a hook," Rose complained. She could make out the riders. My God, there seemed so many. "Johnny?"

"Yes."

"Don't get killed."

Johnny laughed, which wasn't the most reassuring of replies. He moved his sombrero and let it hang down behind his head. He had seen Vin holding a spyglass of his own, and it was trained on him. A breeze ruffled Johnny's coarsely woven shirt. He counted the riders again, and deep in his mind came the troubling thought that he didn't know what would happen when he forced Vin at gunpoint. Leland Rides Horse was another matter entirely.

Rose added the finishing touches to a weapon of her own

creation. She had brought Spanish armor breastplates from the house and strapped them together, cramming them full of black powder. Next she sealed the holes with hardened adobe. An oil-soaked rag provided a crude fuse, and she gave it an extra sprinkle of black powder to keep it burning when the time came to light it. Next she arranged an extra revolver and shotgun on the ground within easy reach. Her hands trembled as she worked. Finally she clenched her fists to still them and quietly voiced the Lord's Prayer beneath her breath. Sitting back on her heels, she closed her eyes, exhaled slowly, and looked up at Johnny.

"There's still time to get back up the canyon," Johnny said, watching her.

The very suggestion seemed to vanquish her fears; she glared at him. "This is our land, isn't it?"

"Yes."

"Let's get them the hell off," she snapped. Determination blazed in her very being. It showed in her eyes and in her bad tone of voice.

Chapo worked his way along the creek bank until he reached a thicket of monkshood that grew thick near the water's edge and up to the treeline. He parted the long stems and watched the horsemen ride through the valley. His gaze fixed on one of the men in the lead, a man who looked like an Apache but wore white man's clothes. His features were shaded by a broad-brimmed sombrero all black with silver stitching, and he smoked a thin cigarillo. Chapo recognized him and the rifle he cradled in the crook of his arm.

The thirteen-year-old brought his revolver forward through the bushes to cover the action. He sighted along the barrel. A shadow flitted in front of him, and Pokeberry Tyler shoved the gun's muzzle in the dirt.

Chapo turned and glared at the old-timer.

"We open up now and the whole game is blowed to perdition," Poke whispered.

"He murdered my father," Chapo hissed.

"And he'll shoot your lights out too or one of his boys will if you go takin' matters into your own hands," Poke retorted. "Ease up, younker. The dance will start soon enough. Then you'll have your chance to tag you a partner."

Poke kept his hand on the gun until he saw the light of reason return to the young boy's eyes. Chapo nodded. A tear spilled down his cheek and he wiped it away on his forearm. Poke eased his hold. "You'll do to ride the trail with, Joaquín Almendáriz. You'll do." Poke crawled out from the monkshood and back to the thickets where his pull rope dangled from the branch of a gray oak.

Chapo stared at the horsemen and numbered each one. Each and every man was responsible for his father's death. He tasted the grit stirred up from the hooves of their horses, heard them talk to one another in soft worried tones. They didn't like the way the canyon closed in on them, and especially the way John Anthem waited for them atop the adobe wall a hundred yards away. Chapo counted each man, and in his mind he shot every one of them dead.

Leland studied the hillsides; he checked the trees by the creek and found nothing to threaten him. And still he didn't like it. He knew the men behind him could handle any situation, but he was worried. He looked aside at Everett's son.

Vin Cotter met his stare, licked dry lips, and wished he had a drink.

"Why is he just standing there? Damn him, why is he standing there?" Vin asked in a voice reduced to a whisper. He looked over his shoulder. Behind him Bert rode with his shotgun ready, as did Jimbo Reasoner. Reasoner seemed almost asleep, but his looks were deceiving, for though his body was slouched forward in the saddle, he was primed and ready to leap to cover at the first sound of gunfire. The rest of the men began spreading out along the floor of the canyon between the hacienda on the knoll and Luminaria Creek. Vin returned his attention to John Anthem. "Why doesn't he do something?"

"We aren't in gun range yet." Leland chuckled. He kicked at a scrub cedar and blew a cloud of smoke from between his thin lips as he guided his horse past the tree.

"Now we are, I reckon," he said when he was fifty yards up the incline. Leland scowled at Vin. "You wanted this, Vin. Well, it's here. So ride straight and stop your trembling if you want me to go a step further."

Vin stared at him in astonishment, but before he could reply, John Anthem's voice knifed through the warm spring air and carried effortlessly to Vin and his men.

"That's far enough, boys," John Anthem called out. "You're on my land. Turn around and head out. Or be buried here, it's all the same to me." Johnny waved a hand in a gesture indicating the men strung out down the incline. "Leave now, boys, and there'll be no trouble for you. All of you can go. You too, Vin. But not Leland. The breed stays."

"I'm special," Leland retorted with a humorless smile.

"You're special," Johnny repeated ominously.

"Brave words for a man alone," Vin called back. His hand drifted to his gun.

"Not alone," Rose said. She stepped into the archway and looked down at the man she had married and never loved. "Just go away, Vin. Leave us alone."

"You'd stand against me?" Vin shouted back.

"You leave me no choice," Rose said, and there was pity in her voice. "It's ended, Vin. Even your father saw that.

No more lies. No more hurting. Go home, Vin. Ride out of here. Do this one thing right."

"I'll show you! The both of you," Vin yelled, his voice growing shrill. "I'll see you dead in the dust." He glanced wide-eyed at Leland, who gestured to the men to ride up alongside Vin. Fourteen men swung their horses around to face Johnny. And still Anthem seemed undaunted.

"This is fine land here," Johnny said in a matter-of-fact tone of voice. "Good for running cattle on, better still for defending. Why, a fella could hide an army along these cliffs and have a clear shot at any blamed fool riding in the open." He noticed the Bonnet men shift uncomfortably and twist in their saddles as they began to inspect the boulder-strewn walls of the canyon. "Sweet water in the creek and plenty of cover too."

The Bonnet gun hands turned to study the forested ground bordering the creek.

"And up the canyon 'round the bend in the trail," Johnny continued, "hell, a man might just run into a whole damn war party of Apaches and never know what hit him until the first arrow sunk home. 'Course, I'd have to be a desperate man to be fighting alongside Mescaleros."

The Bonnet riders were facing three directions now; Johnny had suddenly peopled the entire landscape with a warring host and turned the walls of the canyon into the closing jaws of a trap. "Natchez Washburn found out the hard way. Reckon some of you boys will too."

"We've heard enough out of you," Leland shouted.

"You're right, Leland," John Anthem replied. He raised his right hand, his Colt clenched in his fist. He pointed the hand gun to the sky. It was time to start the dance. He fired once into the air.

The gunmen facing him twisted in their saddles as the shot rang out across the meadow, reverberated up and down the canyon, and eventually subsided. Then silence. Nothing happened. Nothing at all. The men began to relax. It had been a bluff. A bluff. They began to laugh among themselves.

Then the earth shook. A powerful explosion out of sight at the back of the canyon blew a cabin-sized crater in the side of the hill. The longhorns burst into motion at the blast. They hit the makeshift corral fence like a tidal wave and trampled it underfoot. The riders for the Bonnet couldn't see the oncoming stampede but they certainly heard it.

Half a dozen Bonnet men had to fight to bring their startled mounts under control. Two of the men ignored Leland and headed back down the canyon. The clamor of seventy panic-stricken steers and the thunder of their hooves, which set the earth trembling, drowned out any further commands.

Johnny leapt down from the wall and disappeared from sight a moment as Vin ordered the men around him to charge the wall. Jimbo Reasoner led two men up the incline. The Bonnet men opened fire. Slugs bit deep into the wall and sent a shower of dried mud clods into the air.

Johnny picked up the packed armor and held the fuse while Rose touched a lighted candle to the tip. The oil-soaked rag caught fire. Then Johnny tossed the breastplate over the wall and down the incline. The Spanish armor landed about twenty yards down the slope. The front and back plates had been laced tightly together and the armholes packed tight with wadding. The fuse that smoked and sputtered burned its way through the lacing.

Behind the wall, Rose crawled over to Johnny and covered her ears as she lowered her head against his chest. "Do you think it'll work?" she asked, shutting her eyes and gritting her teeth.

In answer, a tremendous blast knocked debris from the wall and lifted a barrier of black smoke and dust and fragments of armor. The air was filled with shrapnel. Men screamed. Horses neighed in terror and rolled over on their riders or bolted down the slope.

"Mama Rosita's gonna hate me for destroying her gift," Johnny shouted as he scrambled to his feet and emptied his gun into the smoke. He dropped the empty gun, and Rose, her ears ringing from the explosion, handed him another. She started reloading the first. Through the smoke Johnny saw Vin and Leland desperately trying to maintain control of the remnants of their force. They almost succeeded despite the gunfire peppering them as Kim Rideout fired down into the valley from his perch among the boulders.

Leland stood in his stirrups and, waving his revolver over his head, shouted at the top of his lungs.

As the smoke cleared, Johnny could see a blackened crater in the slope. Horses and dead men were strewn on the ground where the shrapnel from the exploding armor had cut them to ribbons. He counted two men and their mortally wounded mounts. But the third . . .

"Johnny!" Rose shouted. A heavyset, bearded gunman staggered through an opening in the wall. His clothes were in tatters, his arms lacerated, and blood trailed from his trouser leg. Jimbo Reasoner steadied himself and lifted his revolver. Rose dropped the Colt she was loading and snatched up the shotgun. She didn't aim. There wasn't time.

Johnny, alerted by her outcry, snapped off a shot. Shotgun and Colt fired as one. Reasoner yelped, and fell back over the low wall, his legs kicking straight up and his handgun discharging uselessly in the air as he died.

Johnny emptied his Colt at the riders below. For one brief second he held Vin in his sights but couldn't bring himself to squeeze the trigger. He held his fire and remained motionless a moment too long. A slug spun him around and he dropped beside Rose.

"Oh, my God," she gasped.

Johnny shoved himself against the wall and stared at the

bloody path the slug had gouged across his shoulder. It burned like hell. Sweat beaded his forehead. He felt dizzy for a moment but shook it off.

"Load," he snapped. Then he grinned, to contradict his hard tone. "You traded a life of luxury at the Bonnet for this?"

Rose didn't deign to reply. She let her actions speak for her and handed him a freshly loaded revolver. He took it and crawled to his feet, expecting to come face to face with a dozen armed gunmen.

Leland vainly tried to bring his panicked horsemen under control and point them toward the hacienda wall. He berated the men but his words were lost. The gunmen stared past him in wide-eyed horror as the stampeding longhorns rounded the canyon wall and bore down on them. Massive beasts, each weighing a thousand or twelve hundred pounds with horns like giant curved spears and razor-edged hooves capable of crushing a man in seconds, raced onward. Wild, there was no animal more fiercesome. And these were wild. Shouting commands, Leland pointed toward the knoll and the relative safety it offered and stared dumbfounded as the gunmen wheeled their horses and galloped toward the mouth of the canyon. Worse, Vin Cotter led the rout. He'd had his fill of Luminaria Canyon.

Leland looked up the canyon and saw the steers. The blood froze in his veins. He didn't want to charge the knoll alone. He drove his heels into his stallion and the animal leapt away. Leland angled his horse toward the east wall, running a gauntlet of Kim Rideout's rifle fire. Several of the Bonnet men headed toward the creek, choosing a break in the woods as their avenue of escape from the onrushing herd.

Poke signaled Chapo and they hauled together on their pull ropes. A single strand of hemp rope shot up from the ground, pulling a spikey barricade with it. The rope's entire length was strewn with uprooted cacti and woven with branches and underbrush bristling with three-inch thorns. Chapo wound the rope around an oak tree and secured it. Then he charged through the towering stalks of monkshood toward the clamor of the desperate riders who had hit the barrier.

Bedlam ruled. The thundering stampede. The scream of men and horse buckling beneath the onslaught. The gunfire and groaning and the wounded cries of pain at the barricade. Men, knocked off their horses, staggered, bleeding and blinded, unable to fight. And a boy went among them. A boy with a gun and hatred in his eyes. As Chapo squeezed off round after round, men doubled over and dropped, men were blown back on their haunches.

A slim wiry gun hawk rose out of the dust and brandished a scatter gun. Chapo drew his spare revolver and shot the man in the chest, in the arm, in the stomach. The dying man dropped his weapon. He held his hand palm out and sank to his knees.

Chapo aimed through his tear-blurred vision. "For my father," he cried out. "My father." But the Colt was heavy in his hands and he tried to bring them to bear on the dying man, but his arm had to strain so. Poke reached him, he stepped in front of the boy's smoking Colt. The old man's face was streaked with dust and blood where he had been gashed by a thorn.

"It's over, younker. It's over. Let it be."

Chapo stared at Tyler, and then, sobbing, he dropped his guns and fell into the old man's sheltering arms.

The stampede lost its momentum once the steers cleared the mouth of the canyon. With the whole prairie before them, the longhorns slowed, then spread out upon the plain.

Their sides heaving from exertion, the steers began to graze on the spring grass.

From his hiding place beyond the canyon Vin watched the last of his remaining men vanish in the distance. He shouted for them to stop, but the men were too busy fleeing to pay him any mind. Vin climbed out of the arroyo and looked back at his horse lying on its side, rolling its eyes in pain as it tried to stand on its broken leg. Vin drew his revolver. He hadn't fired a single shot during the entire fight. He felt numb and tired and terribly lost. He aimed at the crippled animal and fired now for the first time. The horse shuddered and died.

He turned then and stopped in his tracks as he saw Leland clear the canyon and head toward him. "Thank God," Vin muttered. He waved his hat in the air in order to make certain that Leland saw him. He started running toward his segundo. And closed the distance between them.

"I was afraid you'd bought it," Vin stammered breathlessly as Leland rode up to him. "We ought to come across another horse before long." He reached up to Leland, expecting the breed to swing him up behind the saddle. He heard the ominous click of the revolver, its hammer thumbed back. Vin retreated a step. "Now see here . . ." Vin Cotter began.

Leland fired. The colt recoiled upward and Vin slammed over on his back, rolled on his stomach, tried to crawl, raised up on his elbows, and for one ridiculous moment remembered another time, in Mexico, with Johnny and a black mare. Leland fired again. The report echoed down the long hills.

28

★

It wasn't over, of course, not as long as Leland Rides Horse was free. John Anthem, Chapo Almendáriz, and Rose had ridden out from the canyon at sunset and found Vin Cotter face-down in the dirt. The powder burns on the back of his blood-soaked coat revealed he'd been shot at close range, and no one but one of his own men had been that close. Behind them in Luminaria Canyon, Kim Rideout and Charlie Gibbs had rounded up the wounded for Pokeberry to try to patch up as best he could.

Chapo removed his hat in deference to Rose as she dismounted and knelt by the man who had been her husband. Johnny climbed down and dropped to his knees alongside her. He hesitated, then gathered Vin up in his arms and draped him face down over Chapo's saddle.

"Take him back to camp," Johnny said. Chapo started to object. John Anthem's gaze hardened. "It's for me to settle this last account," Johnny continued. "It was my right long before it became yours."

Rose stepped close to him. She looked at Vin. "I don't want to dig another grave today. Let Vin's be the last." Maybe she was supposed to feel guilt. She tried. But Vin had written his own story and decided his own fate. She

was moved to pity for him. It was sad. But she still had
Johnny. The man she loved was alive, and she wanted him
to stay that way.

"Leland is probably halfway to Mexico now," she suggested hopefully.

"No. He'll be waiting for me. He knows I'll come,"
Johnny replied.

"How do you expect to find him?" Chapo asked.

"Easy." John Anthem studied the tracks leading off toward Blue Top. "He'll tell me where he is." He turned to
Rose and took her in his arms and hugged her close. "Despite everything, I'm sorry for Vin too."

"I know," she said, and stepped back. Johnny's sun-
bronzed features seemed to sag with fatigue. The lackluster
blue of his eyes betrayed his weariness. He turned and
swung up onto the saddle. His black mare didn't need any
urging, she was anxious to be off.

"*Vaya con Dios*," Chapo said beneath his breath.

"Go with God," Rose repeated.

They watched him until Johnny was lost in the dimming
light.

From the summit of Blue Top Mountain a man could see
for hundreds of miles, all the way to Mexico. The land,
made up of desert mountains and rolling prairie, canyons
and deep arroyos to the west, wore the mark of the hand
of the master creator. The All-Father, Leland thought as he
added a handful of dry grass and wood bark to the flame.
Such was the Indian term. He smothered the flames with
his saddle blanket and yanked it back, loosing a voluminous
cloud of smoke into the air. He continued with the fire for
half an hour and then left the blaze to burn itself out.

Blue Top wore a flat crown of barren table rock roughly
a hundred feet in diameter. Moss grew in and around the
tinajas, eroded pockets in hard rock where rainwater col-

lected. Here, a thousand feet above the prairie, the wind blew cool and clean.

Leland had climbed the mountain by the light of a full moon the night before. It had been difficult, but morning had made the effort worthwhile. He'd enjoyed the sunrise in peace and then begun his signal fire; he knew Johnny would see the smoke. It was impossible to miss. Leland crossed his legs and sat on the hard surface. He thought of his plans, his dreams of controlling the Bonnet. He thought of all he'd endured, taking orders from the likes of Vin Cotter, of being the young man's nursemaid as well as trying to run the ranch. Now everything was lost, because of Vin's foolish behavior.

Rose McCain . . . ah . . . she was a beauty, but the world was big and wide and there were as many women as men. Why throw away everything they had worked for as Vin had done?

"Why?" Leland shouted. His voice returned, asking the same question over and over again. Without answer. He leaned forward and hid his face in his hands and remained that way for more than an hour.

When he moved, at last, it was to unbutton his lace-trimmed shirt. As he undressed, Leland began to chant in a low, melodious voice. He remembered the words but not what they meant. Still he continued his chant.

He discarded most of his clothes and fashioned a breechcloth for himself out of his torn clothes. Then he took a rifle and crawled to a vantage point among the rocks. Anthem would come. And Leland would kill him as he climbed the mountain. Simple. Leland smiled and lay on his belly and studied a distant figure riding at a gallop across the plain. He patted the stock of his rifle and willed Anthem onward. And then he froze, hearing the ominous click of a gun behind him.

*   *   *

John Anthem reached the summit by late afternoon. His legs and arms ached from crawling and climbing up the steep trail leading up from the base. Gun in hand, he peered out from behind an outcropping of pink volcanic rock and stared in surprise at Leland Rides Horse and the man holding him prisoner: Aguila, the Mescalero Apache.

Johnnny climbed out from the rocks and the Apache nodded to him. The warrior held two rifles, Leland's and his own. A hint of a smile crossed the brave's dust-caked features. A revolver lay on the hard surface just within reach of Rides Horse, but the breed wisely made no move. Smoke rose from the ashes of the half-breed's signal fire. Remnants of his once-fine attire could be glimpsed among the coals.

"Aguila, what's all this?" Johnny blurted out. He checked the surrounding rocks, half-expecting a war party to leap out at him.

"I come alone, John Anthem," Aguila said. "*Saaa-vaaaa*! You think I come to fight you? No. But this one will." The Apache gestured with the rifle toward Leland. "I saw his war smoke. He waited to kill you. You give Aguila his life once. Now I do the same for you." The brave started to toss down Leland's rifle, but decided to keep it instead and tucked it under his arm.

Johnny glanced at the half-breed, who continued to stare sullenly at the ground. Then he returned his gaze to the Apache. "Have you thought on my words?"

"I watch long time. See much fighting. It is good to see white men kill each other for a change." Aguila started to retreat. "Your people and mine will live in peace, John Anthem. But first you must come down from the mountain. I will be watching." The Apache backed away among the rocks and vanished from sight. A gust of wind marked his passing.

Johnny squatted down across from Leland, a distance of

fifty feet separating the two men. The half-breed lifted his head and stared at Anthem.

"The air is good here," Leland said. "You chose your land wisely."

Johnny only nodded and breathed deep, caught a hint of pine and the wind-borne fragrance of flowering buds. The sky above was vast and limitless and deep blue. To the north, thunderheads promised a spring shower by nightfall.

Leland dipped his fingers into the ashes, painted two slash marks on his forehead, and drew a black line down along the bridge of his nose, creating the macabre effect of a man with two faces, which indeed Leland was.

"You have come here to die, John Anthem," Leland said. "It was written long ago."

The wind rushed between them, howled in the crevices like wailing spirits in torment. The sun lost its warmth. The wind died, the keening voices with it.

"Reminds me of a fellow I knew who decided one day to see how many holes he could shoot in his head," Johnny finally said as he leaned forward and placed his Walker Colt before him on the rain-scarred stone. His eyes never left Leland. He eased away from the revolver. The two men sat in stillness. Watchful. Sensing the right moment.

And suddenly, motion. Johnny grabbed for his revolver and rolled to his right and heard the report from Leland's Colt. A slug tore loose a chunk off lava rock. Johnnny groaned as his shoulder wound tore open. He braced himself and, lying flat on his belly, thumbed off a shot. Leland charged him, flame jetting from the muzzle of his Colt; .44-caliber slugs shattered stone and went careening off into space. Slivers of stone stung Johnny's face, but he ignored the cuts, squinted to protect his eyes, and fired at his attacker through the showering fragments.

The Colt bucked in his fist, but he steadied it with a two-handed grip, holding ground. He saw Leland falter and try to strike back. The breed took aim; Johnny loosed another shot. Acrid powder smoke blotted out the image of the half-breed. Johnny squeezed off another round and heard answering fire.

Damm it, die. How many times did he need to hit the man? Johnny kept firing, shooting blind at the half-breed, who kept answering shot for shot.

The hammer of Johnny's Colt struck an empty cylinder. The echo of his last shot reverberated. It crashed and boomed again and again and faded like thunder. Johhny shook his head, realizing he was hearing the echo of his own shots, not answering gunfire.

He crawled to his feet as the wind renewed its play among the crevices. Leland Rides Horse was sprawled face-down upon the mountain, his upper torso submerged in the shallows of the *tinajas*. Bubbles rose to the crimson-stained surface of the water. Johnny staggered over to the pool and rolled the half-breed out onto his back. Leland coughed water and turned his head aside and groaned. Pink froth bubbled from two blackish wounds in his chest.

Johnny stiffened as the muzzle of a gun barrel pressed against his side. He hadn't noticed Leland was still armed.

"How many holes . . ." Leland gasped in a faint voice, "How many did the . . . man shoot . . . in his head?"

Johnny stared down at the gun pressed to his side. "Just one," he answered.

Leland managed a horrid sort of wheezing chuckle. He squeezed the trigger. Johnny braced himself. The revolver clicked empty. John Anthem sagged back on his heels as Leland's hands dropped away. The half-breed began to chant, singing, in the tongue of his father's people, the dimly remembered words of a death chant. A minute more and the singing stopped.

Johnny breathed deep, glad to be alive. His arms hung limp at his side. He stood alone on the mountain. For a moment, after all that had happened, the solitude felt good. He looked out across the sprawling landscape, beckoning in beauty, in violence, in storm and brilliant sunlight.

The mountain was peaceful but the dream waited below. The land John Anthem had chosen—that in its own way had chosen him—waited to be lived in with the woman he loved.